TWO FACES OF THE WORLD

THE SEEDS OF WAR

DILOBAR ORTIQOVA

• Chicago •

Two Faces of the World
The Seeds of War
Dilobar Ortiqova

Published by
Joshua Tree Publishing
• Chicago •
JoshuaTreePublishing.com

13-Digit ISBN Print: 978-1-956823-19-6
13-Digit ISBN eBook: 978-1-956823-97-4

Cover Artwork: Sword © pixelrobot Adobe Stock
Historical Image © ZU_09 iStock

Disclaimer:
This is a work of fiction. Names, characters, places, and incidents are the product of the author's imagination or have been used fictitiously. Any resemblance to actual persons, living or dead, events, locales or organizations is entirely coincidental.

Printed in the United States of America

Dedication

In memory of my father Alisher Tuychiev, whose love and care warmed our hearts and whose faith gave us wings . . .

1959 – 2021

Table of Contents

List of Participants

House of Layland

Hagan Layland	Former king of Rhodareen
King Arawn Layland	King of all people, son of Hagan
Ellinor Stavros	Late queen
Prince Asael Layland	Eldest son of Arawn
Lady Calanthe Layland	
Prince Xander	
Princess Eireen	
Prince Noah	
Prince Keon Layland	Second son of Arawn
Lady Ada Lander	
Prince Thaen Layland	The youngest son of Arawn
Tomaso Layland	Arawn's brother
Ailidh Layland	
Prince Sanders Layland	
Princess Isabelle Layland	

House of Ulyses

Taron Griffin Ulyses	Founder of the House of Ulyses
Aodh Griffin Ulyses	Son of Taron
Leon Griffin Ulysses	Son of Aodh, king of the centenarians
Idelisa Griffen Ulyses	Late queen of the centenarians
Leonor Griffin Ulysses	Leon's sister
Estevan Ulysses	
Lady Devora Rose Griffin	

List of Participants (cont)

Witches of the Light

Celia	Moon sister
Ailidh	Moon sister
Idelisa	Moon sister
Abella	Chief of the witches' abbot
Amare	
Charlotte	
Lisette	
Beatrice	
Melani	

Pirates of Incombusto

Aquila	Captain of Incombusto
Cael	
Orrin	
Cosimo	
Belen	

Other influential Houses

House of Stavros	House of Mesman
House of Damen	House of Calhoun
House of Lander	House of Magus

Prehistory

From the very beginning, when the world was created, the earth had become home for all living and nonliving beings. It was inhabited not only by humans and animals, insects and birds, but also a lot of mythical creatures. Among all the creatures, the most beautiful and the most powerful ones were called centenarians.

Centenarians—from caladrius to unicorns, phoenix to thunderbirds, nymphs, mermaids, dwarfs, elves, and many others—varied from one to another. Yet all were unconditionally unique in their own way. These wonderful creatures received their common name because of their ability to live long lives equal to centuries, sometimes to millennia. In comparison to centenarians, mankind was weaker.

For hundreds of thousands of years, while living side by side with centenarians, the people (who were called mortals) faced many wars, famine, diseases, and disasters. How many times had jealousy and greed misled people? How many times had kings started wars, nations gone against nations, families gone against families, fathers gone against sons? History had proved many times that living meant fighting for men, and much would never become enough.

The centenarians, on the contrary, always lived in peace and harmony with every living creature on earth. They tried not to intrude on the humans' world, even though the centenarians had a great influence on the development of every sphere of the people's lives. The centenarians were the founders of the ancient world's great civilizations.

The Ulyses family, the greatest house and ruler of the entire centenarian world, was the founder of their civilization. Despite the fact that, outwardly, the members of the House of Ulyses looked like humans, their family was distinguished by a very rare beauty, sharp mind, and a gift of power and endless life.

In the centenarian world, the creatures cherished Mother Nature as their creator. Their legends told that in the very beginning, there was only darkness. From darkness appeared light, and from the ever-shining light were created the four powers. The powers of the ground, air, water, and fire became the bases of life.

The keepers of these four powers were called the children of Mother Nature. They were not only the founders of life but protectors of all. They were born to keep balance in the world of the mortals and centenarians. But one day something unexpected by all happened. The ever-shining light flared up brightly, and the fifth child of Mother Nature was created.

Quinn, the fifth child, differed from the other children of Mother Nature. His power had no borders. The other four children of nature could not equal him in strengths and skills.

Time flew by quickly. Quinn grew, and so did his power. Unlike the other centenarians, his power increased not year by year but day by day. At the age of eighteen, Quinn had reached his absolute power. No one had lived to see such power until that day. But even for Quinn, the power of nature was too much. It was beautiful yet dangerous. From time to time, Quin lost control over his power. He couldn't hold his strength, and his gift turned into a curse that caused destruction.

The royal family and the other chiefs of the centenarian world tried to help the child to control his power, and the boy was sent to a sanctuary in the centenarians' hidden city, which was called the Moon City. But the existence of the fifth child of nature and the extent of his power intimidated people, and fear made people do such things that afterward they would regret.

The mortals believed that Quinn was a danger to their world. Because of this belief, they made the greatest mistake. As a result, millions of innocents suffered as war broke out between the mortals and centenarians. All the kings of the mortal world created a great army. Together they marched to the Moon City and requested for the boy. Many centenarians fell defending the city walls and all who lived within it. The men betrayed their world. They went against nature. They attacked the city and threatened its child, as well as all the centenarians. Thus, they had to pay their debt with blood.

When people had caught Quinn, he was severely injured, weak, and hardly breathing. But soon everything changed. The people's wish to destroy the fifth child and the destruction they made this way awoke darkness in his heart. Dark power gave the boy immortality. He gathered other centenarians around him. Many centenarians who tasted the power of darkness turned to the side of the fifth child. They accused the mortals of betrayal. The great war between the mortals and the centenarians brought destruction to the world. Death came with a dark shadow and ruined everything on its way.

Quinn and his army spared no life. Despite the humans' betrayal, the centenarian king, by the laws of nature, couldn't let the world balance be destroyed. Therefore, with the help of humans and other centenarians, King Ulyses gathered every living being in the world into an army against the fifth child, and he called them the Army of Light.

With great difficulty, he and his followers were able to stop the war. Quinn could neither be defeated nor could his powers be destroyed. Thus, with the help of three of the most powerful witch sisters, the power of the fifth child was stolen by the great centenarian king and buried under the ground at the center of the Moon City.

The use of dark magic was forbidden for every creature on earth. The city was moved to another place and put under a very powerful spell by the witch sisters, which was so powerful that no one could ever break it. The spell put around the city was an invisible wall: neither mankind nor any evil power could find the city or cross the wall. Because of the sisters' spell, Moon City became the safest place on the planet, and the sisters received the name Moon Sisters.

The stolen power of the fifth child was guarded carefully and could never be reached by anyone. Even the great king of the centenarians could not approach the power's hidden place.

After his power had been stolen, Quinn became mortal. The people and the centenarians gained their common peace and ended the war. All returned to their ways of life before the war. But one day there appeared one who sang a song of the world's end, and the prophecy was told:

> Nature will play a game, a child's
> revenge comes to the scene and
> releases the power, the world will
> never be the same.

Everyone laughed upon hearing such reckless words. The king of the centenarians knew that the spell couldn't be broken, yet his heart was inconsolable.

Chapter 1

You Are Not Innocent!

Autumn 1644

Outside was very dark. The tall trees in the forest fused in branches high in the sky, hiding the night stars behind their heavy leaves. The trees here were as ancient as the land itself. They had stood there for many centuries as big giants protecting the land. Some said they had stood when the world had been created. They had stood to see the great war and witnessed all the mysteries of the world. And they would stand for thousands of years more . . . while the world would stand.

The cold air froze the hard ground, forcing the last field greens to wither under its ruthless breath. The surroundings sank into silence, devastated as if in a cemetery.

Dalir felt himself totally alone and so tiny among these giants of the old forest. The last days of autumn had already reminded that winter was close. All his life, Dalir had lived in the village located high in the mountains, at the very heart of Longwood Forest. It was his home—the place where he first breathed, where he grew up, and which kept all his dearest and saddest memories. It was the place where he had everything once . . . and where everything was lost when he became worthless.

It was his home! The place where he had belonged and would belong . . . always! The deeper he went into the forest, the harder his steps became. Totally gasping, Dalir felt he had aged in those years.

Soon, he reached the place where he intended to go—the place where all his world had turned upside down many years ago.

He had been a lumberman and worked in the forest, as did the majority of the villagers. After an accident in the forest, he had badly injured his right shoulder and hand. He had become a lame who could not return to the forest. He had become useless . . . broken! He had become a man who couldn't hold a weapon, neither for protecting nor for working. That day he'd said farewell to the great giants of Longwood. Since then the iron axe that had once belonged to his father had been buried under the pile of dust in the small hall of his old stone house. After the accident, Dalir spent all his days in the village helping other people with minor tasks, but it was not enough to make ends meet. Luckily, his sister and her husband didn't abandon him and helped him in any way they could.

After a long walk, Dalir stopped at the high oak tree at the edge of an open area like a small field. The trees stood like a wall around it. The shadows of thousands of tree stumps in the field rose high under the light of the full moon. They reminded him of thousands of gravestones. The sight made Dalir shiver. Probably he shouldn't have come to this place. His heart beat fast. He became uneasy. Whispers of the recently started rain echoed over the field. The wind grew stronger.

Standing on the edge of the field, Dalir looked at the sky and closed his eyes. He wished the raindrops could wash away all his troubles. The sudden thunderstorm lit up all the surroundings and scared Dalir with its loud acoustic effect. It seemed the sky felt his troubles and tried somehow to answer him.

"What is disturbing you?" asked Dalir from the sky.

In a while, another thunder sounded even louder than the first one, as if the sky was trying to answer his question. Then he again heard another sound of thunder.

"Third one," counted Dalir.

The fourth one came after it, but this time the lightning hit the old oak tree. Fire burst out, and the tree broke into two. The sound of cracking was even louder than the sound of the thunderstorm. Dalir was in terror. The fire was spreading very quickly. All the trees in the forest started falling. The cracking sound was getting louder and louder . . . Even the ground under his feet became unstable.

Someone called his name. Dalir tried to find the person calling him. He was sure that he was totally alone in the forest. How come he didn't notice the passerby?

"Where are you?" he shouted.

Dalir knew, whoever was in the forest, he couldn't leave that person behind. At that moment a big tree cracked apart from the middle and fell right into the place where Dalir was standing. Disabled, Dalir knew that he had no chance of surviving the oncoming crash, but luckily, his efforts weren't in vain. Dust filled the air. Still on the ground, Dalir tried to manage himself, but a sudden movement grabbed his attention. For sure he wasn't alone . . .

Again he heard his name. Behind the cracked tree appeared a shadow, taller than any ordinary man. Wings widely spread in the air, the man looked at Dalir. Within the black sclera, the shadow's eyes burned in a red flame, and the emptiness was reflected in its pupils.

Dalir sank into those pupils. He was absorbed into the black hole . . . and he fell! He fell, leaving behind the stars . . . down and down toward infinity . . . He fell, leaving behind the comets . . . He fell toward the earth. Closer and closer . . .

Where the azure shining distinguished the border between the sky and the endless blue ocean, he saw the edge of the world. He never had seen such a bewitching and terrifying view in his whole life. He fell . . . too fast. He saw Longwood Forest. How spacious was it? The ground was close. Dalir screamed in horror. But when he reached the end of the fall, there was no crush or brokenness. Instead, the flame widely opened its wings for an embrace and burned Dalir out.

"Devil!" shouted Dalir in panic.

Sweating and gasping, he looked around. He was alone in his room. It was cold inside.

* * *

How could it be a dream? thought Dalir.

What he had experienced was so realistic that he could hardly believe it was a dream. He went to the corner of the room and washed his face with cold water in the basin. It made him shiver. Putting on his wool cloak, he went out. The day was coming to an end. He remembered that he hadn't felt well earlier and had gone to his house to have some rest. He wondered how he could have spent all day in bed. Was it because of a severe change in the weather? Because of the long nightmare, he had a strong headache. The cool air served as a relief for his clouded mind. He looked at the sky and took a deep breath.

The sun, trying to escape behind the big, snowy mountains, reminded him that the day was almost over. Dalir watched the high trees surrounding their village. Among the mountains, at the heart of the long forest, the village seemed like a tiny anthill divided into blocks. In every block, there were five to six houses with their entrances looking toward the common circle yard. All the blocks were located around the big yard in a circle, and at the middle of each circle were big bonfires.

Dalir loved his village. Due to its magical view bestowed by nature, people called the village Sunrose Village. Every morning, under the light of the rising sun, all types of flowers in pink, red, and purple colors created oceanlike waves by moving side to side in the wind. During the sunset, the village was covered in a red-colored blanket, and as it was located very high in the mountains, even the fog sparkled with brilliant pink lights.

Even now, in late autumn, the surroundings looked as beautiful as in early spring. However, it was very cold outside. After darkness started covering the environment, the villagers started lighting up the outdoor and indoor candles. Some women came to the edge of the forest to meet the lumbermen returning home after a long working day. Because of the cold, the people were wrapped up warmly in their capes and cloaks. Some parents called for their children who were playing outdoors.

Dalir approached the people gathered around one of the bonfires on the east side of the village. They greeted him and continued chatting. Dalir pulled his hood closer to his forehead, as if to hide his face from the freezing wind, and held out his hands to the fire. He was watching a group of men returning home from the forest.

In a while, the door of the second house in the next block opened, and a young woman appeared at the entrance. She was expecting a baby and was in her last month. The woman looked at the coming men and smiled, waving toward them.

One of the men waved back at her. He was in his early thirties and worked as a lumberman like most of the villagers. The man quickened his steps and in three jumps reached the entrance of the house. He gave the woman a kiss on her forehead. Afterward, the woman went inside the house and disappeared from sight. The man looked around. His gaze found Dalir's, and putting his axe next to the door, he came up to his brother-in-law.

Dalir respected the man. More than a year ago, he had come to ask for the hand of Dalir's sister, Leah. She was the only person close to him left in this world after their parents passed away twelve years ago. After the accident, his sister and her husband were the only ones whom Dalir could rely on.

"Brother!" the man called him, coming over and putting his hand on Dalir's shoulders supportively. "How are you feeling?"

Dalir nodded and informed his brother-in-law about his better condition. He was feeling well. Probably Leah told her husband about him. The man invited him into the house, and Dalir just noticed that he hadn't eaten since morning. Dalir returned to the house with his brother-in-law to see his sister's smiling face.

"Brother!" Leah widely opened her arms for a hug. "Why weren't you entering? The meal is already ready."

Dalir gave her a sincere smile. The sweet smell of fried potatoes and rice filled the air.

"Hmm! Smells good for a great surprise," he commented.

"Tastes good too!" Leah stated with offense, half smiling.

"I know . . . You have our mother's gift," admitted Dalir.

He directed to the dining corner in the kitchen. His brother-in-law helped Leah bring the meal and other kitchen supplies. After the evening meal, Dalir and his brother-in-law sat to chat for a little while. Leah went to bed earlier.

The evening was cool and silent. However, everything turned upside down when Leah started screaming and writhing in pain. Her labor had started. Leaving his sister in the house with her husband, Dalir rushed to the neighboring block to bring the healer woman. In a while, with the help of an herbal potion, Leah regained some strength. Her husband held her hands to support her. Leah was struggling with all her efforts, her face was washed up with sweat, and between her teeth, she clenched a wood stick.

Dalir couldn't bear to see his sister suffering, so he left the house. He went deep into the forest. He wandered in the dark paths of the forest for a long time. He knew that by that time, his sister might have almost given birth to her child even though he couldn't turn back and go to the house.

The sky was uneasy. It rained and roared, occasionally showing its anger in thunder. Soon, Dalir reached an open area. Watching the thousands of tree stumps on the ground, Dalir knelt near the old oak tree. He was wet from top to bottom, very tired and breathless. Suddenly a very loud thunderstorm broke the silence in the forest. Dalir shivered and remembered his dream.

A long and blue ray of thunder fell from the very rooftop of the sky, creating a zigzag path. It hit the ground several times where the village was located. Some trees started burning. Dalir felt a quake under his feet. He stood up and ran back to the village. The cracking sound was everywhere. Then he heard screams. He heard the people of his village calling for help. He tried to run as fast as he could. However, because of the unstable ground, every step was made with difficulty.

The closer Dalir got to the village, the brighter the light became and the less he could hear the screams of the villagers. When Dalir finally got to the village, it was on fire. Burning trees and houses made it impossible for Dalir to get to his sister. The flame rising higher and higher into the sky blocked the way to her house. His useless efforts to get water from the well failed. Dalir fell down in tears. He shouted and yelled . . . He hit the ground with his fist . . . But all was in vain . . .

When the rain, at last, was able to put out the fire, it was midnight. Nothing was left but ash and stone. There was no village anymore. The fire had destroyed everything. Some houses were still on fire, but no one was calling for help. His head was low on the cold ground, his hands embracing the ashes around . . .

At last, he got on his feet. Dalir didn't know how he found the strength to reach his sister's house. His last efforts brought him to the big hole where once stood a door. The stones of the ruins left by the fire were still hot. The air smelled of burned flesh and wood. Near the burned bodies on the floor, he found the one that belonged to his sister. Dalir sank to his knees in tears and took Leah's body into his embrace.

"L-Le . . ." No matter how hard he tried, he couldn't find the strength to pronounce her name. He wanted to call her, as if his sister could return by hearing his voice. He would call her a thousand times if he could. If only he could see her smiling face once more . . .

He wanted to call her name . . . He wanted to scream . . . to curse . . . He wanted to crush everything . . . the whole world . . . crush it into pieces. If only he could call her name. But all he could utter was a strange noise.

His cry sounded like a song of a dumb man who was never taught to sing. He wanted to call her name out loud, as if she would respond to his call, as if she could be brought back. But every time he tried to utter the name, a strong pain choked him. It stuck in his throat. An unseen sharp knife cut his heart into pieces.

He hugged Leah tightly. Then he did let it go; a very loud yell burst out. With all his strength, all his voice, he yelled— loudly, . . . crazily . . . He couldn't stop. He let the scream shake the surroundings. He let the scream tell the skies and the earth of his sorrow. With a loud scream, he let the world know of his pain. How long he sat among the ruins, holding the burned body of his sister, he couldn't tell.

Gradually his cry turned into a low sobbing. The surroundings were as quiet as a graveyard. Only Dalir's cry was heard. Then another strange voice grabbed his attention. It was a cry. Dalir wasn't the only one in whose tears the ground sank. He wasn't alone!

Dalir raised his head and looked around. With all his efforts, he tried to understand and catch the source of the cry. Was it an adult, or was it a child? Dalir couldn't believe his ears. Did his loss draw him mad? Or was it a miracle, a blessing sent from the heavens? Dalir wasn't sure.

Soon, fully recovered from his pain, Dalir clearly could hear the cry of a newborn. The cry grew louder. Unbelieving his ears, Dalir followed the cry. Moving the stones and half-burned wooden beams, Dalir reached the area that had once been the inner hall of his sister's house. Among the piles of ruins, he noticed the tiny body of a newborn child, moving back and forth on a stone floor and crying loudly. Next to him was the body of the healer woman. Dalir ran toward the child. His heart in pain, he sobbed.

"Dear God! Merciful! You are mighty . . . ," were the whispers of prayer uttered by his lips.

Dalir bent over to take the child into his arms. The child also noticed the approach of a stranger. He stopped crying and looked at the unfamiliar person next to him. Their eyes met. Instead of lifting the child up, Dalir stepped backward and fell onto the ground.

"No! No!" he shouted in terror.

Shaking and breathing heavily, Dalir watched the one who again burst into cries after seeing him back away. After being abandoned by an adult, the child's cry became even louder.

Dalir remembered his dream. How could he forget it? He wanted to rise on his feet and run away—far, far away . . . But his legs wouldn't obey. He stood in one place, totally numbed. Then he took a step toward the child.

He himself couldn't explain why he was still among these ruins. The child calmed down the moment he saw the man standing over him. He held out his tiny hands toward Dalir and uttered strange sounds as if he wanted to talk. Dalir lifted the child up from the ground. In his consciousness, he knew he was holding the son of his beloved sister. He was so small and innocent. He was totally alone in this ruthless world. He couldn't feel his mother's love, and Dalir was responsible for this child. Yet Dalir could not accept the boy as his nephew.

"No, you are not innocent," he whispered.

The child looked at him as if he was surprised, wondering what the stranger was talking about. Dalir recognized the child's eyes. He had seen them before. In his dream. With an innocent smile, the devil was looking at him!

Chapter 2

Expected Day

Incitydoor. It was a city located on a big peninsula surrounded by high mountain ranges on three sides. Fairy gardens, various buildings, lakes, fountains, big markets, and roads as many as the roots of a tree gave the city an unnaturally beautiful view. Incitydoor had been the capital city of the Layland kingdom for many centuries. It was the heart of Rhodareen.

Arawn Layland was the fifty-sixth ruler of the kingdom, the heir of the Layland Dynasty and king to all people. The king's castle was located in the east part of the city. It was separated from the neighborhood by the vast River Duur and connected with a long bridge that led to the castle's main gates.

Despite the weather becoming very cold in recent days, the severe autumn couldn't spoil the people's festive mood. On this day, the city had become even more beautiful. The people of the city had decorated their houses, buildings, and public centers with different types of autumn flowers—like crocus, begonia, gladiolus, snowdrops, and many others. From early morning the musicians had been playing traditional music. All the women in the city wore flower headbands on their heads, and the children were laughing all the way, chasing each other and playing games.

After the sun's first lights fell on the city, all the people directed toward the palace's main gates, holding bunches of gladiolus in their hands. All were in a hurry to get on time to the chapel and to find a better place to see the wedding ceremony of the king's niece and the heir of the centenarian throne. It promised to be the wedding of the millennium.

Even though the groom with his escort hadn't arrived yet, the people of the city had already stayed in a long queue to look at the centenarian king.

Griffin Leon Ulyses was the third to inherit the throne of his father after his great father. The great father of King Leon, Griffin Taron Ulyses, had fought together with the ancestors of King Arawn Layland against the dark power a thousand years ago. Together they had built a world where people, centenarians, and all other creatures started living in peace and harmony without fear and hesitance. Today the two greatest dynasties of the world decided to strengthen their alliance by uniting the two families with royal marriage.

The second highest tower of the castle's west wing was given to the princess of Rhodareen. The chamber's high ceiling was decorated with hanging golden roses. Flowerpots filled with crocus, red dahlia, and carnation were put in every corner of the room. Long candles were lit on the round table in the middle of the room and next to the princess's bed. The crackling logs in the fireplace illuminated the room by staining it with a reddish light.

However, inside was cold and dark . . . It was everything that Isabelle had been feeling—that and emptiness . . . It was already morning, yet Isabelle was still in bed. She was staring at the little sunlight entering the room through the fat curtains. She couldn't sleep since yesterday. It was her wedding day—the most expected, most promising day, but less wanted by Isabelle. A sudden knock on the door disturbed her thoughts.

"Isabelle, it's Nihan. I am entering the room."

After introducing herself, a woman of about fifty opened the door and stepped inside. She was Isabelle's maid, and she had taken care of her since childhood.

"Oh, my dear goodness, you are still in bed. Time to get ready, my princess."

The woman approached big windows and parted the heavy curtains aside. The room brightened at once. Isabelle grimaced and covered her face with the blanket. The woman looked through the window and smiled. From the windows of the princess's room, one could see the beautiful view of the bay. Far on the horizon, the sails of the royal ship could be seen. The maid came to Isabelle and started pulling her blanket.

"They will soon be here. It may take an hour or a little more. We need to hurry."

"Nihan, can you please give me some more time?"

"Covering your face with cushions will not postpone anything. You are getting married to the great king, you will be a queen of two worlds."

With the strong insistence of her maid, Isabelle stood up, approached the mirror, and sat on the stool. Two other maids straightened the beddings while Nihan took care of the princess. With gentle movements, Nihan started combing the princess's hair.

Isabelle looked at her reflection in the mirror. Her long golden hair made curls around her shoulders. She was a twenty-five-year-old lady with emerald-green eyes. Her maid liked to call Isabelle *hilalim*, "my moon," because of her white skin and beautiful eyes, the light in her gaze, and her tenderness. Isabelle sat in silence for a long time, looking at the mirror, and after a while, she replied to the last words of her maid.

"Great king . . . I am getting married to a 158-year-old man who lives forever." Isabelle exhaled a deep sigh and closed her eyes.

"Oh, my dear, you know well that centenarians live long lives. The more they live, the less they get older. Probably he is a fine young man full of strength and grandeur in his 150s." The maid smiled.

"Yes, he is," Isabelle confirmed her maid's words. "Time almost stops for centenarians after they reach the age of eighteen. Lucky them . . ."

"You did see him, didn't you?" asked Nihan while helping the princess get ready.

"It was a long time ago."

"You will be happy with the king. You will like him," said Nihan.

But the princess objected to her maid, "I promised to hate them my whole life. All of them."

Nihan turned Isabelle to herself. Her words made Nihan worry. "You can't build happiness with hatred in your heart."

"I hate the centenarians! They took from me the most precious person. I am afraid I will never be able to overcome my hatred and my fear, especially toward the king!"

"Oh, Isabelle . . . ," the maid said sighing.

"I saw what they are able to do. I was there, Nihan. The day of the tragedy, I saw them."

"Isabelle, you were a little girl," said the maid to the princess. "You can't be sure what had happened was real."

Isabelle nodded, confirming that she knew what she saw, and it was a terrible truth that couldn't be changed. No one could deny it. Isabelle looked down at her fingers.

"Who cares about my happiness? My life is a sacrifice for my king, for my father . . . for everyone."

"Oh, my dear child," said Nihan with pity. She felt sorry for the princess.

Isabelle turned toward the mirror. She didn't want this marriage ever to happen. But her uncle, the king to all people, arranged this marriage with his ally. Isabelle had no choice but to obey.

"Peace for all people . . . Let them be happy," said Isabelle with a deep sigh.

"Isabelle, do you hate me also?" asked the maid in a sad voice.

"What? How can I hate you?" said the princess to her maid with astonishment. "Nihan, you raised me. You took care of me. You replaced my mother for me. I love you very much! You are very precious to me," said the girl to the old woman with tears in her eyes.

"In that case, promise me! You will be happy with the king. Whatever happens, you'll do everything to be happy."

Isabelle threw herself toward her maid and embraced her. Nihan also gave a warm hug to the princess. Soon, the doors to Isabelle's room opened, and the other maids holding the bride's wedding dress and accessories entered the room. In a while, Isabelle was clothed in a white wedding dress covered with pearls. Her headdress was covered with white snowdrops, and the long veil covering the long skirt of her dress lay on the ground.

"What a beautiful bride you have become," said Nihan, smiling at Isabelle with tears in her eyes.

Soon, Isabelle got ready for the ceremony. She sat on the edge of her bed and waited for the announcement. At last, footsteps were heard outside her room, and someone knocked on the doors.

"Isabelle, are you ready? Can I come in?" asked the man.

Isabelle recognized the voice at once. Her father was waiting for her outside. Nihan went toward the doors and opened them.

"Where is my princess?" shouted her father and looked at his daughter. "You are so beautiful." Her father kissed her daughter's forehead and hugged her.

Isabelle's father, Tomaso Layland, was the king's only brother. He was King Arawn's most trusted man and was sixth in line to the throne after the king's sons and grandchildren. Tomaso looked at her daughter.

"I hope you are happy, Isabelle?" asked Tomaso with great hope.

Isabelle looked straight at her father and gave him a light smile.

"You will be very happy," promised Tomaso to his daughter.

Soon, a young man appeared at the doorstep of Isabelle's room. He was holding a bunch of white flowers. He approached Isabelle and knelt beside her, handing the flowers to her.

"My dear little princess, my congratulations on the happiest day of yours!" said the man. Then he rose up and bent over to whisper to the princess, "We still have time to run away, my princess. Only wish for it!"

"Get lost," said Isabelle, smiling through tears, and took the flowers.

The man opened his arms widely and embraced Isabelle. "Be happy, little sister," he said to Isabelle.

Isabelle tried to hide her tears. Sanders was not only her brother but her best friend. He was Isabelle's protector, her soul mate, and one she trusted more than anyone else. Isabelle embraced her brother farewell. She knew very well that after leaving her room, they would not have another chance to say goodbye to each other.

The royal carriage went slowly among the crowd saluting their princess. Isabelle tried to calm down. The noise of the drums was distractive. It was everywhere. The people were playing drums on the main street and the two second biggest roads that led to the chapel's gates. When the carriage turned left at the beginning of the main street, the noise became louder. Isabelle could hear the joyful hollers of the people.

When the chapel bells started ringing, Isabelle understood that they were very close to the destination. At the main gates, the coach stopped, and Isabelle went outside. Her brother, Sanders, helped Isabelle come down. The sun was shining brightly, and all the people gathered from two sides of the red carpet were happy to welcome their princess. From all sides, flowers were being thrown.

Isabelle remembered the stories of her mother about fairy princesses and princes, about beautiful wedding ceremonies, from her childhood. Isabelle could hardly believe the view that appeared beside her came, in reality, from her dreams.

With the music of playing instruments, Isabelle entered the chapel. Her father, Tomaso, was walking next to her, and together they directed toward the priest through the long road. From both sides of the road, the ceremony's guests were standing to greet the bride.

Holding her father's hand, Isabelle slowly stepped forward. For a moment her gaze fixated on the chapel's ceiling. From two sides, the flags of two kingdoms hung over each row of the seats.

On the left side, she saw the flag of the Layland House, where the picture of the sun crossed with two swords was illustrated. The swords belonged to two brothers. They were the first men who gathered all people together and led the army against Quinn and the followers of the dark power a thousand years ago. After the victory, the people made the brothers their kings and gave them the name Layland—"Protector of Men."

On the right side, Isabelle could see the row of the two different flags of King Leon's house, hung side by side. In the first flag, a picture of a mystical beast was depicted. A griffin! The creature—which had the head, wings, and forelegs of an eagle and the body of a lion—looked frightening.

Isabelle believed that if the creature from the flag were real, it probably would lash out at the people. The main reason King Leon had the mystical beast's image on his family flag was that it was the protecting spirit of their house. The people believed that the centenarian king's roots were deeply related to the mystical creature and the king's family name came from his great ancestor: a mystical half bird and half lion—the griffin.

The second flag of King Leon's house was even stranger as it consisted of only black color that was bordered by a golden line of infinity signs. The black-colored flag was a symbol of darkness. It reminded the bearers of the flag from the House of Griffin that inception belonged to the darkness. Darkness existed before light was created and would always exist for eternity. The color also represented power. Dark power, beautiful yet destructive, presented the might to all who bore it. It was the power that King Taron Ulyses had banned many years ago. The griffins bore the symbol of darkness so as not to forget their origin. The sign of infinity showed the edge of the power. The edge that did exist in an indefinite dimension only. The thought that their world was surrounded by darkness made Isabelle even sadder.

Then she looked at the groom, who was waiting for her at the chancel. She tried to avoid his gaze and looked down at her skirt. Isabelle tried to swallow, but something hard was stuck in her throat. When Isabelle approached the chancel, the priest advised both King Leon and her to kneel.

Isabelle sat down, and the wedding ceremony started. She could hear the priest reading a prayer and going around them with a little bell. After finishing the prayer, the priest burned a strange herb and added it to the water in a chalice. He handed the chalice to Isabelle, and she took a sip. The priest repeated the same ritual with the centenarian king. After the two of them took a sip from the chalice, the priest asked the bride and groom to rise and look at each other so he could announce them as one family. Isabelle stood up and turned toward her husband, but when she looked at King Leon, she became dumbfounded.

How many times she had imagined the day when she would appear beside the king of the centenarians, looking at him with hatred. How she wanted to show her feelings to the king, wanting him to know the truth . . . But all she could do, standing in the chapel and all covered in white, was to stay on her feet.

Looking at the fine young man with a noble and serious look, she couldn't say anything or think about anything. She had never thought that all her efforts would be in vain beside the feeling of fear. Isabelle squeezed her palm to get rid of her trembling. All the horror of the fact that she realized about her marriage became real.

With all her thoughts, Isabelle misheard the priest's announcement. She came to her consciousness only when King Leon bent over and gave her a kiss. Isabelle was scared to fall. She felt the ground under her feet about to vanish when his lips touched hers. She looked at him with eyes wide open. Leon was a tall and handsome man with dark-brown hair, green eyes, and a piercing gaze.

Leon also noticed the trembling of his bride when he took Isabelle's hand.

"Isabelle?" He watched her. "We have to go," Leon stated calmly and turned toward the chapel's main door.

Isabelle did not say anything but obeyed the king. Together, holding each other's hands extending forward, the two of them left the chapel. She felt how his strong hand squeezed her palm. His touch was burning her skin. When the big doors of the chapel opened, the people greeted the newly married royal couple with screams and yells, throwing bunches of flowers into the air. When Isabelle approached the carriage, King Leon held the door.

"We will meet at the palace," the king informed Isabelle.

Isabelle dared to look once again at the king. She couldn't read the king's thoughts from his expression. When the doors closed, Isabelle sighed with relief. The carriage set off.

Chapter 3

The Worst Son

What a wonderful morning, thought Thaen sitting on his cozy sofa in the corner of the room.

He took a sip from an old bottle of wine. Thaen went to the window and moved the heavy, dark-red curtains aside. The sun was shining brightly. He watched the blue sea behind the high walls of the old fortress. The sound of cawing seagulls mixed with the noise of strong waves striking the shores of Perle de la Mer Island in the English Channel.

The island was located between Guernsey and St. Anna Islands in the northwest of France. It was a very small island. All the island inhabitants were military personnel of King Arawn Layland's royal army. About five hundred soldiers were in service in the fortress.

The youngest son of the king, Thaen Layland, was sent to the fortress to serve. After his brothers, Prince Asael and Prince Keon, and the sons of his first brother, Thaen was fifth in line to the throne of Rhodareen. At his early age of twenty-five, Prince Thaen looked almost like his lord father, King Arawn.

Thaen had his features—dark hair and brown eyes—but he was uglier and thinner. For more than three years, the prince had been spending his days and nights in the fortress. Thaen had been called to the capital city four times since he arrived at Perle de la Mer. It was a requirement from an heir to participate in the summit held on behalf of strengthening the fortress defense. His father, Arawn, used to say that future kings must know how to rule their people as well as how to defend them. The future was unpredictable, life was ruthless, and no one ever knew who would be the one to wear the crown.

Perle de la Mer was very important to the king. Its location helped the king to track the northern lands. On one hand, Thaen liked to be away from his father's capital city. The father-and-son relationship was not at its best. The king loved his son, but it was not enough for Arawn to be proud of him. Despite the fact that Thaen was quite smart and loved reading a lot, the king's youngest heir was weak. Because of health problems, Thaen had spent most of his childhood surrounded by healers. He never was a good warrior. He never was a winner. He always used to be behind his brothers. The princes were ahead of him in everything.

Keon was the best fighter. He was the winner of every tournament held in the capital while Thaen used to lose every battle. Only Prince Sanders, his cousin, the son of Tomaso Layland, could fight with Keon as an equal opponent. The king's youngest son had always stood in the last row of the participants while his brothers received all the applause for their victories.

However, Keon was irrepressible. Most of the time, the king had to send his men to the far borders of his kingdom in search of his second son. Wherever there was a fighting contest, Keon was the first in the line of volunteers.

Contrary to Prince Keon, Prince Asael and Sanders, in addition to their good fighting skills, were distinguished with their sharp minds. King Arawn loved being accompanied by his eldest son and his nephew, especially when he was on a hunt. They were good companions.

Thaen got used to being in the last place regarding importance. Arawn always wanted too much from him—that much that his son could never give in return.

The door opened, and a man in armor entered the room. He was a senior officer at the fortress.

"Your Grace!" he called for his master.

Thaen raised his hand high and then threw the wine bottle onto the floor with all his strength. The splinters of the broken bottle scattered all around.

"Damn you, Herv!" shouted Thaen. "The closed door is for knocking!"

"My apologies . . ." The man looked down.

Commander Lothar appeared behind the soldier. He knocked twice on the heavy door and entered the room with a wide smile.

"Don't get mad at the poor man. I urged him to be quick!"

Then he looked at the officer and made a signal. The man closed the door from outside. Lothar went directly to the corner and sank into a cozy armchair. He was a tall man in his middle age. He was the royal troop's chief commander at Perle de la Mer, responsible for all military actions occurring in the English Channel. Lothar had mentored Thaen during his stay at the fortress for years. They had become very close. His sharp mind and critical thinking ability made Lothar one of the best military men in the realm. He was a nephew of Lord Harvin Calhoun, the first military man and head of the royal arms.

From a young age, Thaen had admired Lord Harvin, the uncle of Commander Lothar, and wished to be like him. Lord Harvin Calhoun was born to bear a sword. He was a man of honor. He was the chief warlord of King Arawn. Lord Harvin showed undoubtful courage during the war against the savages of Skin Islands in the North Sea. His participation in the religious wars that occurred in Central Europe was significant, and yet the war, being held for more than twenty-five years, had to end soon.

"What brought you up here in such an early hour of the morning?" the prince asked, interested.

"What could a bored man do in your chamber, Your Grace?" Lothar answered the question with another question. "Came to talk! Besides, the sun is up. Not that early! What were you celebrating?" Lothar hinted at the remains of the bottle on the floor.

"Do I need any reason to celebrate?" Thaen answered rudely.

"You have been drinking too much for the last few months. The king won't like your new habit," Lothar expressed his worries.

"The king has many worries to think about. This one is out of importance." Thaen sighed. He went to the shelf and took two wine bottles, handing one to Lothar. "Would you like to join me?"

Lothar grinned and approached Thaen. He took a cup from the top shelf and poured wine into his cup. Thaen opened the lid of his bottle and drank directly from it.

"You could have attended the wedding of your sister," added Lothar while taking a sip. "And you decided to stay on this damned island with soldiers. You are missing such great fun."

"Didn't want to see the smug face of my father. Probably he is proud of his work. He made a great deal with the centenarian king." Thaen chuckled. "It's so like him."

"They are strong allies. We need it." Lothar looked at his cup. With two sips he almost emptied it. He took the bottle and filled the cup again. "You could've found other interesting activities there."

"Decided to save myself from unpleasant conversations with unpleasant men." Thaen emptied his bottle.

"It's a pity that you can't enjoy your time listening to the latest achievements of Prince Keon. It would bring you great pleasure," said Lothar, trying to tease the prince. He knew well Thaen's unbearable hatred of being compared to his brothers.

"What a shame," the prince said with sarcasm.

"I heard about the recent engagement of Keon," continued Lothar. "The Landers are now favored by the king—"

But Thaen cut his words. "If you came to congratulate me on his stupid achievements, you can shut the door from behind!"

"Aren't you happy?"

"My brother quickly recovered from his recent loss!" said Thaen gloomily.

His brother was engaged to the girl from the Damen family. However, soon after the engagement, the girl died. Some stated that the girl was poisoned. The Lander family took advantage of the tragedy right away and offered their daughter to the second son of the king. His brother Keon's wedding ceremony with a Lander girl was expected to be the second-largest wedding of the year that had to occur right after the wedding of his cousin Isabelle.

"I am sorry for Lady Damen, a daughter of a great house. She was too young . . ."

"Too tiny, too ugly. Unpleasant woman . . . Great house? For sure . . . unlucky she was," stated Thaen indifferently.

"Death does not choose by age," Lothar said sighing.

"A tragedy for the Damens is luck for the Landers," Thaen said smirking. "At least my brother is happy. I heard the Lander girl is pretty enough."

"Yes, she is," admitted Lothar. "What about you? You are quite lucky too to have Lady Catherine Stavros as your bride."

"The worst son of the king got the best pearl of the kingdom." A satisfactory smile appeared on Thaen's face.

He was promised the only daughter and the heir of Lord Raymond Stavros of Southbrent. The House of Stavros was one of the richest houses of Rhodareen and was related to the king's family. Lord Stavros was a cousin of late queen Ellinor, Thaen's mother. Catherine was a beautiful young woman with a great family name and endless inheritance.

"She is a real rose of Rhodareen."

"You could've seen her if you attended the wedding of your cousin," said Lothar.

"Maybe later, some other day . . ." Thaen approached the tower's open windows.

"Alas, you are missing such entertainment." As a master and a teacher, Lothar wished his ward only the best, but the way how Thaen tried to avoid his family bothered the man.

"Izzy could be a great queen with her kindness, the greatest queen of two worlds . . . hopefully!" Thaen said.

As the only female member of the royal family, Isabelle was precious to all. Isabelle was the only one whom Thaen loved and cared for among all his relatives.

"She will be!" Lothar confirmed Thaen's words.

Thaen looked at Lothar. "Let's drink to new beginnings!" He raised his bottle high.

Lothar also raised his cup to support the prince.

While the two of them were celebrating the occasion in Thaen's chamber, the other soldiers were training in the yard. The guard opened the fortress's gates for those who returned from a morning run on a rocky wasteland of the island.

In a long row of threes, the soldiers crossed the gates. On the east wing of the fortress, a few soldiers were gathered under the canopy tent. They were watching how a junior officer was playing draughts with the freshman of the fortress. The young soldier came to the fortress two weeks ago for the service. He dared to make a laugh of the two officers playing draughts earlier this morning. The eldest one got angry at him and offered a game to the newcomer. This was the fifth game, and the newcomer emerged the winner for the fifth time.

"This is unfair. You are cheating!" shouted the officer.

"Sir, these are not cards. So many witnesses around us. I would never dare," responded the boy with a smile.

"Boy, you couldn't beat me fairly, for sure! Impossible! How did you do it?" The officer was angry at his bad luck.

"You did see me playing! Just admit I am good at draughts, sir!"

One of the soldiers watching the game stretched out his hand to his fellow. "So where are my coins?"

The second one standing next to him took four coins and gave them to the soldier. They bet on who would win the next game. The one who supported the officer lost.

Another soldier standing around added, "The smallest one stepped on the foot of the best one! What a shame."

"My lady mother used to say, 'The best fighters are not the best thinkers,'" added another one.

The young soldier chuckled at the words of his peer. He was proud of himself for giving them a nice game. The other officer standing over his head slapped the soldier at his nape.

"He wants to say, you are weak! Fool!"

"Hey!" shouted the soldier. "Watch your hands!"

At that moment Herv appeared at the doorway of the main building. He stepped out into the yard. The soldiers removed the game board.

"What are you doing here?" asked Herv.

"Nothing! Sir!" shouted all the soldiers at once.

Herv turned around and was about to leave when the junior officer once again slapped the nape of the soldier for fun.

"Hey!" shouted that one, turning at his offender.

Herv returned and looked at two of them, who pretended as if nothing had happened. At that moment one of the guards on the watchers' tower shouted for the commander.

"Ship on the horizon! Ship on the horizon!"

Herv ran to the top. When he reached the watcher's tower, the guard handed him the spyglass and pointed to the small shadow, fifteen inches high, of a black ship to the north of Perle de la Mer. Herv looked through the glass. The ship with black sails was sailing toward the island. Its sails had a drawing of crossed swords in a fire around a white circle.

"Why are these savages not in their caves?" wondered Herv. "Guard! Ring the bells! Ring the bells!" Herv shouted.

The watcher pulled the bell's long ropes.

"All men to the wall! Move the cannons to the crenels. Everyone! Get prepared!" Herv urged the others.

The soldiers ran to the top of the fortress walls holding their swords. The two groups of soldiers hurried to get in a row at the front yard of the fortress. Four soldiers pulled the heavy gates and locked them after.

"Get prepared. Don't shoot without command!" Herv ordered, and he rushed to Prince Thaen's chamber.

Thaen and Lothar were sitting around the table. With a loud laugh, Lothar wiped his teary eyes.

"I didn't know about your dream of becoming a great man that history will remember for centuries . . . But how?" Lothar kept laughing.

"You don't believe in me?" asked Thaen, feeling insulted.

"I do believe in you, but I can't imagine how it is possible in this damned land," said Lothar.

"All I need are reliable men," assured Thaen.

"You know I am with you wherever you go. You have me. But it won't make you great." Lothar put his cup on the table. The two of them had already finished a few bottles of wine. "History remembers the great kings and heroes. You are not the king . . . and definitely won't be."

Thaen gazed at Lothar. "Are you sure?" he asked.

"Yes, man!" stated Lothar with confidence. "You are fifth in line to the throne. The line may become longer once Keon introduces his own heirs to the world. And hero? Damn . . . we are living in peace. The protection of ordinary men passes to the hands of the centenarians."

"Did I say I want to protect the miserables of the world?" Thaen had hardly finished his words when they heard the bell ring from outside.

Lothar ran to the windows to see what was happening outside. "What the hell, why are they making that noise?"

"Lothar!" Thaen tried to stop him.

"What?" Lothar had already reached the door.

"I am summoning a meeting," said Thaen. He looked at Lothar with a piercing gaze, as if he was checking him.

"What kind of summon?" wondered Lothar. "Why?"

"I said I want to change history. I'll change the world," Thaen said smirking. His words sounded mysterious.

Lothar tried to understand his thoughts. At that moment the door opened, and Herv rushed in, hardly breathing.

"Your Grace! Commander Lothar! There is a ship on the horizon. It bears the symbol of the Arsandars of the Skin Islands. The soldiers are ready to fight!" informed Herv.

Lothar didn't like seeing the Arsandars' ship on the horizon. The inhabitants of the Skin Islands were wild people. For hundreds of thousands of years, those people had denied the reign of their king. They were uncontrollable savages without a god and beliefs who could easily be sold out for miserable coins. His uncle, Lord Harvin, had fought against those people for many years, and the savages had been defeated. But they were like insects. Even totally destroyed from the entire root, the Arsandars always managed to survive and multiply in number.

Lothar looked at Thaen. What could it possibly mean? The prince assured him about a summon at the moment wild people were about to invade their sea territory.

"How many ships did you count?" asked Lothar, still watching the prince. Then he turned to Herv.

"Only one, sir!" answered Herv.

"Good! These bastards will regret daring to swim into our shores." Lothar went toward the sofa and took his sword from the ground near the table. "What about the cannons?"

"Everything is ready," still standing at the doorway, Herv answered.

However, Lothar had hardly reached the boy when Thaen stopped him.

"I would not hurry to get into a fight with the savages," said Thaen to Herv. "Go and tell the officers not to fire without my command," he ordered.

Herv didn't know what to do and waited for Lothar's command.

"Thaen, what the hell are you doing?" asked Lothar with both anger and horror.

"I already gave you a command, soldier!" Thaen said to Herv. "Close the door from behind."

When Herv left the room, Thaen looked at the impatient Lothar awaiting his explanation in one corner.

"Don't look at me like that. I've told you what I want. These savages are my allies, and with them, I will build a new world. I want you to follow me as your leader and your king . . ."

"Thaen . . . what are you talking about? What are you doing?" Lothar couldn't hide his astonishment.

"You made a promise at the gates of Rhodareen to serve me. You promised to do whatever it takes to conduct your duty with honor." Looking at Commander Lothar, Thaen felt he couldn't trust the man.

"I made a promise to serve the king and the kingdom. My promise was made to the throne." Lothar's breaths became heavier, his face expressions gloomier.

"You are my friend, Lothar, and I want to rely on you!"

"You can rely on me in everything, but I won't sign on to what you are asking me."

"You don't know yet what I am asking you," Thaen said laughing.

"I know!" shouted Lothar. He approached Thaen and grabbed his collar. "What you are doing is treason! Stop before it's too late. I beg you!"

With one strong movement, Thaen released his collar from Lothar's hands. "Lothar!"

"Thaen, I know you. You won't do that! Don't do that," Lothar kept begging. "Why not drown this damned ship with its damned people?"

"I told you, I need allies," Thaen interrupted him. "Strong allies."

Lothar became numb. He shook his head and stepped farther from Thaen.

"No, this isn't right!" Only these words he could hardly utter. He couldn't believe that Thaen could betray his own family. He looked at Thaen with disgust. Then he turned toward the door and went with fast steps. He wanted to leave the room and warn the others. He had to put Thaen under charge and prevent him from making a mistake.

But Thaen caught him before he could reach the doorway. Thaen closed Lothar's mouth with his one hand and struck the man's heart with his other hand, using a knife he kept at his waistband.

"I am sorry, my friend," whispered Thaen. "When I will be king, I must be sure that everyone is on my side."

Lothar fell, choking in his blood.

"I thought you were a smart man," said Thaen, looking at the dead body of the commander. "Alas!"

Thaen then left the room. He met Herv at the veranda at the fourth level of the tower.

"Your Grace!"

Thaen only nodded to the officer.

"The enemy's ship is coming, Your Grace. What will be the orders?" Herv asked Thaen.

"The Arsandars are not enemies anymore. They are our allies," answered Thaen.

His words made the soldier worry. "Where is Commander Lothar?" inquired Herv.

His question irritated Thaen. "Too nosy, you are," Thaen answered rudely.

"Your Grace—"

"He is fighting his own thoughts. Give the old man some time."

Thaen watched how the ship turned its nose to the berth. Another junior officer was passing by close to the veranda. Thaen stopped him and gave him the order to open the gates.

The soldier looked down and shouted to the guards, "Open the gates!"

The head of the guards standing in the yard wondered about the prince's command.

He repeated the order, "Open the gates!"

Four soldiers ran to the gates and started pulling them. Herv watched how his fellows opened the gates. They were waiting for the guests, as Thaen informed. He felt something was wrong. He watched Thaen while Thaen was looking at the opposite side.

Unnoticed, Herv went to the prince's chamber. He slowly raised the handle of the door and pushed it. However, he couldn't open the door fully as something was stuck behind it. From the small aperture of the door, Herv looked inside the room. Scared, Herv backed away. The dead man's two wide open eyes seemed to be looking straight at him. In a rush, Herv closed the door. His breath quickened. The enemy was coming, and they had opened their gates to welcome death.

For a second Herv thought about what he had to do. Thaen belonged to the royal family. He was an heir. One day he could become the future king of all people, and this man ordered them to let the savages in. With his palms, Herv covered his face. He tried to concentrate. Then he ran.

He ran as fast as he could, shouting out loud, "Close the gates! Close the gates! Treason! Close the gates!" And still he ran.

Thaen looked around to see who dared to contradict his order—that one coming to the veranda still shouting, urging the men to close the gates.

Herv didn't pay attention to his master. "Prepare the cannons!"

The soldiers first looked at Herv with astonishment. Thaen himself was confused to see the man of such a low rank finding the courage to act against the will of his lord. The confused soldiers at the gates started pushing the heavy gates back. Another soldier standing next to Herv received a subtle sign from his lord.

Thaen gave the order. The man was fast. Herv fell lifeless in the arms of the traitor. The enemy was already inside the fortress. The others, too confused, could hardly understand the situation, then the noise of a cannon gun grabbed their attention. In seconds, part of the south wing battlement collapsed. The fortress was under attack.

Chapter 4

Useless Gift

Little fairy, little fairy,
Fly to my window, I'll sing for you
Little fairy, little fairy,
Don't be afraid, I am a friend to you.
I'll give you love, I'll give you a smile
I'll give you all the shining stars . . .

"Move aside, you stupid child, or I'll give you a good beating!" shouted an old man riding a one-horse open carriage to the girl walking on the edge of the main road. "Sing at home to your folks, *chanteuse*[1]*!"

The old man's shout frightened the girl, and she jumped onto the pedestrian road. The paper bag that she held fell out of her hands, and all the goods inside rolled away. For a while, she stayed still in place and looked at the carriage until it disappeared out of sight.

The girl said, "*Stupide!*[2]*" She was thinking about the carriage driver that passed by. Then she looked at the little creature with golden wings flying around her. "Isn't he?" she asked.

For her early age of seventeen, the girl was tall. Her brown eyes were shiny. Her skin was white as snow, so her friends used to make fun of her, saying she was as transparent as water. She wore a long, blue dress with a long, black two-sided apron. Over the dress, the girl wore a hooded black cloak. Her hair was hidden under a dark-

---

1 * *chanteuse* (Fr.)—a female singer

2 * *Stupide!* (Fr.)—Foolish!

blue bonnet. The girl crouched and started collecting things from the ground and putting them back inside the paper bag.

"Bread, one apple, two apples, third one . . ." she counted while collecting them.

When she bent to take the other apple from the ground, a little boy in very odd and dirty clothes took it and ran away. The girl looked after the running boy and smiled.

If you'd asked for it, I would give it to you. But you didn't, thought the girl regarding the boy thief.

The girl raised her right hand to the air toward the boy and whispered, "Return to me! *Yal!*" She waited for a little longer and repeated her words, "*Yal . . . Yal . . .*"

But to her great disappointment, nothing happened. When the girl tried to spell once again, someone called her name, and she turned around to see who it could be.

"Amare! Here you are! I was looking for you. Where have you been?" asked a girl her age. She wore similar clothes like Amare did. The dark-blue dress with a long two-sided apron was the uniform of the house they belonged to.

"Charlotte!" Amare called her friend. She was happy to see her friend.

"What are you doing here?" the girl asked Amare.

"A beggar stole my apple. What will I say to Mother Abella?"

Amare's friend Charlotte looked toward the place where Amare pointed out. There was no boy on the street. He was gone long ago. Charlotte raised her right hand and uttered the spell that Amare had tried before.

"*Yal!*" said Charlotte, and a small red apple appeared on her handbreadth.

"You are a witch!" yelled Amare to tease Charlotte. At the same time, she was a little angry at herself as she failed to use the spell.

"Oh, look who's talking," Charlotte said, smiling at her friend while handing her the apple.

Charlotte knew how Amare was desperate for magic. She had been training her skills her whole life but in vain. Despite the chief witch saying the girl was special among all other witches, Amare never had succeeded in using any spell.

"You could be easier with those poor beggars. Just one apple doesn't make you rich, but for them . . . ," continued Charlotte.

"It is not because I am greedy about the apple. Stealing is not good. Besides, I just wanted to test my skills. You know . . . I am useless."

Charlotte felt sadness and anger in her friend's trembling voice.

"You will be able to spell, just give yourself a little time. Let me show you what I bought from the market today. Look! It is so beautiful," Charlotte said, taking a red ribbon and bouncing it in the air.

"It is beautiful, but where are you going to wear it? We almost never take off our bonnet. Even if we do, very rarely. As I said, never . . ." Amare took one end of the ribbon.

"I can wear it under the bonnet. If no one can see it, it doesn't mean I can't make myself happy," Charlotte said smiling.

"Will you let me try it for some other days?" asked Amare.

"No, of course, I won't," Charlotte teased her friend and took the ribbon away.

"But I am your best friend," Amare begged her friend.

"Still," objected Charlotte, putting the ribbon back to her pocket. "Let's go, we need to hurry."

The two girls went down the street and directed to the east. Soon, they reached the gates of Mr. Bastien's old house.

"*Bonjour,*[3] Mr. Bastien!" shouted Charlotte to the old man who appeared at the gates.

There was a small stall near the gates. Different types of herbs and flowers in baskets were on the stall shelves.

"Good day, Mr. Bastien," said Amare with a smile.

"Good day, my dear girls," the old gardener welcomed them. "Come inside, I'll show you new seeds."

The girls thanked Mr. Bastien and crossed the gates. Through the narrow road under the wall, the girls directed to the inner yard of the gardener's house. Followed by the two witch sisters, Mr. Bastien unlocked the door that led to the second garden. It was a big garden with a high glass ceiling and surrounded by crystal walls. Green trees and different flowers rose high. The sweet scent of flowers filled the surroundings.

---

3 * *Bonjour.* (Fr.)—Good morning. Hello.

The girls walked into the garden chatting happily. Soon, the gardener's wife came to greet the girls. Small in height, the tiny woman with bold hair widely opened her hands for a hug. After the warm greetings, Charlotte handed Mrs. Bastien the list of the necessary herbs for the abbot.

Mr. Bastien sat on a bench in the corner of the garden, next to the door. He put on his glasses and started carving. He started this carving work of a small butterfly from wood a few days ago. He didn't have much time to finish it earlier. The girls ran toward Mr. Bastien when they saw his work.

"Oh, Mr. Bastien, you have already finished it!" screamed Charlotte.

The old gardener smiled. He carved the last line of the butterfly's wing. "Ready?" said Mr. Bastien and put it on the widely opened palm of Amare.

"It is so beautiful," whispered the girl.

Charlotte looked down from behind Amare's shoulders. "*Pardon,*[4*]" said Charlotte, taking the wooden craftwork from her friend's hand. "Can you give it to me?" She looked at the butterfly and whispered, "*Noji ree . . .*"

The girls stood still, waiting for the miracle. They were afraid of doing any movement, even to take a breath. In seconds, the wooden butterfly became alive. It flapped its wings. The girls screamed with joy when the butterfly flew.

"I did it! I did it!" screamed Charlotte.

"You did it!" jumped Amare. She was truly happy about the success of her friend.

The wooden butterfly rose high. It jumped from one flower to another, enjoying the sweetness of the flower petals. Mr. Bastien looked at the girls with admiration. He loved magic. He loved how the girls from the light house came to his garden and spelled. He loved to see the world from different angles. He could spend hours with the girls, carving them different shapes of animals. Soon, Mrs. Bastien brought out two baskets full of all the abbot's requested herbs.

"I marked all that I could collect for you from the list, except one. We haven't left the wild salvia in our garden." Mrs. Bastien handed the baskets to the girls.

"Thank you very much, Mrs. Bastien," said Amare.

---

4 * *Pardon.* (Fr.)—Sorry.

"Please don't worry. We'll look for salvia in another place. We'll find it," said Charlotte. She raised her hand to the sky and whispered, *"Nadhes yal . . ."*

The butterfly returned and sat on Charlotte's hand. Then it turned back into an ordinary wooden toy.

"Thank you for your present, Mr. Bastien," said Charlotte, putting the butterfly inside her bag.

The girls went out holding big baskets. As soon as they reached halfway to the abbot, small raindrops started falling down.

"Raindrops." Charlotte looked up to check the dark clouds. "It is going to rain heavily, let's run!"

The two friends ran together along the road under the rain, and at the end of the street, they turned right and entered the gates of Saint Daman Abbot located in the corner.

The abbot served as a saint house for the witches of light in the Selestat commune located in the northeast region of France. It was a school where the members could learn the language of Mother Nature, astronomy, and medicine together with witchcraft. The place provided a sanctuary for centenarians who were seeking help from outside. The two girls, totally soaked under the rain, sighed with relief when they entered the abbot and saw other sisters rushing back and forth in the long corridors.

Although the abbot looked like a small building with a high front tower, it was quite big inside with many corridors, rooms, and several gardens. They called it an optical illusion. With a help of a spell, the witches of the abbot could create a sanctuary for centenarians laid over a long distance.

In the inner yard of Saint Daman Abbot, located in the east wing of the old building, an old woman in a long, white cloak was walking. The yard was small and surrounded by arched walls all around. After having a little walk in the yard, the woman stood and looked up to the sky. Her head was covered with a hood over a white bonnet. She looked to be over fifty. Afterward, the woman knelt and picked up a yellow leaf from the ground. She exhaled a deep sigh.

This year promises to be colder and severer than the previous ones, thought the woman. She took another leaf from the ground. All her thoughts disappeared at once when two girls entered the yard and called for her.

"Mother Abella!"

The woman looked at them. She rose up and went toward the girls. Mother Abella was the eldest one at Saint Daman Abbot. She was the keeper of the light community and was responsible for all the young readers at school. Mother Abella gave a bright smile to the girls. With a slight gesture, she showed the girls the arch that led out of the garden. The girls followed Mother Abella to the next hall.

"How was your visit, girls? Have you found all that you needed in the market?"

"Yes, almost," answered Charlotte. "Except wild salvia. Mr. Bastien hadn't left any. He said that he will go to collect them next week."

"Good. Maybe we'll send a servant to the neighboring village. We don't have much time. We have to close the gates when the last leaf falls. You better go and check the others. Is there anything missing too?" Mother Abella pointed to the other members of the abbot returning from their tasks.

"Yes, Mother Abella." Charlotte turned away and went toward the east side of the building.

Mother Abella directed to the opposite side. She wanted to have some privacy in her own room. Then she stopped, noticing that Amare was following her instead of going with her friend Charlotte. She looked as if something was bothering her.

"Do you want to ask me something, Amare?"

"I am sorry, Mother Abella. I don't want to take much of your time, but there is something that I am worried about."

"I am listening to you."

"I am already seventeen, but my gift has not yet been awakened."

Mother Abella looked at Amare, waiting for the girl to continue her sentence.

"You said I am special. However, no matter how I tried, there is no magic in me."

"You need to give a little time to yourself. It will come."

"Witches obtain their gift from birth. Even Melanie spells well at the age of five."

"Amare, I know what I said to you. You are special, and it is not a lie. You will understand me. At the right time, it will come to you," the old woman tried to reassure the girl.

"I want to study together with the other girls. Maybe it will help me obtain my power," Amare interrupted the eldest witch.

Mother Abella continued her talk in a calm voice, "There is no need to go to common class. You should keep studying how to control yourself. It will help you to control the power—"

"The power that I don't have . . . Why don't you let me join the girls? I want to learn how to spell." Amare was very anxious. She could not understand why her custodian hadn't let her study magic all these years. The feeling of being useless was killing the girl. "Maybe you should let me study with the other girls."

"No!" uttered Mother Abella strictly. "You are impatient. You must learn how to control your emotions."

"You don't understand. Maybe this is my chance to obtain the power! Please, Mother Ab—"

Amare wanted to beg her more to allow her to attend the common classes. However, the old woman didn't want to listen to her and interrupted her speech.

"You have a task! Go and help the other girls to finish today's work. After that, go to your own class."

Mother Abella turned away and left Amare alone in the empty hall, letting her know that their conversation was over. Amare stood alone for a while, then she wiped away her tears and directed toward the east side, where Charlotte had gone. After finishing all her tasks, Amare went to her classroom.

In a small room with closed red curtains, Amare sat for several hours. She was sitting on the floor in the middle of the room. She moved the table with a chair aside when she entered the room in the afternoon. Her eyes were closed. She could hear the caws of crows outside her window.

"You need to concentrate! You need to be patient . . . Be patient."

Amare took several deep sighs. No matter how hard she tried, she could not calm down after her conversation with the eldest witch. She could not understand why the witch didn't want her to learn witchcraft. Was there anything the old woman hiding from her? She could not find any answers. For many years Amare had sat in a room alone, staying in her study room for hours after her special classes.

"Please don't stay till late hour!" asked her teacher while leaving the classroom earlier that day.

Amare reread the materials that she and her teacher had learned for the day. Then she moved her books aside, blew off the candles, and sat in the middle of the room. Mother Abella told her to control herself, to learn how to listen to the silence.

She remembered well when, a few years ago, she had approached Mother Abella and told her that she was ready to join the other girls. Mother Abella had told her to concentrate and ask what she could see and what she could hear. They had been in the main square of the Selestat commune with the other readers. Amare could not understand why the old woman was asking to tell her what she could see as everyone could see what was happening around her. But she had started telling Mother Abella what she had heard and seen.

"I see a craftsman. I see people celebrating harvest day. I see children playing ball in the next corner, and I can see carriages with horses. There is a musician playing a recorder . . . and I . . ."

Amare had kept counting everything in order. But Mother Abella had stopped her and said that she was not ready to join the others and she would never be ready to join them as her mind was disturbed by all the noise around. She couldn't find privacy among those people. She couldn't control her mind. Amare opened her eyes and looked at the window.

"You are disturbing me," said the girl to the cawing bird outside her window. Again she tried to concentrate but couldn't. Amare got angry and screamed in the empty room, "Dear God, what is wrong with me?"

She stood and opened the door. Amare was expecting a conversation with one of her principals next week regarding her success, thoughts, and beliefs, but she couldn't stay longer in the study room alone and went to her own room.

On the way back to her room, she stopped near the common class where her friends were learning witchcraft. Amare envied them very much as they could spell very well, knew how to properly use their power, and were familiar with the different types of potions. They were real witches. The only common class Amare was allowed to attend with her friends was history class, where together they studied the legends of the past—about the great war, the heroes of their world. But Amare was more interested in witchcraft that she was forbidden to learn.

Mother Abella told her that Amare had power of unseen strength that once was owned by three sisters. It was a rare gift as well as a curse. Before studying witchcraft, first, she had to learn how to control the power given by nature. Thus, the power of the mighty witch was blocked in order for the girl not to harm herself or the others around her.

Amare went to her room and sat at the corner of her bed. She took an old notebook under the blanket of her bed and started to read. It was a notebook wherein Amare wrote down all types of spells that she had learned from her friend Charlotte.

She looked at the candle on the table in the corner of the room and said with a whisper, "*Roon eib!* Give the light!" Nothing changed. "*Roon eib!*" repeated Amare. "*Noi! Noi*, you, stupid candle! You are supposed to light on."

Amare sighed deeply. At that moment the door to her room opened, and Amare saw her best friend, Charlotte, at the doorstep.

"Charlotte! Thanks to Mother Nature. I was dying here alone." Amare jumped up, ran to her friend, and pulled her inside. "Come! What was new for today?"

"Can you give me space? You are making me breathless," Charlotte said laughing. "If the principal finds out that I am teaching you magic, she will kill me."

"I am sorry, but you are my only light," begged Amare.

"I know," Charlotte said smiling. "Let's have a seat."

"So what have you learned today?"

"Don't rush me! Today the principal was angry at us. While we were waiting for her, Beatrice made the principal's chair disappear, but she couldn't return it. Even the principal could not break her spell. She had to give a lecture on foot."

"Really? How come?" Amare said smiling.

"You know Beatrice, she has problems with conjuring in the right way."

"Yes, of course, she has. And my skills are worth not even half of hers."

"Amare—" Charlotte tried to object, but Amare stopped her.

"Don't say anything. It is better not to talk about it," she said with self-pity.

"Hey, don't be upset. It is the other issue. Have you talked to Mother Abella?" Charlotte took her friend's hand supportively.

Amare nodded. She looked at the notebook in her hands. "The old witch hates me. If she wanted, she could help me with my problem. She is powerful. She can do everything."

"Don't be a fool, Amare. She has no reason to hate you." Charlotte wished she could help her friend.

"There is no other explanation why she doesn't want to help me. The word *impossible* doesn't exist for Mother Abella."

"Okay, she hates you!" confirmed Charlotte.

"Everyone hates me!" complained Amare to her friend.

"Hey, I like you, fool girl! Don't forget!" Charlotte wanted to cheer her friend up and started tickling her.

"Stop! Stop! Please, I hate tickling! Stop! I hate you!" screamed Amare.

"Good! I like you!" Charlotte said laughing at Amare. "Hey, silly! I can give you my ribbon to try if you stop complaining."

"Really? Will you? I have already stopped." Amare smiled at her friend with her mouth wide open.

"See?" Charlotte also smiled and took out the red ribbon that she had bought from the market that day.

Amare took off her bonnet, and her friend made her hair into a pigtail with the ribbon. The girls started giggling and playing together. In a while, the girls put their bonnets back on and went downstairs to join the others for the evening meal.

Chapter 5

Feast for the Kings

With joyful laughter, the guests' pleasant conversations, and the sounds of musical instruments—the great hall of Incitydoor Palace, with three big windows looking to the inner backyard with a lake, was bright and shining. Thousands of candles lit above were sparkling in color. The hall was decorated with flowers and candlelight. In every five steps along the wall, statues of all the kings from the Layland Dynasty were put in a row. The marble floor was so clean and shiny as it reflected the beautiful design of the ceiling. The ceiling was high and covered with carvings of angels with wings. The atmosphere inside was uplifting.

Isabelle, sitting very high on the bridal throne, was watching the special entertainment for the evening. Dozens of dancers in red, making movements in time, were going around in a circle. Their faces were covered with golden masks. The long, red skirts of the girls' dresses reaching the ground fluttered every time they made a turn. Their long, curly hair spread over their open shoulders jumped in the air. All the dancers had the flower crocus tied to their wrists.

In the middle of the great hall, another girl was dancing on a big, round stand. The stand was decorated with flowers and held in the air by two kneeling servants. From two sides, the guests of the event—relatives of the bride, members of the two royal families, government officials, and others—were watching the entertainment. Some were chatting nicely in the corner, and some were having a feast. The long table near the windows was full of different types of meals.

Sitting alone on the throne, Isabelle took a golden cup of wine and sipped from it. She was very nervous and could hardly contain herself not to run away from her own wedding evening. While taking a sip, Isabelle watched one by one every guest present in the ceremony, including the servants.

In one of the hall's corners, her brother, Sanders, together with Keon, was talking to the ladies of the court. They all were enjoying their conversation. Keon was accompanied by his bride from the House of Lander. They were a lovely couple, and their marriage was next in line. Keon made a bow to the ladies, asking them to excuse him. Lady Lander, too, showed her respect to the others, and they went to meet other guests, the other members of the House of Lander.

Isabelle watched his brother. One of the ladies laughed at Sanders's words and with slow gestures took his hand. Sanders put his cup on the table and followed the lady to the middle of the dance area. The other ladies continued their conversation merrily. Sanders was a tall and charming young man. If there was no age difference between Isabelle and Sanders, everyone would think that they were twin siblings. However, Isabelle had been modest and shy from a young age. The absence of her mother had made a big impact on her self-confidence, leaving scars on the little girl's soul.

Compared to a timid and vulnerable princess, Sanders was a sociable, cheerful boy who easily could get into relations, making new friends . . . He was surrounded by the attention of the ladies in the court, always. Sanders was the king's dearest nephew. He had always been distinguished by his braveness and strength. For Isabelle, Sanders was a friend—the most loyal, the most reliable. She loved her brother.

When the dance was over, Sanders went to meet another honorable guest of the wedding ceremony. Lady Catherine Stavros was chatting with her siblings. She was happy to see the prince. Isabelle noticed it. Sitting high, Isabelle felt herself like a lone watcher of the tower. She also noticed this: Sanders, too, was happy to see Catherine. But there was something more than a cheerful welcome of old friends.

Lady Stavros's groom was absent from the wedding. Prince Thaen was far, far away at the moment, in his fortress on the island of Perle de la Mer. However, no one in the palace knew that the lady's heart belonged to Sanders, not to the king's youngest heir. Only Isabelle was aware of Catherine and her brother's true feelings.

Their relationship had started long ago, before Sanders had been sent to war against the wild people of Skin Islands. Isabelle was the one who had delivered the lovers' secret messages. For her, it had seemed fun to see her brother's flushed face and hear her best friend's shy giggles. She'd felt herself the most trustworthy person in the world. Isabelle had been very happy to see Catherine next to her brother.

However, everything changed when Sanders had been sent to the war. Isabelle heard that Sanders had fought bravely, standing side by side with Lord Harvin. The battles had been difficult and dangerous. The last message sent from Perle de la Mer had brought great sorrow to her family. Rhodareen had lost its ships in the channel, and Sanders had disappeared. For quite a long time, all had believed that Sanders was dead.

Fortunately, he returned home alive and in good health. However, her brother had lost his right to look at Catherine. Lady Stavros's hand had already been promised to the king's youngest son, and their wedding was waiting for an appropriate time to be celebrated. Thaen's marriage couldn't be held before Keon's and Sanders's.

Isabelle felt sorry for her brother and Lady Stavros in the same way she felt sorry for herself. When the king of the centenarians had first met Isabelle in the castle of Incitydoor, he had let Arawn know about his intentions. Isabelle was young, yet she dared to reject the mighty king. Many noble houses had asked for her hand. For anyone who won her hand and heart, Isabelle was a real treasure. But Arawn was so eager to get in his hands such a great ally that he promised her hand to the centenarian king and rejected any offer that came from the other houses.

Isabelle watched her brother's dance with Lady Stavros until it was disturbed by Calix Mesman, one of the young nobles who dared to steal her brother's dance partner. Then Isabelle's gaze was fixed on the furthest corner of the great hall, where her father, Tomaso Layland, the minister of the king's state, was. Together with the king, King Arawn Layland, and his elder son, Prince Asael, the heir of the kingdom, they were having a conversation with Leon Ulyses. After a while, King Arawn Layland and Leon Ulyses decided to have a private talk and directed to the hall's right wing, leaving behind the other lords. They went to a special room for guests on the other side of the great hall. While watching her uncle with her newly married husband going for privacy, Isabelle wondered what else they had left to talk about as all agreements had been made before the wedding.

When King Arawn approached the room's tall and heavy doors, the two servants bowed to their king and pulled the doors. Arawn entered the room, and Leon followed him. The room was wide and well furnished. The air was saturated with the scent of autumn flowers. Arawn looked at the servants and nodded, letting them know: the king needed not to be disturbed by other guests. After the doors were closed, Arawn looked at Leon.

"Please, have a seat," proposed Arawn to Leon, pointing to the big, red-covered armchair with a gesture. "I say again, so honored we are, King Leon! So honored!"

"Honored too," replied Leon with a smile and sat down on the armchair.

In seconds, the two servants guarding the room from outside opened the doors. The third servant entered the room, pulling a stand with wheels. He approached the round table close to Leon's and Arawn's seats. The servant took a silver tray and put it on the table. Arawn Layland took two golden goblets filled with red wine and handed one to Leon. Leon thanked him, taking the goblet from the king's hand. Arawn bypassed the round table and sat on the opposite armchair to his guest.

"The two houses had never had any contradictions in the past. Hopefully, we all get to benefit from the new ties of our families," said Arawn to the centenarian king.

"The House of Ulyses will support the king and his family. I promise in the name of all centenarians," said Leon Ulyses.

"I do believe in you. Griffins always had been men of their word."

"Appreciate your trust," Leon thanked him.

"Regarding the agreement . . . ," Arawn started with hesitation, but the centenarian king interrupted him.

"No worries about the treaty. I already signed," Leon said to the mortal king. "In more than two weeks, my people will start moving Arimaspians to the northeast lands. The territory of the Riphean

Mountain, with all the gold reserves, passes to your hands. Send your people to the mountain. My people will be in the northeast foothill. They will move the habitants and hand the place over to your people's command."

Sitting on his cozy seat, Arawn smiled with satisfaction. How long he had dreamed of getting this land. The Riphean Mountain was believed to have one of the richest freshwater reserves because of its cold and snowy winters. Uncounted treasure was hidden in the mountain's underground caves.

Its main inhabitants, the Arimaspians, loved gold more than anything else. They were blindfolded when talking about the gold. These one-eyed people of the north could not resist gold and were the most daring and fearless creatures. Whenever they saw a shining and sparkling thing, they would go to steal it, and now the king of the centenarians granted to Arawn the treasure that the Arimaspians had spent centuries collecting. These unusual creatures troubled both people and centenarians much, especially the House of Griffins. Maybe this was the reason Leon didn't hesitate to give the lands away when Arawn asked for the Riphean Mountain.

"Ten thousand warriors of *braaf* will join your troops in Vatika early in the spring," continued Leon. "Everything in accordance with our agreement," finished the centenarian king.

Arawn didn't expect Leon to agree to sign the Royal Treaty without requesting any change to its contents. However, the centenarian king did an unexpected step, which was totally unusual to his principles. Leon Ulyses accepted all the conditions of King Arawn. He was ready for everything for this marriage. Even ten thousand men from the centenarian army were about to be sent to the mortal royal force camp in Greece to serve under Arawn's commandment. The soldiers of the centenarian military force were enlisted from the nation of Ifri.

The Ifrans took their roots from the southwest lands of Africa. These cavemen received their name according to their lifestyle. The Ifrans were half mortals. However, not much they had in common with mankind. Humans loved the sun and couldn't bear the darkness. Spring gave them hope, and winter terrified them. However, compared to mortals, Ifrans didn't prefer either cold or hot weather. Mostly they lived in caves and were good at night vision. They were trained in special camps located all over the hot continent.

The bravest and the strongest Ifrans became braaf—the main military force of the centenarians. After graduating from the special training schools, braafs were sent to their new destination point to fulfill their duties. Courage and honor were the main values of braaf men. Ifrans were believed to be the most diligent, most loyal in the world, and Leon provided braafs under the king's will.

He understood well. Arawn was eager for the strong army. Many centuries ago, his ancestors had shown courage in the great war. All the mortal kings had put their swords on the doorways of Incitydoor, showing their greatest respect to the House of Layland, and promised to rule their countries under Layland's commandment. His house had gained power. The first Layland king had had strong allies and trusted people. However, life went on.

Year after year, the territorial division weakened the House of Layland and strengthened the power of other houses. The kings whose ancestors once showed unconditional obedience to the great king took power into their own hands. The throne became just a symbol to the people—a reminder of history, nothing more. The relationship between the Layland House and all the other kingdoms was held in traditional respect, but the king could no longer influence their domestic and foreign policies. His lieges could start war unexpectedly, destroying the neighboring lands.

People always craved power. Land expansion, treasure increase, and slave gain made small people feel great. All Arawn Layland could do was find a better solution for both sides who participated in the war.

Obviously, the strongest kingdom helped the king to deal with the best solution. It was clear as day that the king had lost his power to his people. King Arawn was afraid of his people. He was afraid of his throne's complete destruction. Trust had left King Arawn. His niece's marriage to the centenarian king gave birth to a new hope for Arawn. Even if Leon wouldn't provide safety for his house, at least the new ties would serve as an alarm to others.

"The army will be accompanied by Estevan, my cousin," added Leon.

"I met him earlier this day. Another noble son of Griffin House!" King Arawn praised him. "If you could know how grateful I am, Leon. You are very generous."

"Please don't mention it. I did it all for our new queen."

Arawn knew his niece Isabelle was very precious to King Leon. However, the reason was unknown. Leon needed neither the power and influence nor to prove his dignity or generosity. He had everything. Being king to the centenarians meant being king to the whole world.

"Izzy," King Arawn said about his niece, "may be silent or annoyed, very stubborn. But she is young, still a kid . . . I hope her ignorance in royal affairs will not bother you."

Leon put down his goblet and addressed King Arawn in a firm tone. As everyone knew, the centenarian king was a man with honor and dignity, but he was proud. He couldn't tolerate disrespectful attitude whether toward himself or his family members.

"I don't want to be rude. But from now on, Isabelle belongs to the centenarian world. She had become Ulyses. Her manners should not bother you. I hope you will show proper respect to Queen Isabelle."

Arawn noticed that the centenarian king didn't like the way he was talking about Isabelle. "See . . . she is my niece. Still hard to accept that she is no longer under my care," said Arawn, justifying himself.

"It's true, but I will appreciate it if you address her properly," required Leon with a smile.

The king didn't object. Instead, he smiled and raised his goblet high in the air.

"Well then, let me drink for the sake of the groom and bride. Health to your house," Arawn Layland wished.

"Health to your house!" Leon said, raising his goblet as well.

After finishing the wine, the two kings decided to join the others in the great hall. The guests were still enjoying the evening. Leon approached the throne where the bride was sitting surrounded by the ladies of her own house. She had a nice conversation with Lady Calanthe, the spouse of Prince Asael. Ten-year-old Princess Eireen was flaunting next to her mother. Leon made a bow to his queen, inviting her for a dance. Isabelle held his hand, and together the groom and the bride went to the center of the dancing area. The musicians stopped playing their instruments. Every dancing couple directed to their place.

Once again the king bowed to his queen. The queen sat in deep reverence. With the first step made by the royal couple, a new piece of music began playing. Leon held Isabelle's hand. He did not take his eyes away from his queen. The king's gaze was fixed on Isabelle, desperately wanting her to look at him, but the queen looked at the marble floor under her feet.

Leon remembered her differently. Their roads had first crossed twelve years ago, when Leon had visited Incitydoor for a five-year assembly of the world leaders.

After the tragedy had occurred in 1622, when the second end of the world had been barely prevented, all the kings had signed a new Trust Treaty under the Peace Treaty signed in 532, after the great war. On the basis of the new treaty signed in 1622 by the great kings, every five years, the king of the centenarians, with King Layland—including other supporting kings of the mortals—had agreed to gather in Incitydoor.

Even a thousand years later, wherein the one who desired revenge for the past lived—the one who wanted to end the world division between the mightiest and the mortals, the one who believed in the existence of the prophecy—the people and the centenarians had to trust each other and support and share the world for common peace.

During the third assembly, Leon had taken a walk with Arawn Layland's two sons—Prince Asael and Prince Thaen—together with the king's nephew, Sanders Layland. He remembered well how a girl with a joyful scream had appeared behind them. She had been trying to catch a rabbit. Few handmaidens of the young Isabelle had tried to help their lady. Sanders had called his little sister to introduce her to the guest. He had been at his early age of sixteen then. At thirteen years old, Isabella had sat on a curtsy clumsily. It had been her first experience of attending the world's trust assembly.

When had Leon asked her to join the walk, the little lady had gladly agreed. Leon had enjoyed the girl's presence. Isabelle had been a very cheerful, kind, and sincere person. However, everything had changed when she'd gotten to know the person to whom she had been introduced was a centenarian. Worse, he was king to them all. Leon had noticed how the girl's face had changed. He'd seen mistrust in her eyes. She had apologized, informing them that she couldn't continue the walk together with the lords for some reason. And with that excuse, Isabelle had made a curtsy and left the company of the men.

After their short conversation during the walk, Isabelle had tried to avoid any meeting with Leon. Since then, he had never seen the old Isabelle—the cheerful girl with shining eyes. The new Isabelle who appeared in front of him was different: silent, serious, and with cold eyes. Her look was so cold it seemed like she looked at Leon but never saw him.

Leon had been very hopeful that Isabelle would change her attitude after all these years, but nothing had changed. And on this day of their wedding, dancing along with Isabelle, Leon did not take his eyes away from her. The music sounded beautiful, and Isabelle's gentle movements were charming. Isabelle tried to look happy. She tried to show the highest level of respect to her husband, but all she did was try.

After the long-lasting wedding ball, Leon's escort accompanied the newly married king and queen to the bay. When the carriage stopped at the fort, Isabelle saw a very big royal ship. The ship looked beautiful and magnificent. King Leon held out his hand, offering to support Isabelle. She let him lead her to the ship. When they got on board, King Leon showed Isabelle her royal cabin. The cabin was decorated with taste; it looked very luxurious and rich with different room ornaments. While Isabelle was looking at the golden-striped red curtains around the bed, King Leon approached her.

"I have a small gift for you, my queen," said the king, holding her right hand. He took a thin golden bracelet and put it on Isabelle's wrist. The bracelet had a little red ruby in the middle.

"It is beautiful. Thank you," said Isabelle to the king.

"This bracelet will always keep you safe. You shouldn't take it off," said Leon.

Isabelle nodded and thanked the king once again. Then she walked away to the other side of the cabin. The king watched Isabelle for a while attentively. With a knock on the door, the queen's maid asked permission to enter the cabin. When Isabelle saw her maid at the doorstep, she could barely hide her joy and relief.

"I will leave you alone for a while. You two take your time," said Leon and left the room.

"Nihan! Thank goodness! I missed you." Isabelle threw herself toward her maid as soon as the door closed.

Nihan looked at Isabelle and apologized for coming in at an inappropriate time. The two of them sat on the bench near the royal ship's small window.

"Oh, Nihan, I was afraid that we mistakenly left you in Incitydoor."

"If I am not mistaken, we are still on the shores of Incitydoor," the old woman said smiling.

"I know, yet I am happy you are here. You are right on time."

"How are you, my little princess?" Nihan asked Isabelle.

"A little tired," Isabelle admitted.

"How is your king? You have talked to the king. Isn't he rude? Is he nice to you?"

"Yes, he is nice, very attentive, and . . ." Isabelle looked down at the floor.

"And?" asked Nihan, trying to make Isabelle speak.

"Oh, dear Nihan, what am I to do? What am I to do with all this?" Isabelle merely cried.

"Isabelle, what happened? Please tell me you are fine!" begged the old woman to Isabelle.

"I can't pretend like everything is fine. The more I see him, the more I am afraid. His presence terrifies me, Nihan. The thought of living in the lands of the centenarians is killing me."

"My dear . . ." Nihan gave Isabelle a warm hug, feeling sorry for her.

"I believed I could bear everything and overcome my fears. I thought it would be easy, but it is not."

"Isabelle, look at me," said Nihan, putting her hands on the girls' shoulders. "I understand your fear. I understand your heart . . . I know it is not easy. No one said it would be, but you've become a member of his family." Nihan continued to encourage Isabelle, "He will love you. His people will love you. He promised to care and to defend you. Give the king some time, and you will see, love will come to you too."

"Oh, Nihan!" Isabelle hugged her maid even tighter and cried.

Nihan didn't move and let Isabelle cry in her arms. She wanted the queen to calm down. After a while, Isabelle raised her head and started wiping her tears.

"Now . . . how are you?"

"Much better," Isabelle said, smiling through her tears.

The day had been very tough for Isabelle. All the traditions and rituals of both royal families tired her. The old woman understood it well. Nihan buried Isabelle's face in her own palms.

"My dear, you need to have a rest. I'll go upstairs."

"Don't leave! You may stay with me, in my cabin."

"Oh, dear . . . I better go. The king may return. Then it would be inappropriate," said Nihan.

"Please stay with me," Isabelle begged her maid. Tears again appeared in her eyes.

Nihan looked for a while at the young queen and gave a sigh. "Fine, I'll stay with you till you fall asleep."

"Nihan, my father promised me. You also made a promise. Was it true? You won't leave me alone, will you?" the queen asked her maid.

"How can you think I could leave you alone? I'll always be with you," said Nihan with a wide smile.

Isabelle smiled back at Nihan. However, she couldn't find relief in her maid's words. Even though the maid approved her joint voyage to Adahhar—the capital city of the centenarian kingdom, Alaasouad—Isabelle feared. What was promised might not be real.

"Now, come and have a rest!" said Nihan, leading the queen toward the bed.

Isabelle fell asleep as soon as she reached the bed. The day had been full of events, and the queen couldn't stay on her feet anymore.

When Isabelle woke up, she looked around. The queen didn't find Nihan in her room. She was alone in the royal cabin. Inside was cold and dark. Almost all the candles had been burned out long ago. The only light source in the room was a small candle left on the table near the cabin door. Isabelle put on her long, red velvet mantle with a train. She opened the door and went out to the long and narrow passageway. Isabelle was looking around when suddenly a maid's voice frightened her.

"Yes? Who is here?" asked Isabelle, turning around. Then she saw a woman sitting in a low curtsy. "I didn't hear what you said," Isabelle told the maid.

"May I help you, Your Highness?" the woman asked again. Afterward, she rose and looked straight at the queen. "I am Miray, your personal maid. I will be happy to be useful to you, Your Highness."

Isabelle looked at the woman standing beside her. A small, aged woman with a sincere smile, she looked very old and tired. Her gray hair was hidden under a wide, white bonnet. Isabelle believed that an old woman with a lot of wrinkles on her face and hands must have been serving the House of Griffins for many years, if not centuries. While looking at the old woman, Isabelle doubted her new maid's helpfulness.

"Yes," said Isabelle unwillingly, as if she didn't want to bother Miray. "I need candles to be lit. It is quite dark inside . . . and also cold."

"I'll bring you ale and renew the candles."

"Good," Isabelle said nodding.

"Let me send after the watcher, he will check the fireplace." The maid bowed to the queen and asked permission to leave.

"Yes, of course," said Isabelle. "Wait. Miray, correct? Please send Nihan to me. I need to see her." After giving her orders, Isabelle decided to enter her own cabin.

However, her new maid, Miray, stopped the queen. "Forgive me, my queen, for daring to say. I am afraid calling your maid Nihan into your cabin is impossible."

"What do you mean by impossible?"

"The person you want to see is not present on the royal ship. Your previous maid stayed in Incitydoor."

"Are you telling me that Nihan is not here?" The maid's words astonished Isabelle. She could hardly believe her ears. She doubted whether she had heard her words correctly.

"Forgive me." Miray lowered her head. Her gaze was fixed on the floor. "From now on, I am your new maid. I will be happy to serve you, my queen."

"Nihan is my maid! She must serve me! She must be here!" shouted Isabelle at the maid.

The queen got very angry to hear that her trusted person had been left in Incitydoor. She could not believe that she had been lured. Nihan had lied to her. Everyone had lied. Isabelle threw herself into her cabin. For seconds she walked back and forth in her room. Her steps became heavier, her breathing harder. Then she looked at the old woman who was still waiting for her queen.

"I must see the king. Lead the way!" ordered Isabelle to the maid.

Miray obeyed her queen. She bowed, turned around, and went along the narrow passageway toward the stairs. Isabelle said nothing but followed her maid. She made a very strong effort not to fall in tears. She was going to see the king.

On the very top deck of the royal ship, King Leon was sitting in his great cabin with large windows. Despite the moon being at its zenith, he could not sleep at all. With his left-hand fingers, he was playing with an ink pen, stabbing it at the papers on the table. With his other hand, he was holding a moon-shaped silver locket. A sudden knock on his door brought the king from his thoughts to reality. When he gave the approval to enter his cabin, the door opened. The king saw his bride on the other side of the door, and he stood up to welcome her.

Isabelle entered the room and sat in reverence. All her inner world was turned upside down. Trying to hide her negative emotions, Isabelle went toward the big windows. Outside was as dark as black resin; nothing could be seen from inside. Staying beside the windows, Isabelle looked at her hands. The king was waiting for her to explain the reason for such a late visit, hoping that the queen was feeling well.

"I apologize, my king. I shouldn't have come to you at such a late hour," said Isabelle with a tremble in her voice.

"I do believe you had an urgent reason, my queen."

"Yes, I do," replied Isabelle in a hurry. "My king, I came to ask you to turn the ship back. We must return to Incitydoor . . ."

"What must we do?" asked the king with great surprise. He tried to read the thoughts of his queen. What could be so urgent that would make the queen wish to return to the lands of the mortals?

"Return home. We must . . . Please . . ." Isabelle tried to calm down but could not deal with her feelings.

Leon waited awhile for the queen to continue. But Isabelle stood still, and he noticed that she was about to cry. His surprise intensified.

"My queen, I apologize, but can you please explain the reason for your sadness and why you want me to turn back the ship?"

"I can't explain. It is important to me. Give the order to return the ship back home! For me . . . ," begged Isabelle.

"We have already passed the halfway of two borders. I can't just give such a meaningless order to satisfy your childish caprice unless it is reasonable."

"It's about my maid, Nihan. She had to travel to Adahhar. We had to go together," Isabelle burst out.

When the queen pronounced the name of her maid, King Leon understood why she was so impatient to return to Incitydoor. He remembered that the queen's father, Tomaso Layland, King Arawn Layland's first adviser, had approached him on the given matter. Isabelle had made only one request to accept her marriage with King Leon.

She had asked the king to allow her maid, Nihan, to travel to Alaasouad together with her. However, her request had been rejected. Leon had agreed to accept any other request and condition from Isabelle except letting Nihan enter the capital city of the centenarian kingdom.

King Leon had his own reasons for refusing his future queen her only wish. When Tomaso Layland informed Leon about his daughter's wish, the centenarian king had asked for a meeting with the maid. He'd had to know who would accompany the future queen of the centenarians.

What the king had seen bothered him. The woman had been cursed in the past. A long, wavy, reddish burn line had been drawn from her right shoulder till the end point of her right thumb. It was a line left after the mark of a curse. The curse mark that she had received was one of the most ancient symbols. The mark could be received only by those who participated in the spiritual ritual of witches. A volunteer served the witch as an instrument for conducting a very terrible thing using dark magic. Most of all, it required blood. The mark helped one to return to the world of living together with a dark spirit after the suicide. But those who returned were cursed, for there was no place for the dead among the living.

Tomaso had told the king that many years ago, after the great tragedy, the maid had been believed to be dead, but she had returned a year after the tragedy. She couldn't remember anything but one name—Isabelle! She had remembered only little Isabelle. After the death of her mother, Isabelle had been all alone, and Nihan had taken care of the girl. For his daughter's sake, Tomaso had not sent Nihan away.

But Leon couldn't let the old woman go to Alaasouad. Such cursed people were neither allowed to go to the great city of the centenarians nor could they walk freely on the land of both mortals and centenarians. They were sent to the Lonely Tower in the south, a special place where they were usually kept. Leon had promised not to send the woman to the Lonely Tower, but he couldn't allow her to go with them either. Tomaso Layland had promised to inform her daughter about the king's decision. Yet Leon believed the first adviser could not keep his promise, and probably his daughter was unaware of the outcome of the two men's conversation.

Leon Ulyses looked at the table. He was silent for a while. Then he sighed deeply and talked to Isabelle, trying to be as polite as possible.

"I am afraid I need to refuse your request, my queen. Your maid can't cross the borders of Alaasouad, in the same way the ship can't turn back to Incitydoor."

"Please, I beg you. Let her step into the land of the centenarians. There is no harm from increasing the passengers' number by one."

"That is impossible."

"It was the only condition that I requested, and you agreed. You made a promise. Please . . . ," asked Isabelle with tears in her eyes.

Her words made the king's look even gloomier. On one side, he felt sorry for the queen; on the other side, he was angry at the Layland family due to the condition they had put him before his bride.

"I never give a promise for things that can't be realized, and if I do so, I keep my promise. Always!"

"But you did. You made a promise!"

"Isabelle, I didn't. And I ask you to stop accusing me with a lie." Leon tried to control his temper, but the queen's words made him angry.

"Lie? But my father approached you on this matter. He talked to you . . ." Isabelle didn't want to give up. She was desperate.

"Yes, he did, of course, and I refused his request," Leon answered rudely. However hard he was trying to stay calm, he couldn't hide his irritation anymore.

"I am not asking you to give me the whole world. I just want Nihan to be with me."

"You have become the queen of two worlds. You can't ask what already belongs to you."

"Is this your answer? I can't believe I was made to marry you with a lie," said Isabelle with regret.

"All your complaints, you can address to your lord father, my queen."

"Oh, I will tell him too, if you don't mind and give the order to return the ship to Incitydoor," said Isabelle, raising her voice.

Leon didn't want to have their conversation anymore. "As I informed you before, there is no need to turn the ship back. You can write to him. The new maid will provide you with ink and paper," he concluded. Then he rudely opened the door of the cabin, letting Isabelle know that he didn't wish for her presence anymore.

The king's words and his indifference made Isabelle upset and angry at the same time. She clenched her fists. She wanted to tell the king how she hated him, hated all his race, and how deep her regret was of their marriage. She didn't say a word. Instead, Isabelle turned around and left. She went straight to her own cabin.

The new maid had already put new candles, and inside was bright and warm. At the corner of the cabin, small particles of ash from the burning wood were flying out of the fireplace. On the table near her bed, Isabelle saw a plate with freshly cut fruits, black bread, and a bottle of hot ale with a silver glass near it. Everything was prepared for her return. Isabelle went toward the table and threw everything to the floor in anger. She sat down and started crying out loud. All around her was wild and different.

Miray, the new maid, worriedly ran into the cabin when she heard the noise. But when she saw the queen crying on the floor, she decided to leave her alone with her own thoughts and pain. She believed it was best to let the queen cry and get rid of her bad emotions. Eventually, the night would promise to be as long as their trip.

Chapter 6

Debt of the Cursed

"Pull the ropes! Pull the ropes! We are all going to crash!" screamed the ship's first mate to his crew partner. "Pull the ropes!"

The storm was very strong. Big waves were throwing the big vessel from side to side. The crew members could hardly stay on foot. The people, soaked in salt water from head to toe, fell and rose again. All of the crew's efforts were to keep the ship moving into the waves for as long as possible. The first mate hurried to the back side of the ship to take down the sails. On the way, he stopped the young boy passing by him.

"Go and check the safety ropes! Check everyone! Hurry!" shouted the man.

The boy ran all over the ship, checking the ropes around the waists of the crew members. He fell several times. The more times he fell, the harder it was to rise up again. He swiped his face with his hand to move aside his golden hair. With the other hand, he was holding the rope tied around the mast. Because of the large waves, so much water was dumped aboard, and it started weighing down the vessel.

"Take down all the sails! Take them all!" shouted the first mate.

The boy looked up and saw that the tallest sail mast in the middle of the ship had started leaning to the right side. Everyone on the ground hurried to help the ones who were working hard up on the mast. The boy hurried to climb up through the ropes. When he got up to the very top of the mast, a sudden strong noise of cracking wood drove his attention.

The front top sail of the ship broke down and fell. Those who were working down on the board tried to escape the crush of the falling mast in vain. At that moment, a strong thunder roared near the boy. He looked around. Dark clouds started encircling the vessel. All who were below started screaming and hurrying in horror to climb up on the mast through the ropes. The board of the ship had already disappeared among the black clouds. No more waves were seen around.

"Help! Please help me!" screamed someone from below.

The boy could hardly hear the voice because of the storm's noise. A few meters below, he saw a girl climbing up. She had no strength left to hold on. The boy started climbing down to reach the girl. When he closed the distance between them, he extended his hand to help.

"Give me your hand!" shouted the boy.

"I can't! I am slipping down!"

"No, Hester! Hold on! Don't let it go!" screamed the boy. "Hester, you can do it! Just give me your hand!"

The boy tried hard to reach the girl, but because of the strong wind, all his efforts were useless. He called her name several times. The boy couldn't see the girl's face, but her dark-blue hair the color of the night was flying in the wind. She was holding the ropes tightly.

"Hester! Look at me! You need to move on! Please give me your hand!"

"I can't!"

The boy, with all his effort, attempted to get closer to the girl, but the clouds around them thickened. Soon, the knees of the girl disappeared behind the clouds. A sudden vision that the boy saw in the clouds scared him. He could not scream, nor could he call for his sister's name. He wanted to warn Hester but was unable to utter any word. A big, black shadow behind the clouds approached Hester from the bottom.

The girl felt a touch. Something very cold grabbed her toe and pulled her down. The girl screamed and drowned in the clouds. The boy couldn't believe that he lost the most precious person in the world. Then a very light thunder hit the place where the boy was standing. Because of the pain, he couldn't hold the rope anymore and let it go. He fell . . .

* * *

Again, he felt something hit him. The boy felt pain on his right cheek.

"What is going on?" he asked. Someone was holding him tightly. "Let go! Where is Hester? Is she alive?"

"Stand up, boy!" the one holding him started shaking his shoulders.

"What do you want?" The boy, still with closed eyes, tried to get rid of his restrainer.

"Wake up, you fool! Captain wants to see you!" said the man to the boy.

The boy opened his eyes and looked at the one who woke him up.

"Cael, it's me! Belen!"

"Belen?" asked the boy with astonishment. He was sweating because of his nightmare. Cael saw the broad smile on his friend's rectangular face. He was staring at Cael with pure hazel eyes.

"Yes! You got it at last!" said Belen to his friend.

Though Belen was softer and kinder in comparison to the earnest and persistent son of the captain, Cael and Belen had a strong friendship built in the years that they had spent on Cael's father's ship. Belen was much older than Cael, and Cael admired him and loved him like his own brother. Even though they had a significant age difference of ten years, everyone on the ship called them twin brothers. The two of them were inseparable. Both of them were good fighters. Both loved jokes and board games. They were the mood of the ship.

"Where is Hester?" Cael kept asking, still worried.

"Are you asking about your sister? She is at home. In Samaria," answered Belen.

"In Crete?" wondered the boy.

"Yes. Where else can she be?" Belen couldn't understand why his friend was acting so weird.

"Then it was just a dream." Cael, a seventeen-year-old boy with curly golden hair, sighed with relief. "Why are you here, Belen? And what time is it?" he asked his friend.

"It is still dark outside. The moon is at its zenith," answered Belen.

"Are you kidding me? It is midnight!" Cael got angry at his friend as he woke him so late at night.

"Your father told everyone to get prepared! We have reached the destination point," continued Belen.

"Already?" asked Cael.

They had been traveling on the ship for months, and he couldn't believe that they finally managed to reach the shores of Valona at last.

"Yes," nodded his friend. Belen's smile widened. "This is the last trade, and we are going home."

His words made Cael smile too. He liked thinking about his home, and the acknowledgment of the end of their long, hard journey in the seas cheered him up. He rushed to the main deck. All the members of the crew gathered at the deck to send their captain to the last errand.

The night was cold and misty. Small raindrops were falling from the sky's rooftop. The waves were striking the banks of the old city Valona. The city was located on the bay of Vlore. From one side, the coast of Valona was washed by the Adriatic Sea. From the other side, the city was embraced by the long range of the Ceraunian Mountains. At the beginning of the fifteenth century, the city was captured by the Ottoman Empire. Since that time, the city had been known as Avlonya and become one of the main port cities of the Turks' empire.

As it was a late hour, the city streets were empty. The firelights put in some city corners had gone out long ago. Only the lights of the full moon in the sky occasionally illuminated the surface of the earth when the black clouds were chased away by the wind.

The captain of the old pirates' vessel *Incombusto*, Philipp Aquila, was wrapped tightly in his coat sitting at the nose of a small boat. Two of his men were lowering the boat down to the sea. Philipp Aquila was a tall man in his midforties with a short beard. His hair had turned pale long ago. His face, covered with a lot of scars, was already aged. The stern look of the captain was stiffened on the bay of Vlore. Even though the man looked very calm, his inner world was raging.

He strove to the shore. When the bottom of the boat touched the water, the sailors pulled the ropes from two sides of the boat and released it from the main ship. At the front bow of the *Incombusto,* a young pirate boy with curly golden hair was watching how his father, the captain of the ship, was swimming toward the banks of Valona.

Cael had asked his father to take him to the island with him. However, Philipp Aquila had ordered him to stay on the ship together with the other crew members in any case. He had to meet an important person. He had been waiting for this same night for many years. This night was expected to be very special as Captain Aquila and all his crew members, including his seventeen-year-old son, were about to receive their long-awaited freedom.

Aquila closed his eyes and took a deep breath. All he could think about at that moment was his home in Crete Islands.

This is over! We did everything. We will be free. We must be! Soon, we will be at home, Aquila said continuously in his mind.

When the small boat landed at the banks of the city, the sailors got off and started pulling the boat onto the land. One of the sailors, who was ten inches taller than the captain, took a long rope and tightened it around the fat wooden stick on the bay.

Orrin Pearce was Philipp Aquila's most trusted man. He was a giant man with a brutal look. His strict and cold gaze was frightening to all other crew members except the captain of *Incombusto.* Aquila had known Orrin for many years and trusted him more than anyone else. Even his own son, Cael, could be under his suspicion, but not Orrin. Aquila owed his life to his old friend. He was the only one who could stand up for his captain till the end of the world.

After tightening the boat, Orrin took out his heavy, half-moon-shaped sword and looked at his captain. Aquila nodded to his men. Orrin and the other pirate, named Cosimo, bent over the boat and lifted a heavy locked chest. Together the three pirates directed toward the small hill lying to the right of the shore.

When the three men approached a big, leafy tree near the cliff, Aquila walked to the other side of the tree. He found a small circle-shaped hole with half-moon carvings on the tree. Afterward, he took a small, round stone mallet with a long handle. The head side of the mallet had the same carvings in the shape of a half-moon, the same as the ones carved in the hole on the tree.

Aquila put the carved side of the mallet into the hole on the tree and pressed hard. The mallet went deep inside the hole. When he heard the clicking noise from inside, the captain of *Incombusto* turned the mallet around by its handle. In a second, the sand under their feet started sinking, opening a pathway to the hidden staircase that went down under the tree. Orrin lit the flambeau torch, and together all three men with the big locked chest disappeared under the big, leafy tree near the hill.

Their journey wasn't very long. Soon, Captain Aquila and his two men reached the basement. The end of their passage brought them into a cave located under the ground. The cave was not very big but with high ceiling. The bottom of the stairs and the flat area located on the other side of the cave were connected by a narrow path that crossed the middle of the cave. The right side of the passage was being washed by the waters of the underground lake. The cave's walls and the underground lake's borders were covered with flowstones. The passage's left side was full of big, upward-growing stalagmites. Long and sharp stalactites hung all over the cave ceiling.

The flambeau torches put along the passage brightened the cave, and the crystal pool spars at the bottom of the lake were shining under their lights. The end of the passage abutted on a small, round, flat area also lit by flambeau torches. When the men reached the small area at the end of the cave, Orrin and Cosimo put the chest on the ground and waited for their captain's next order.

"Now we have to wait," said Aquila to his men. "We will wait for the witch." Aquila looked around. The cave was cool, and the captain felt a cold wind striking his face. *The cave must have some unseen holes*, thought Aquila.

The person they had to meet in the cave had to come soon. The three men did not have to wait long as their guest appeared beside them in a moment.

"You are late!" said a woman's voice, making those present turn around.

Aquila noticed a shadow hiding behind the tall and fat stalagmite in the corner of the flat area.

"We were waiting for darkness," answered the captain, taking one step toward the one hiding behind the stalagmite.

"Good," uttered the person and went out to the light from the shadow.

Aquila saw a young woman, approximately in her late twenties. She was wearing a long, hooded black cape over the crimson dress with a leather belt tightened around her belly. Her chestnut-colored hair was hanging down in curls under her hood. She looked straight at the captain's eyes with determination.

"Show me the chest."

The woman kept looking at Aquila, checking him. The captain felt uncomfortable from her look and shifted his gaze to the other side. Her brightly celestial-colored eyes were penetrating. Aquila gave a signal to his men. Orrin and Cosimo moved the chest toward the woman and, with a strong effort, opened its heavy lid.

The woman approached the two men and looked at what was inside the chest. The chest was full of small golden sparkles. The woman bent over and took a handful of sparkly dust. After that, she raised her hand and dropped the sparkle dust back into the chest.

"We searched all seas," said Aquila to the woman. "No other golden dust of Kaia left behind. We took them all."

The golden dust of Kaia was magical dust that appeared under the water. According to the legends, only one night in a year, when the earth got frost during the winter solstice, the mermaids of the great ocean sang a song. That night the moonlight reached the bottom of the ocean. The underwater sand reached by the moonlight turned into golden dust. Some called the phenomenon "moon tears"; others believed it to be the soul of the earth and called it the "golden dust of Kaia." Its properties were as peculiar as its origin. The dust had strong magical powers. With a special spell, one could make things disappear. The dust could be used to create portals, connecting far distances.

"Yes, this is what I needed. You did a great job," replied the woman with a smile. Then she gave a stern look at the two other pirates, letting them know that they could already close the chest's lid.

Orrin and his partner raised the heavy lid from the ground and moved it on top of the chest. The woman stepped toward the captain and handed him a folded fabric.

"What is it?" asked Aquila.

"Look at it."

Aquila unfolded the fabric with hope. Could it serve as the sign confirming their freedom? He tried to hide his happiness. However, his expectations did not justify themselves.

"A map?" exclaimed the captain with astonishment.

The two of his men were also surprised to hear what their captain uttered.

"Yes, this is a map," confirmed the woman.

"It can't be!" said Aquila with anger. "You can't send us to another mission. We did all you wanted. You promised our freedom!"

"You will receive your freedom! First, you must bring me the silver leaf of Vu Ula. The map will show you the way to the land of Mahv," said the woman to the captain.

Her words made Orrin angry. He clenched the handle of his sword in his right palm.

"Mahv is a cursed land!" Orrin interrupted the conversation between his captain and the woman.

"Going to Mahv means real death," said Aquila looking at the woman. "No one can reach its shores."

"But you will!"

"No!" refused the captain. "I will not go to the death mission and will not take my people there."

"Be careful. It would be better to think before rejecting my offer," the woman warned him.

"My people are waiting for the freedom you promised in exchange for sea golds. We served you all these years by collecting the sparkle dust."

"I appreciate all your efforts," the woman said calmly.

Aquila understood that the woman had no intentions to free him and his people from their duty. He knew that they had to go to the land of Mahv. And after their return, she would find another task to keep Aquila and his men under her rule. At that very moment, the captain wanted to take her life out with his sword. He stood beside the woman and looked at her eyes with hatred.

"Get lost with your appreciation!" said Aquila, ironically smiling at the woman. "This is the final point. My people will receive their freedom, whether you want it or not. Good luck with your trip to Mahv." Aquila looked at his men. "We are leaving."

The captain of *Incombusto* turned toward the passage. Orrin and Cosimo followed him. However, after taking a few steps, they stopped where they stood as the woman burst into an evil laugh. All three men turned around and looked at the woman.

"Do you know what is interesting about people?" asked the woman with a deep sigh. "You offer them a job. You give them opportunities. In exchange, you believe, you can win their loyalty. You believe they will serve you because of their wish, not because of fear." While speaking the woman walked back and forth, playing with her curls with one hand.

Aquila tried to understand what she was thinking about. He listened to her as if he wanted to be able to read her thoughts.

"But in the end," the woman said, her face saddening, "they betray you. All they do is wait for the right time to escape. And when there is one, they run away as a dog does when you take off its collar." The woman looked at the men. Her gaze was cold and her words full of anger. "Betrayers!"

Suddenly the skirt of her cape burned out, spreading fire around. Captain Aquila and his men started running away, but the flame reached them in seconds. The three men fell down screaming in pain. Their skin became black, turning into ugly forms on fire.

"You may have forgotten what happened six years ago," continued the woman. "But I did not. Don't forget, I saved your miserable lives."

She watched her victims roll on the ground from side to side, scratching and hitting their faces and bodies, trying to get rid of the pain. The fire was killing them very slowly, melting their skins.

"I thought you were different. I was assured you were special. I believed in your loyalty, believed you would remember what I did for you." The woman bent over the burning man. With her right hand, she grabbed the captain's chin and forced him to look at her.

Aquila gave another moan of pain.

"Do you know the cost I paid to save your souls? If you want to return to hell, go ahead! But first, bring me my silver leaf!" Then the woman pushed him back to the ground and took a few steps backward.

In a second, everything disappeared: the fire, the pain . . .

Aquila looked at his people. Their faces were still grimaced because of the recent pain they felt, but they had all stopped screaming. Orrin tried to stand up, holding his sword, but couldn't get to his feet and fell again. All three men had no strength to make any movement. The witch approached the men and dropped the map beside Aquila.

"I am giving you three months. The sooner you finish the task, the sooner you will receive your long-awaited freedom. Don't think you can circumvent Celia," said the woman, mentioning her own name. "I will know your every step."

The woman directed toward the big stalagmite and disappeared behind it. The chest also disappeared with her leave. Aquila sat on the cave's cold ground for a long time. After a while, he and his men stood up and decided to leave the cave. With a strong effort, the captain of the *Incombusto*, with the other two pirates, reached the cave's entrance.

The cold night wind struck their face, chilling their skin. Staying near the big tree at the cliff, Aquila looked at the whole bay. He closed his eyes, trying to remember the day of the tragedy—the day he lost his ship, the day he lost his freedom, the day life itself was lost. He opened his eyes and once again looked at the bay, at the old city of Valona. His thoughts brought him to the day that had caused a significant change in his life.

* * *

Six years ago, in 1638, Aquila and his crew stepped onto the ground of Valona with great hope. He searched for the patronage of the Ottomans' king. For many years, barbarian pirates had lived under the protection of Turks and received support for the existence of their groups in the Mediterranean Sea.

Aquila needed a safe house for his people, especially for his family, so he and his crew came to the shores of Valona to meet the person who could organize the meeting between the Ottomans and the centenarian pirates. When they arrived in Valona, the port was bombarded by the Venetian fleet. As a consequence, the whole city was destroyed by fire. Ships sank into the sea, drowning thousands of people under the water. Houses turned into ash on fire. Aquila heard the screams of dying men and women, their shouts for help. There was no place to run, no chance for salvation.

Despite the cold night, Aquila felt the heat of the fire of the doomed day. He looked down by the bay and saw people trying to find an exit from the chaos. And he saw his son, Cael, only eleven years old at that time, running toward him.

The sudden noise of a cannon grabbed the attention of the old captain, and in the next few seconds, one of the cannon balls hit the place where his son was standing. Aquila felt strong pain in his chest. Then he saw his own death. He fell. The pain forced him to kneel. All the parts of his body—his face, his eyes—were burning. He couldn't breathe. Aquila heard his own yell.

Then everything stopped. Time stopped. A young woman approached the old captain of *Incombusto*. She eased the pain. She gave Aquila a second chance. She gave him a new life and took his promise to serve her loyally.

Aquila accepted all her conditions without a word. In exchange for his loyalty, the woman saved his life and the lives of his people. At that moment, when all pain was gone, when the death was gone, Aquila stood up to see the ruins of Valona: the fire and the death of hundreds of thousands of people except his own crew members, except his own son. He remembered how his son, Cael, rose up in astonishment and in horror. The eleven-year-old boy could not understand what was happening around him, yet he was alive. He was safe.

* * *

Watching from the cliff the scene from his past, tears appeared in the captain's eyes. Aquila was sinking into his own terrifying memories when Orrin disturbed him.

"Captain," said Orrin, "we should return. Soon, it will be morning. Our people are waiting for us."

Aquila nodded to Orrin. He knew he had no choice but to obey the witch and hold his destination toward the land of Mahv. He owed the witch everything he had. Aquila knew he was still breathing because of her. He was alive, and he had to fight for this life, whatever happened.

As soon as the three men reached the bay, they got on the boat and sailed in the direction of the *Incombusto*. When the boat reached the *Incombusto*, the captain and his two men got onto the big ship. Everyone was waiting for their arrival with great hope. But when the crew saw their captain's face, all felt that something went wrong in Valona.

The captain's look was gloomy and severe. Even Cael was frightened and didn't dare to say a word to his father. No one could foresee what had happened down in the cave; they could only guess.

Aquila had neither the strength nor desire to stay on board and give an explanation to his crew. He only ordered his men to set the sails and went straight to his own cabin. Orrin's and Cosimo's conditions weren't better in comparison to their captain's either. All understood: their thoughts about freedom had turned into a dream. How long they had to dream, no one knew . . .

Chapter 7

Ally to the King

Despite the late November, the day promised to be warm. A maid approached and opened the big wooden windows of the royal cabin. The scent of salty seawater spread around the room immediately.

The air was fresh and chilling. The sun was shining brightly in the sky. The queen's set of clothes was neatly put on the chair. The breakfast that had been brought several hours ago had almost cooled down. Despite it being already late morning, Isabelle was still in bed. Three maids were waiting next to the bed for the queen to get up. Not one of the maids dared to talk to Isabelle. They all were aware of what had happened the other night. The queen had been very upset on the night of her wedding day.

Soon, the door of the royal cabin opened, and Miray entered the room. She looked at the other maids. The three women looked at Miray. One of them grimaced, and the other one shook her head as if she wanted to say that all their efforts were useless. Miray sighed deeply and approached the queen's bed. She tried hard to sound nice and polite.

"I hope you had a good night's sleep, Your Highness! It is almost afternoon. Please let me get you prepared for going out."

"You better leave me alone," Isabelle replied in a rude manner to her maid. Afterward, she covered her head with a blanket. She didn't want to see anyone on the ship, especially the king.

Miray and the other maids once again looked at each other.

"My dear queen, soon lunch will be served. Till then, you may enjoy the day on the deck. The weather is great today. I am sure you will like it," continued the old maid.

Miray's words irritated the queen. Isabelle was in a bad mood and wanted to yell at the old woman. However, she did not say anything.

Miray waited for the queen's response in vain.

"Forgive me for saying this, Your Highness," Miray said at last. "I understand your feelings. But the king's will is to see you at the day feast. This is his order."

The maid waited for a little while for a response.

When she did not get one, she continued, "Otherwise, the king will have to come to see you. Please, Your Highness . . ."

Isabelle didn't want to get up, but after hearing Miray's words, she decided to appear at the lunch. Most of all, she didn't want the king's presence in her room. Meeting him among the other members of the royal ship was better than seeing him when she was all alone. In addition, Isabelle knew Miray was a servant. Even if Isabelle was their queen, Leon was their king. The old woman had no choice but to obey his orders in the first place, not hers.

When the queen sat on the edge of her bed, one of the maids brought her a basin with warm water. While washing her face and hands, the queen looked at the maid. The young woman didn't raise her head to look at her queen. However, her cheeks turned red immediately. She was very shy. Miray approached the queen and introduced the maid to Isabelle.

"Her name is Hannah," said the old woman.

"My pleasure to serve you, my queen!" uttered the woman with great effort.

"This is Asel, and next to her is Jael," Miray introduced the other maids to the queen. "They will serve you as well as I, Your Highness," informed the old woman.

"Our pleasure to serve you, Your Highness," said the other two maids while making a bow.

Isabelle looked at all the maids. They were young, nice, and polite. They helped the queen to get ready to appear before the guests. As Miray said, the weather was great, but it was a little chilly. Isabelle went to the main deck. The strong sulfury scent of the sea filled her nostrils and gave her a little pain. A slightly windy and sunny day was as pleasant as the first small drops of snow.

At the forecastle deck, Isabelle saw a canopy tent. Several ladies in beautiful gowns were sitting under the tent and chatting with a cup in their hands. Isabelle looked around. She noticed the king on the sterncastle deck of the ship, staying near the wheel. He was surrounded by several men and having a conversation with them. When Isabelle saw the king, her breaths came faster. Her hands became shaky. Isabelle still couldn't overcome what she had to live through the night before.

The queen tried to avoid the meeting with Leon, so she turned around and directed toward the ladies. First, Leonor, a woman sitting in the corner, noticed Isabelle. She went to meet the queen halfway. When she crossed the distance between them, Leonor slightly bowed, showing her respect to the queen. Leonor couldn't half sit in reverence as she was expecting a child. Her belly was quite noticeable.

"Your Highness!" said the woman with a kind look. "I am pleased to see you here. You made us glad with your presence. I am Leonor."

"I remember you," said Isabelle warmly. "We met yesterday, at the wedding celebration. You are my sister-in-law."

"I am happy to see you in our family, Your Highness!" The woman's smile was bright and sincere.

Leonor was the king's only living sibling. She was married to her cousin Estevan Ulyses. He was the second heir of the centenarian throne after her brother, King Leon.

"Would the queen like to join the ladies for a tea feast?" Leonor asked Isabelle.

The other ladies had already stood up and were waiting for the queen. Isabelle slightly nodded with a smile and approached the other ladies. All women curtsied in reverence. Leonor once again introduced the ladies of the House of Griffin to the queen.

Lady Devora Rose Griffin approached the queen to greet her. She gave the queen a light hug.

"What a beauty you are," said the woman.

Lady Devora was a fine young woman. She was the eldest of the centenarian royal family and mother to Estevan. Unlike mortals, centenarians showed the highest respect to the elder family members despite their position in the family.

Isabelle tried to be nice and smiled during her conversation with the other ladies. She hoped that no one would notice her trembling and sadness. Moreover, Isabelle felt that these women's presence was not as scary as she had expected.

Leon was still on the sterncastle when he first saw Isabelle since the night before. He leaned on the handrails of the ship. Estevan joined the king. The two of them watched the ladies for a while. Leon didn't take his eyes away from the queen. It seemed she was having a nice and quite interesting conversation with the other ladies.

"I almost forgot she laughs too," said Leon in a low voice.

"Did you say something?" asked Estevan as he misheard the king.

He was brought up together with Leon. Their fathers were brothers. The years had built a strong bond between Estevan and Leon. They were brothers who depended on each other like two sides of a sword. Leon trusted him a lot, and Estevan proved his loyalty to his king and kingdom.

"Leon?"

The king shook his head. "No, nothing!" Leon answered Estevan and called for one of his servants.

Isabelle was enjoying her tea with the other ladies when Miray approached and informed her that the king wanted to see her at the sterncastle deck. Isabelle said nothing. She followed her maid in silence. Leon was waiting for his queen at the nose of the ship. His gaze was fixed on the rising waves over the board.

"You wished to see me, Your Highness?" Isabelle asked in a low voice, trying to hide her inner fear.

"Hope my queen had a good rest and regained her strength," Leon stated coldly. "You are no longer upset, aren't you?"

Isabelle shook her head. "No, Your Highness, I am feeling well." Isabelle didn't dare to show her true feelings to Leon.

"Good . . ." Leon kept watching the waves raging and roaring around the centenarians' royal ship. "I hope my queen had had enough time to think about our conversation yesterday, hadn't you?" asked Leon.

"Hm," Isabelle nodded. She wished she could escape his presence.

"Isabelle . . ." Leon continued after a little pause, "Yesterday your behavior was inappropriate as the queen of the centenarians."

"Inappropriate?" Isabelle struggled to understand what Leon wanted to say.

His indifferent and open conversation bothered the queen. She couldn't believe that the king asked for her presence in order to reprimand her. She believed she didn't do anything wrong. All she did was ask the king to bring her maid, whom she loved like her own mother.

"I don't understand, Your Highness. Could you please explain? Is making a single wish a mistake? Or does the queen have no right to request for a promise made by men?"

Leon shook his head. Then he looked directly at his queen. Isabelle stepped backward as if avoiding him. His piercing gaze seemed to be able to see into her soul.

"Becoming a member of the centenarians' royal family is not easy. On the contrary, it can be not only difficult but also very dangerous. You disrespected me, and you dared to show your disagreement with my decision in front of others. It was a great mistake."

"Your Highness . . ." Isabelle clenched her skirt in her fist. "I felt myself deceived, betrayed, and abandoned by those whom I love. I would understand if you considered human feelings as a weakness, not a mistake."

Leon noticed that the queen was tense. He could feel her trembling. For sure, his presence bothered the queen. Isabelle was not ready to enter the centenarian world. She became a tool in Arawn's hands. Leon Ulyses was also an accomplice in this case. It was he who wished to take the girl to his own world. Leon leaned over and took Isabelle's hand. His touch burned her hand like lightning. Her heartbeat quickened. However, Isabelle couldn't free her hand from Leon's grip.

"Remember," Leon said in a low voice, "you are the queen, and you must know what your position presents by itself. The queen is the main ally of the king. She is a reflection of his power and the stability of the kingdom's domestic political condition. If the queen betrays the king, then all will. My enemies are everywhere. They watch your every step, always . . ." Leon tightened his grip. "No one must get to know your true feelings. Whether you fear me or hate me, don't show it to anyone. Do you understand?"

Isabelle hastily nodded. She couldn't take her eyes off Leon. Could it be possible that Leon was aware of her true feelings?

"Good!" said Leon. "It's almost time for lunch."

Still holding Isabelle's hand in his palm, Leon went toward the stairs. Isabelle was helpless to do anything but obey. Soon, everyone followed the king and queen to the main hall. The afternoon meal was ready.

While walking next to Leon, Isabelle didn't dare to raise her head. All the way down to the hall, she was thinking about Leon's words. The king was right. Isabelle knew, from the day of their marriage, she had come to the middle of the universal circle. From that day on, everyone on earth started watching her every step. She couldn't fail anyone, especially herself.

Her heart was uneasy, even though the queen tried to look calm while walking down to the main hall together with the king. No one around noticed the cover on the queen's face except the king. In the common hall, everyone gathered around the long and round dining table. Following the king and queen, all the other guests found their seats. With the permission of the king, the feast started. Everyone enjoyed the lunch. Isabelle watched the others who were chatting merrily, remembering funny moments of the prewedding preparations.

After lunch Leon headed to his cabin with Estevan as he had to discuss imperial issues. The ladies decided to occupy the teahouse on the lower deck of the ship.

Wishing to be alone for a while, Isabelle went to the main deck of the ship. Staying alone at the nose of the royal ship, she gazed at the waves below. The waves were high and strong. Their loud, raging sound devoured the surroundings. For Isabelle, those waves were the reflection of her inner world. Since the announcement day of her marriage, she had lost her peace.

Isabelle sighed. Her thin, white fingers clenched the icy-cold handrails of the ship. The mortals had used her as a bargaining tool and abandoned her when "the desired" was achieved, and for the mighty king of the centenarians, Isabelle became a golden trophy that would decorate one of the empty shells of his palace. Leon's words couldn't persuade Isabelle. Weak and powerless mortals couldn't be an ally to the king. The girl who had nothing to offer to support the king's position on the throne couldn't be equal to the king who ruled the world. She didn't belong to the world of the centenarians.

Staying alone on the deck, Isabelle prayed to the only god to whom she gave her oath. She prayed to her god to end her misery in the lands of the centenarians and to one day let her return home to her dearest Nihan and her father and brother. The queen made a wish, and only the waves knew what kind of wish was buried at the bottom of the queen's heart.

Chapter 8

Meeting in the Forest

It was already late evening. The path went through the jungle forest. The narrow road was illuminated from both sides with tiki torches. Almost two hours had passed since the ship had arrived at the port and Isabelle made her first step on an unknown land. She was a little tired, but even so, she was afraid to look weak.

The forest ended when they reached the silver arched gates at the end of the road. It served as a passage between two long walls to the inner garden. The arch was very high and had beautiful rose carvings. At the very top of the arch was a carved symbol of the sun embracing the new moon inside. The two columns holding the arch had the same rose carvings at the bottom. The shape of a tree had been carved in the middle of both columns. They had two angels leaning on it, their wings widely flapped outward. And at the top of the arch, right below the sun, the edge of their wings was bound together. The angels were surrounded by stars. The walls were built of silver bricks and had strange writings on them.

Isabelle couldn't read the writings. The people had forgotten the language long ago. It was believed to be the language of nature, also known as a dead language. Isabelle moved the curtain of the carriage further to better see the view. Isabelle, together with Leonor and Lady Devora, was inside the first two-wheel carriage being pulled by servants. Three other carriages, with ladies inside, were following the carriage of the queen.

The inner garden looked to be as old as the forest beyond its walls. The last lights of the sun couldn't reach the ground of the garden because of the tall trees. The lights from the tiki torches were not enough to shine bright in the dark night.

Isabelle smelled the scent of sweet narcissus with the heavier and smokier smell of old oaks mixed together with the smell of the wet ground after the rain. Although it was late, the sound of birds nesting up high on the trees was loud. Isabelle noticed round, green nests hanging on the trees. All the nests, circular with a diameter of sixteen inches, were built up from leaves, with small windows in the shape of stars and wooden doors. The windows were lit. Isabelle noticed several flying creatures with sparkling, transparent wings. They were as tiny as her handbreadth.

Leonor, who was sitting next to the queen, leaned toward Isabelle and whispered, "Keepers of the forest. Night fairies. We call them *nuri.*"

Isabelle looked at Leonor with a smile on her lips. "Amazing," said the queen to her sister-in-law. During their long trip, Isabelle had gotten used to Leonor. She was a friendly woman with a kind heart.

At the vanguard of the long royal escort, King Leon was marching together with his cousin Estevan and political adviser Lord Byron Caldwell.

Lord Caldwell looked old enough to have lived several thousand years. His steps were short, his movements slow. His gray hair had begun to go bald. He was talking about politics. What was going on in the world of the mortals worried the old centenarian.

Estevan was listening to him, or at least he was trying to look attentive to the old one as a sign of respect to his age. Leon said nothing about his old adviser's beliefs. Occasionally he would stop and turn to look at the carriage where the queen was. Soon, the walkers reached the open meadow located in the middle of the ancient garden. King Leon stopped and waited for a bit.

When the carriage approached their group and stopped, Leon offered his hand and helped the queen to get out. Holding his queen's hand, Leon led Isabelle to the front of the meadow. Beside Isabelle appeared a wide area full of greenery. The long crystal stairs led down to the bridge over the river through the green meadow. At the center of the meadow was located a four-story crystal castle with green gardens on the right and left wings on every level. Around the castle were different tree-shaped silver sculptures with carvings. Behind them, a lonely mount was towering over the castle.

"Welcome to Nur-adamantas," said Leon to his queen. "This is the Castle of Crystal Green."

Isabelle said nothing. She walked beside the king toward the castle. Earlier that day, the king had informed everyone that they were going to stop for a few days and stay in a centenarian city located deep in the forest.

The queen found the place fabulously beautiful. It was a very quiet place, far from the bustle of big cities. The population of the city was small. When they reached the castle, the servants pushed the big, heavy gates to let their masters in.

Inside, Isabelle saw the inhabitants of Nur-adamantas. They gathered in the inner yard to welcome their king and queen. After the greetings, Leon and the others directed to the hall. In the middle of the hall, there was a tree surrounded by stones laid in the shape of a rhombus around the tree. The open ceiling of the hall that connected the two levels allowed the tree to grow tall. The tree branches hanging down went deep into the ground accreting with roots. Water was falling along the wall where the stairs leading to the upper levels of the castle were. The flow of the waterfall went down to the small inner fountain under the stairs. Isabelle watched in admiration the mesmerizing beauty of the castle's construction.

Leonor apologized, informing the others about her wish to go straight to her own room to have some rest. The long sea trip and being on the road for several hours had been tiring for a pregnant lady. No one objected to her wish.

Soon, everyone was invited to the great hall of the castle, and the long, tiresome day ended with a delicious evening dinner.

Isabelle went upstairs. However, despite the long trip and hard day, Isabelle couldn't fall asleep at night. She spent the whole night turning around. The room was cool. In the corner of the room, on the opposite side of the balcony, a small fireplace was lit. When Isabelle stood and approached the balcony, it was almost morning. Yet stars were shining high in the sky. The cold autumn wind brought the scent of the forest into the room. Isabelle noticed a lot of flying fireflies below in the garden. Their night dance in the garden was mesmerizing. Then she noticed a shadow in the sky. A big eagle was making circles high above. It was hard to notice the eagle at first sight.

Isabelle moved the white, translucent curtain of the balcony's doorway. She was afraid to be noticed by the bird. Hiding behind the curtains, she watched the eagle for a while. After a few turns in the sky, the bird disappeared behind the lonely mountain. Soon, the first rays of the sun looked down. The colorful sunrise brought brightness into the dark sky. For a while, Isabelle stood on the balcony and admired the beauty of the surroundings. She didn't notice how the time had passed.

After a knock on her door, Miray entered the room. The other maids followed her with a bowl of hot water and fresh clothes for the queen.

"You are already up, Your Highness! Hope you had a good night's sleep."

Miray moved the stool near the carved wooden console mirror. All the furniture in the queen's chamber was made of wood. The whole Castle of Crystal Green was made of wood. The carvings of pictures and ancient symbols gave the forest castle an unnatural, at the same time mysterious, beauty. The opposite wall of the balcony was covered with evergreens. Neatly cut ferns were all over the wall. It was cut from the middle with a horizontal row of white iberis. Below the iberis, the purple phlox, surrounded by light-green hostas from both sides, went down the row.

Isabelle washed her face in the hot water brought by the maids. Soon, the queen prepared to go out. Downstairs Isabelle found Leonor. She was chatting with her mother-in-law on the veranda, the entrance of which looked out to the lake in the saffron fall crocus garden.

"Your Grace!" Lady Devora welcomed the queen.

Leonor put her cup on the small, round table near the bench they were sitting on.

"Had a good rest?" asked Lady Devora.

"Hardly can say. I can't sleep in totally new places," answered Isabelle.

"This is your home now. One of them. Soon, you will get used to it."

"May I offer to have breakfast in the garden. The day is fine today," proposed Leonor to the women.

"Would be great," Isabelle agreed with Leonor.

Lady Devora made a signal to the servants waiting not far for them. They hurried to prepare the breakfast table for their ladies.

"What about the king and his men? Won't they join us?" asked Isabelle, wondering if the king would object to it.

"The lords already had breakfast," answered Leonor. "My brother and Estevan went hunting early in the morning."

"It is their most beloved activity," added Lady Devora.

Isabelle said nothing. On the contrary, she was glad to hear that the king wasn't in the castle.

"This place holds the dearest memories of our childhood. Hope you will fall in love with this castle too."

"This place is really a fairyland. How often do you visit the castle?"

"We haven't been here since . . ."

Leonor started to speak but couldn't finish her words. The memory of the past bothered her, and she changed her mind about saying what she wanted to. Anyway, it wouldn't be appropriate to talk about that to the queen.

"Forgive me, Your Grace."

"Since the great tragedy!" finished Lady Devora instead of Leonor. "Why remember the past, especially if it brings sadness? Let's go to the garden. Probably the servants had already prepared everything."

Lady Devora made a gesture toward the direction of the garden, at the same time letting the queen know that they would follow after her. Two other ladies of the House of Griffin joined them at breakfast.

At that moment, far from the castle, King Leon and Estevan were walking in the forest, searching for traces of animals. Estevan sat down and touched the ground with his right hand. The grass on the ground had been trampled on. He noticed the traces of a forest deer around. Next to him, Leon took his bow and checked the bowstring, pulling it several times. Three servants were waiting behind them with spears.

"They went east," said Estevan and rose on his feet.

Leon approached Estevan and watched the traces that he showed. He patted Estevan's shoulder. "Good," admitted Leon. "Improving your skills as a huntsman?"

"Did you think that I have been sleeping all these years spent in Camp Braaf?" Estevan said grinning. "I trained a lot while you were enjoying your cozy throne day and night."

Leon smiled back. Estevan was a brave man. Leon was proud of his brother. He was a hardworking person. Most people would admit that he acted as a kid. Estevan loved jokes. Sometimes he would be too careless in choosing proper words while talking to others. His frankness bothered others. All in all, he belonged to the royal family, and everyone expected proper behavior from the king's cousin. But Leon liked Estevan the way he was. Leon and Estevan had always had a close relationship. Their relationship mostly had an informal base when the king and his cousin were in privacy.

"I never dared to think like that," admitted the king. Leon hung his bow on his shoulder.

Estevan showed the way, and together they directed to the deep of the forest.

"By the way," Estevan continued their conversation, "do you really believe that you made the right decision?"

"What do you mean?" Leon wondered about his cousin's words.

"I am not judging you and your agreement with the mortal king, and I am not even surprised regarding the Riphean," Estevan confessed. "I myself do not like the Arimaspians. They betrayed us. They betrayed your father," he continued. He stopped and looked at Leon. "Twenty years is not that long to forget and forgive. But braafs . . ."

Leon sighed. "It is not what you think it is," he said.

Estevan approached the king and put his hand on his shoulder. "Brother . . . you are giving him an army. And braafs . . . they are not just soldiers. What do you think he is going to do with them?"

"He needs protection. I gave only what he asked for," answered Leon.

"But what if he turns them against us?" Estevan believed that providing the mortal king with the army was unthoughtful from the king's side. "Did you consider this option too?"

Leon laughed at his cousin's words. "Only the mortal king believes that the army belongs to him. He doesn't know. Even being under his command, the braafs will always belong to me."

Estevan looked at Leon with surprise. He didn't expect it from his brother to neglect the treaty.

"But this is cheating," said Estevan. He waited for Leon's response.

"I never trusted the king!" answered Leon shortly. "Don't judge me, Estevan. I never trust mortals."

Estevan sighed. "In that case, I'll say, you made the right decision," Estevan supported his brother. "I won't judge you."

Leon bypassed his cousin and approached the high bushes next to the chestnut tree and looked for other traces.

"Leon," Estevan called for his brother after fighting with his thoughts for a little while, "is it possible that Layland thinks the same way as you do?" he asked. "As well as braafs belong to you, the queen may also belong to him. What about your trust in Queen Isabelle?"

Estevan's thoughts had reason. Leon understood well that the queen could be used by Layland for political purposes. Since their wedding night, the queen had tried to avoid privacy with the king. On one hand, Isabelle didn't try to win the king's trust. Her acts were natural. Or was it a special way of winning the trust of the king? Leon didn't know.

He looked at Estevan. "The queen shouldn't bother you," he said. "Did you invite me for hunting or for talking?" asked Leon.

"You know I like doing both of them," Estevan said smiling. "Anyway . . . don't trust the queen in everything," he warned Leon.

"I won't," said the king.

Even though Isabelle was his wife, they belonged to two different worlds. Leon had lived long to see the extent of mankind's devotion. He saw the edge of their patience and where self-benefits brought treachery. In this life, he could trust only himself and no one else.

Estevan noticed another trace. "This way," indicated Estevan to the others, and they directed to the east.

Leon walked slowly behind him. The three servants followed their masters. Following the traces, the king and his men spent an additional couple of hours in the forest.

"Won't you play a bet on who will first kill the deer, brother?" Estevan decided to break the silence at last.

"No need, you still will lose," the king assured him, yet his offer seemed tempting.

Estevan didn't want to step back. Leon's words heightened his desire to win.

"What will be the reward of the winner?" asked Estevan, moving the branch of the high bush next to him.

"I should admit that you lost your fear in front of your king," Leon said laughing, checking another trace left on the ground.

He raised a broken stem of the plant left on the ground. Probably the deer stopped in this place earlier that day to eat grass. Estevan bypassed the bush and went toward the tall pine tree. He bent over then raised his hand, urging others to be silent, as if he noticed something.

Leon stopped and looked at Estevan. His cousin waved to him, asking him to come closer. Not far from that place where they were standing, next to the big willow, a deer was grazing alone. From time to time, the deer raised its head and looked around, as if it felt their presence. The long, branchy antlers of the deer towered high above its head. It stretched his neck up to get the leaves of the old tree. Estevan took his bow and put the point of the arrow on the arrow shelf. He sighed deeply and pulled the string.

The deer let the leaf go and looked at the other side of the tree. At the time the deer jumped aside, Estevan released the arrow. With a painful scream, the deer fell. Estevan and Leon also jumped in their place. Leon took his sword and got prepared for anything unexpected.

Estevan's arrow missed what it was aiming for. A long iron spear stuck out from the chest of the writhing deer. The king's cousin also raised his sword in the air. They were not alone in the forest. Leon looked toward the place from where the spear was thrown. In seconds, a tall creature of nine feet jumped out from behind the trees. It approached the dead body of the deer. The creature struck his own chest with its fist, indicating triumph, raising his front hooves several times. It bent over and pulled the spear out of the deer's chest.

Estevan lowered his sword and uttered with astonishment, "A centaur?"

Soon, two other centaurs appeared around the caught trophy. Leon noticed shadows of other centaurs. He suggested that approximately dozens of them were hunting in the forest. No one in the green forest of the Nur-adamantas had been able to see centaurs for the last hundred years. These beautiful creatures avoided any encounters with the other species that lived around. They were wild creatures that had a secret life hidden from everyone.

Leon himself had heard about the centaurs of Nur-adamantas from his mother when he was a little boy. Their mother queen used to tell bedtime stories about the beautiful inhabitants of the green forest to Leon and his sister, Leonor, but he had never had a chance to see any of them in real life. His mother told him that the centaurs were wild hunters. They were distinguished by their aggressiveness and mistrust of the surroundings.

Another centaur, standing next to the hunter, raised the deer by holding its antlers. The astonished servant of the king took a step toward the centaurs. The rustling of the leaves grabbed the attention of the forest creatures. The one who killed the deer first noticed the intruders on their lands. Angered, the centaur bellowed at them and galloped toward Leon and his men. It raised its hand and waved its spear in the air.

Estevan clenched the hilt of his sword in his hand. Centaurs were believed to be strong and ruthless in battles. However, when the distance between them and the creature shortened, Leon went forward and, with all his strength, drove his sword into the ground and knelt.

The centaur stopped a few steps away from Leon. It bellowed at Leon and hit the ground with its front hooves several times. Despite the centaur threatening Leon with its spear, the creature didn't attack the one without a weapon. The centaur puffed with anger while watching him sitting on his knees. Leon raised both his hands in the air, letting the creature know of his peaceful intentions. The other centaurs that approached the intruders also watched him, trying to understand the reason for their invasion.

"*Aros,*[5]*" said Leon in the old Welsh language. He slowly rose to his feet.

According to the queen mother's tales, Leon had heard that the centaurs of the Nur-adamantas belonged to Karadans root, whose ancestors lived in northern lands. When their home was destroyed during the great war, all the centaurs, as well as many Celtic tribes, were moved to the south from Galloway Forest.

"*Aros yn dawel,*[6]*" Leon repeated to the centaur, calling him to calm down.

---

5 * *Aros.* (Welsh)—Stay.

6 * *Aros yn dawel.* (Welsh)—Stay calm.

Estevan also drove his sword into the ground. The servants repeated what their masters did.

"*Fy enw i yw Leon Ulyses,*[7*]" Leon introduced himself. "*Rwy'n fab i Aodh Ulyses, ŵyr Taron Ulyses.*[8*]"

The centaur looked at him with mistrust.

"*Nid ydym yn elynion!*[9*]" continued Leon. "We are not enemies to you!"

For a while, the forest creatures watched them carefully. Then the centaur stepped back. He lowered his spear and bowed to Leon.

"*Y brenin!*[10*]" uttered the creature.

The other centaurs also bowed to show their respect to the king. Leon pulled his sword from the ground and put it back into its scabbard. He took a few steps back to let the creatures know about his intentions of leaving them alone. The centaurs took their trophy. They left the hunting field and disappeared behind the trees. At last, Estevan sighed with relief.

"I thought we would end in this forest and lose our souls forever. Yet what a scary creature these centaurs are," admitted Estevan.

"We invaded their territory. Good thing we were able to avoid the fight," said Leon.

"You are right," confirmed Estevan. "Let's continue our journey. Maybe we still have time to check our luck."

"Still want to hunt?" surprised Leon. "I thought you were ready to turn back and run," he teased his cousin.

"You wish! Nevertheless, I don't want to return with empty bags," admitted Estevan.

Estevan went ahead. They wandered around the forest for an additional hour, looking for an animal. During the time they had spent in the forest, Leon and Estevan were able to hunt two wild ducks and western capercaillie. At last, they gave up on finding any big animal to hunt and decided to return to the castle.

Midway toward the edge of the forest, one of the servants stopped. He noticed some noise behind the bushes. The others also heard the noise when they stopped. Estevan took his sword and

---

7 * *Fy enw i yw Leon Ulyses.* (Welsh)—My name is Leon Ulyses.

8 * *Rwy'n fab i Aodh Ulyses, ŵyr Taron Ulyses.* (Welsh)— I am the son of Aodh Ulyses, grandson of Taron Ulyses.

9 * *Nid ydym yn elynion!* (Welsh)—We are not enemies!

10 * *Y brenin!* (Welsh)—The king!

approached the bushes. Leon also got prepared. The servants raised their spears.

Estevan was very hopeful for luck. He got close and moved the edge of the bush with his sword. Suddenly a little wild shoat ran out behind the bush. The shoat ran under Estevan's feet and knocked him down.

"Damn!" shouted Estevan when he landed on his lower back and cut his hand on his own sword.

One of the servants tried to catch the shoat.

"Leave it!" shouted Leon.

Estevan tried to stand up, but he threw himself aside when he noticed a wild boar of four and a half feet in front of him. The fierce mother of the shoat attacked Estevan for scaring its child. Estevan waved his sword but couldn't get the boar. One of the servants threw their spear but missed the animal. Leon rushed to take a spear from the hands of another servant and threw it toward the boar. The wild animal fell down growling. Estevan raised his sword high and aimed at the boar's neck. His strike was hard. The animal stopped moving. Estevan and Leon looked at each other.

"And here is our trophy of the day!" said Estevan.

Leon observed the body of the animal. "Let's take it to the castle," said the king. "We have to return already."

The servants pulled the spear and tied the boar's legs with a rope. As soon as they finished with the animal, Leon and his men turned toward the castle. The little shoat followed them on the way to the castle. From time to time, it stopped and gave a long, longing cry for its mother.

While listening to the screams of the wild shoat, Leon thought about life. How ruthless could it be? Hunt was an amusement for him. But from now on, the orphaned shoat would have to live and survive on its own in the wild forest. Would it survive till next spring, or would it be buried under the snow of the coming severe winter? No one knew. Leon hurried the rest, leaving behind the wild shoat. Soon, they reached the edge of the forest. The trees became thinner, the day lighter. They were already home.

Chapter 9

Anything to Promise

After breakfast, Isabelle wanted to look around the castle. Leonor gladly agreed to walk with the queen. The weather was pleasantly cool. A long, narrow road along the crocus garden led to the lake with water lilies floating on its surface. Soon, Leonor got tired because of their walk. She was almost in her last few months of pregnancy. Isabelle proposed to Leonor that they had a seat by the lake, feeling sorry for Leonor due to her condition.

Around the lake was laid a stone wall of sixteen inches high. Pink and purple phlox plants were growing all over it. The two ladies approached the bench near the lake. The other side of the lake was a land of huge trees that had grown old for millennia.

"I never could imagine that such beauty does exist in reality," said Isabelle.

"How I missed being here," Leonor sighed.

Isabelle closed her eyes and took a deep breath of fresh air.

"This is a place where you can find peace of mind and soul, Your Grace. A place that heals everything."

"I think I could stay here for quite a long time," Isabelle confessed.

"Totally agree with you. If there weren't family obligations, I could have stayed here forever. All of us."

"What about the king?" Isabelle inquired.

"His heart belongs to this land. All that keeps him away is his duty to his family and the world. The throne is like a chain for my brother."

"What kind of man is he? I mean, is he a good king?" Isabelle inquired.

Leonor nodded to the queen's question. "I guess he is. After all, I don't know any other centenarian king, not mentioning my father," said Leonor. Her gaze was fixed on the lake. "Of course, he is very good, kind, and the right one. I like him like my brother and my king. But if Estevan would do what my brother did for his family, I would never forgive him. Even in the afterlife."

Leonor's words confused the queen. Isabelle didn't know what to answer or ask her sister-in-law. Leonor noticed that she had said unnecessary words to the queen. She turned red, ashamed of her words.

"Oh! I apologize, Your Grace, for what I did say. I didn't mean that he is a man with a bad personality. I just disagree with some of his decisions."

"You actually scared me, Leonor!" Isabelle said in response and smiled.

There was a little pause between the ladies. Isabelle first decided to break the silence.

"Honestly, may I ask you, Leonor?"

"Whatever you would like to ask, Your Grace," answered her sister-in-law.

"I know that the king was married previously. What happened to his family?"

"Haven't you heard about it before?" Leonor was amazed.

"Just rumors. I am not sure that I have heard anything. There are a lot of gaps in the stories."

"You probably have heard about the tragedy," Leonor suggested.

"The one that Lady Devora was talking about?" Isabelle asked.

Leonor nodded. "Twenty-two years had passed since the day we were betrayed by one of the moon sisters," said Leonor.

Isabelle nodded. She knew what story Leonor wanted to tell her queen.

"She, the one who betrayed us, was the youngest sister of the twins Ailidh and Idelisa. My mother was the keeper of the dark heart, and the safety of the red heart was under the responsibility of the mortals. The heart was given to your mother, my queen."

Isabelle kept listening in silence. She was aware of the fact that the world belonged to centenarians as well as the mortals. The four children of nature were responsible for the balance and peace in the world, and they ought to protect the heart of the earth. The heart had two sides: black and red.

The black heart was a symbol of darkness and was a reflection of life for all mythical creatures. The red heart was a symbol of blood and reflected the world that belonged to the mortals. The heart was kept at the bottom of the Lonely Mountain in the land of the Ifrans. When the great war ended, the mortals demanded for the red heart to be given under their protection. The people still were angry. The war had brought a lot of destruction. They wanted to keep the power of the earth in their own hands. They couldn't let centenarians have all of it, so the heart was divided into two parts.

For centuries, the queen of the centenarians was the keeper of the black heart. However, the red side of the heart was kept in the highest tower of the Incitydoor. The position of the heart-keeper was given to the queen of the mortals and passed from generation to generation, from one queen to the next one that belonged to the Layland Dynasty. When the last queen of all mortals, wife to Arawn Layland, passed away because of serious illness, Isabelle's mother became the keeper of the heart. The heart was moved to Ardoran, the city that was under the command of Isabelle's father. Isabelle was three years old when the one who betrayed the world attacked the city to steal the red heart. Her mother died protecting the heart.

"We all lost someone in the war," Leonor continued. "Leon had to choose. His family was on one side of the cliff and the world on the other side of it. He chose to save the world and sacrificed his family, his queen and his heirs."

Isabelle said nothing. She seemed to be drowning in her own thoughts. At that moment, Leonor noticed two silhouettes passing behind the trees on the opposite side of the lake. Their steps were slow.

"Here they are!" exclaimed Leonor to the queen.

The king and his cousin Estevan went straight toward the ladies. Three other men were following their lords. They carried the catch. When they approached, Estevan bowed to the queen.

"Ladies! You are enjoying your morning walk, I see!" said Leon with a smile.

"I heard you went hunting, Your Grace," Leonor tried to be polite.

Leon confirmed.

"We had a great catch," added Estevan.

"Oh my goodness, Estevan! What happened?" shouted Leonor as she had just noticed the wound on her husband's hand. "You are bleeding!"

Estevan waved his hand. "Nothing worth worrying about, my lady," said Estevan, trying to hide his injured hand. "I only got knocked by the wild boar," said he, raising his tone and giving special significance to the last word.

Leon laughed when he heard his cousin's words. "Did you mean 'wild shoat'?" Leon asked to tease Estevan. "Leonor, don't worry. Your husband got what he deserved."

"Brother! Don't be so cruel." Leonor gave her brother an offended look. "He needs treatment," she said.

With permission from the king, Leonor and Estevan headed to the castle, supporting each other. Leon gave a signal to servants, and they took the body of the wild boar to the backyard kitchen. Then he looked at the queen, whose relaxation and good mood had vanished with the appearance of the king and the leave of Leonor. He couldn't help but notice the changes happening to his queen in his presence. However, Leon didn't feel offended. On the contrary, the queen's behavior amused him.

Thinking about their last conversation, Leon made a decision. He couldn't let Isabelle get away from him this time.

"I hope you are enjoying your time in Nur-adamantas, my queen," Leon suggested with a half smile.

Isabelle nodded. "Yes, Your Highness! The place is as beautiful as in fairy tales." Isabelle turned her gaze to her fingers. Even if she couldn't like the place, would she confess?

"Good! My pleasure to hear that. If you don't mind, my queen, I need you to follow me," stated Leon and turned around.

He didn't wait for the queen's response, not giving her a chance to protest. Isabelle didn't know what the king wanted and went after him without a word. Leon led Isabelle to the other side of the lake. Soon, they reached a path that went through the high trees.

In a while, Leon and Isabelle entered the ancient garden separated from the main castle territory with high walls. The path became narrower. In fifty yards, the turn went into the backwoods. The crystal stairs were laid till the very edge of the ancient garden. The deeper they went, the less light there was. The big leaves of the trees closed the sunlight. When they reached the bottom of the stairs, Isabelle and Leon came to a small, open area. Isabelle could hear the noise of falling water.

"Where are we going?" Isabelle asked impatiently at last.

"You'll see," Leon answered her question shortly.

Behind the big, leafy tree, at the edge of a narrow river, a small boat was waiting for the two of them. Leon helped Isabelle to get onto the boat. Isabelle sighed with relief when, finally, she was able to have a seat. She didn't expect that they were about to walk such a far distance. Her feet were aching, and her throat was tormented by thirst, but she did not say anything.

The narrow river went directly into a cave under the lonely mount. They swam in silence for a while. The cave tunnel was dark. Leon lit a tiki torch that was attached to the nose of the boat. Soon, the boat reached the cave's underground lake with a low edge ceiling. Isabelle felt the cold chill her body. The inside of the cave was also lit with several tiki torches. Strange writings were carved on the cave's side ceiling.

"This place belonged to our gods once," said Leon. He directed the boat toward the shore. "Our great kings started the passage of their life from this holy land. These writings tell our history, how we gained our life, how we found ourselves, how Mother Nature blessed her children . . ."

"I am aware of the history somehow," Isabelle interrupted the king. She couldn't understand the reason for their arrival at Nuradamantas and why they were in that small, strange underground cave.

"You must know the sacred place of your family. It is not about history only," said Leon.

Isabelle didn't want to argue.

When the boat reached the shore, Leon helped Isabelle get out of the boat. Isabelle noticed a doorway carved in stone in a further corner of the cave. The doorway led to a narrow path that went up. Granite stairs were laid throughout the way. Leon offered his hand to support Isabelle. The stairs were high, and the way up was long. Soon, the stairs ended. In a small hall opposite the stairs, there were two elevators with an elaborate system.

"Please," said Leon, helping Isabel to climb up the elevator.

When they were ready to go up, Leon pushed the lever arm. The elevator quickly went up. At the very top, when the elevator stopped, a new passage led toward the wooden doors. It was the entrance to the first level of the high tower atop the lonely mount. It was a tower for the watchers. Leon took Isabelle to the open balcony on the last level of the tower. From the tower, the moon, the stars, and the whole world were visible like on a palm.

"This place is called *Luna si Steaua*, 'the House of Moon and Stars,'" explained Leon. "The tower was built by the Romanians. It is believed to be the closest place to the heavens. Here, our people became close to their gods."

"The view is beautiful from this high," answered Isabelle.

"I have spent my childhood in the Castle of Crystal Green. This place is special for our family. We are standing in the place where my parents joined their bonds, where they gave a promise to each other," said Leon. He looked at Isabelle.

Isabelle tried to hide her gaze from the king.

"I am sorry that our marriage started with a lie," continued Leon. "I am sorry you were disappointed in me. Here I want to make a promise. From now on, I will never let you down. I will keep my every word. Always! This I promise to you."

"But I don't have anything to promise," said Isabelle.

"Promise to trust me," Leon requested. "Be always on my side. That will be enough."

Leon's words were sincere. All he wanted from his queen was her trust and support.

Isabelle didn't know what to answer. She only nodded. She went to the edge of the balcony and kept looking from afar. Her acts were clumsy. Most of all, Isabelle was afraid of privacy with Leon Ulyses. The moment Leon opened his heart to his queen, Isabelle wished to run away, far away . . . She was afraid of her own thoughts. She was afraid to go against her own principles.

Leon knew well that Isabelle would always agree with him, would always follow her king, but her heart definitely was aiming for the opposite direction. He knew, despite Isabelle standing beside him, her thoughts and heart belonged to another shore, wherein he wasn't at all. And not knowing the reason for her neglecting attitude, Leon would try to reach her distant shores. Always . . .

Chapter 10

Iggnos Odivar

Early in the morning, Amare jumped up to the window shield and looked outside.

What a wonderful day! She thought while watching old Selestat.

Amare was eagerly waiting for this day. Today was the last day of autumn, one of the greatest days of the year that was celebrated by both mortals and centenarians. It was a common holiday for all living creatures on the earth.

During the great war, people lived in fear and faced many difficulties. For years the war had brought destruction, and hope had left everyone. Even after the end of the war, famine and sicknesses took many lives. Winter became a reminder of the old cold days of the terrible past. The coldest season of the year always used to be the hardest period for everyone. Thus, with the proclamation of King Taron Ulyses and other mortal kings, the last day of the autumn had become a holiday that was annually celebrated worldwide. They called it *Iggnos Odivar* ("The Last Day"), or *Igzui Odivar* ("Fall Farewell").

It became a special day when people said goodbye to autumn and greeted the winter smiling widely and praying to overcome the difficulties of the coldest season of the year with ease. On this day, everyone would go outdoors and celebrate the holiday together by singing merry songs and sharing special holiday meals with neighbors. Everyone would bring to the center of the city or village what they had at home.

The door of the common room opened, and a tall girl with a lot of wrinkles on her face ran inside.

"I found it!" shouted the girl, holding a golden brooch in the shape of the sun.

She ran toward her little sister, Melanie. She sat down beside her and fixed the brooch on the right chest area of the little girl's white tunic.

All the girls were wearing long, white, long-sleeved tunic dresses up to their toes. Their shoulders were covered by long, hooded white cloaks. They wore flower headbands on their heads made of Vendela roses, white phalaenopsis orchids mixed with lisianthus, and fresh seeded eucalyptus. All the girls had similar golden brooches in the shape of the sun fixed on the right chest area of their tunics. The golden sun, with thick and wavy rays around the circle, was the main symbol of the Selestat Light House.

"Where did you find it, Beatrice?" asked Amare turning toward the girls.

"Under her bed," said Beatrice. "Melanie is so careless," she added.

When Beatrice finished her work, Melanie ran toward the tall mirror with a wooden frame in the corner of the room and looked at her own reflection. Satisfied, the girl smiled widely.

"Oh, I can't wait till the parade starts," Charlotte said impatiently. She straightened her headband.

Amare approached the mirror. Her long, dark-blue hair laid in curls over her shoulder reminded one of the clear night sky.

"Girls," the elder witch who appeared at the doorway of the common room called for the other sisters in a serious tone. "Get prepared. Prayer will begin soon. All go to the great hall for gathering," she said and left the room.

"Lisette is so strict, as always," Charlotte said sighing. Then she ran toward the mirror. "Let me look too," asked Charlotte, gently moving Amare aside.

"You are beautiful," said Amare to her friend.

"I know," Charlotte said, laughing and giving Amare a warm hug.

Soon, all the girls directed toward the great hall in a row of two. The prayer started with the blessings of Mother Abella. During the prayer, the girls sat in a row under the high ceiling of the great hall.

The long wooden benches located between the columns were carved from the roots of Golau, the sacred tree of light.

In the place of honor, under the thick, branchy tree next to the giant hall windows, stood Mother Abella. While praying to Mother Nature, Mother Abella begged for the blessing and mercy of their god. At the end of the morning prayer, all the sisters of the Selestat Light House approached the Golau tree that was behind Mother Abella. They pressed their palms into the basin below the tree. The rose-red color mixed with honey was sticky on the tips of the fingers. With prayers on their lips, each of the girls left their mark on the tree that symbolized their belief.

After the prayer, the girls went outside the abbot. The streets were full of people celebrating the last day of autumn. A big, round table was decorated around the old oak tree at the center of the commune. It was filled with different types of food, yet there were still people carrying baskets toward the table. Close to the center, in the corner of the street, several men were playing musical instruments like the chalumeau, musette de cour, and tambourine.

Near the big, red gates of the next street, a young man was singing a serenade to his beloved under the tunes of the lute. Next to Mr. Bastien's store, children were joyfully screaming and jumping around the old man, who was sharing nice wooden gifts that consisted of different shapes of carved animals, birds, butterflies, and many others.

Holding each other's hands, the girls went to the center of the commune. Amare took a round-shaped cake with nuts and had a bite.

"Hmm . . . so delicious!" said Amare with satisfaction. "Do you want a bite?" She handed another one to her friend.

Charlotte screamed with joy when the sweet bite of the cake melted in her mouth.

"Bonjour, Mr. Bastien!" Amare shouted to the old man while passing by the store.

The old gardener greeted the girls warmly. The children playing in front of his store started jumping around the girls.

"Charlotte! Charlotte, please show magic!" the children begged Amare's friend.

"Charlotte, you could show them the magic that you recently did with the light," Amare suggested.

"I only tried it twice. I may not succeed." Charlotte loved to spell. However, she was afraid to disappoint her little friends who were eagerly waiting for the miracle.

"Charlotte, please!" The children kept pulling the girl's hands, urging her to cast a spell.

"All right, I will do my best," Charlotte agreed at last.

She turned around and took a thin branch from the ground. "*Roon eib!*" the girl uttered.

When a tiny light lit up at the end of the branch, Charlotte blew on it. She caught the tip of the light with her fingers and pulled it further. The light lengthened, creating a long, thin line like a golden thread. When Charlotte waved her hand in the air, the long thread went up into the sky and turned into tiny sparkling particles. Amazed, the children screamed happily and started running under the golden rain falling from the sky.

Happy about her friend's success, Amare watched her own hands while clapping. Would she ever be able to cast a spell? Amare hid her fears under a bright smile. She hated her own hands, her useless hands . . .

"Oh, they started playing instruments in the main square! The show is about to start."

Charlotte's words disrupted Amare's thoughts. Only now did she pay attention and hear the sounds of lively music.

"Let's hurry up!" Charlotte pulled Amare toward the main square.

The people of Selestat already stood in the middle and danced in unison to the music. Holding each other's hands, they went around, occasionally jumping and clapping before changing places with the other dancers. The stream of dancers quickly attracted the girls, and Amare and Charlotte found themselves cheering and laughing in the middle of the square among the crowd. They happily participated in additional two music pieces before being called by Beatrice.

Leaving the dancing area behind, Amare hurried after the girls.

"Wait for me!" Amare shouted to her friend, who was running a few steps ahead of her. "Charlotte!"

"Hurry up!" Charlotte urged Amare. "She already started her stories!"

The girls ran toward the bridge. On the day of Iggnos Odivar, and many other holidays, Mrs. Bastien loved to go to the small yard behind the bridge. She loved to sit on the old wooden bench and tell different stories. Children listened to her stories with great admiration. Charlotte and Amare also loved the old woman's stories. Most of all, the girls favored the story about the great war between the centenarians and the mortals. Despite the girls knowing her stories by heart, they ran to the bridge whenever Mrs. Bastien started telling them.

Charlotte and Amare passed by Mr. Bastien's store and directed to the south. When they reached the destination, Mrs. Bastien, surrounded by dozens of children, was at the center of everyone's attention. The girls sat behind the children of ages six to eight. Even though the children were quite small, Charlotte and Amare could hardly see Mrs. Bastien from their seats because of all the headbands.

"It was their third victory . . . conquered with a great effort . . . ," continued Mrs. Bastien. "The cost was the life of many innocents. The king gathered his army and went east. He knew that the end was not close. Even after so many battles, Quinn still had power. Worse than that, he managed to gain even more supporters after his great loss in the Pamir Mountains. Whispers were everywhere. Darkness was calling . . ."

Charlotte squeezed the part of her skirt in her palm. It seemed her consciousness took her back to the past, like she was watching the whole event with her own eyes.

"The men who followed Quinn's tracks were chased by dark shadows in their dreams. Screams were everywhere . . ."

"I can't listen anymore." Amare covered her ears with both her hands.

"What are you doing? You'll miss the most interesting part." Charlotte grabbed Amare's hands. "Put them down!"

The girls fell silent when one of the listeners in front of them turned at the girls with an angry shushing face.

"On one of the coldest nights of February, the king and his army came out in front of a vast valley. Snow particles were slowly dancing in the air. The icy snow crunched under the feet of the soldiers . . ."

"Oh, it's the Dolorem part," whispered Amare.

The girls were so engrossed in the story that they didn't notice Mother Abella's approach. Mrs. Bastien first saw Mother Abella and nodded to her old friend. Mother Abella didn't want to interrupt Mrs. Bastien and made a signal to the girls to follow her. The girls were upset as they couldn't stay till the end of the story.

"Mother Abella," Charlotte broke the silence while following the chief sister of the saint house. "All that Mrs. Bastien told can't be true, can it? And if the prophecy is real, then what will happen to us? What will happen to our world?"

"Should you trust all the nonsense that you hear?" Mother Abella answered the question with another question, walking slowly.

"But it is our history, our past . . ." Charlotte didn't want to give up. "Books teach us . . ."

"Books were written by writing fans, silly chroniclers, not by the ones who created history. The eyes of the creator and the eyes of the observer see the same thing differently." Mother Abella stopped and looked at the girls. "Don't waste your time on silliness. Go and join your sisters!" ordered the chief sister, going away.

Amare and Charlotte went to the east from the central square and joined the other members of the abbot. When the last rays of the sun painted the wide sky scarlet, its borders met the first messengers of the night in the far distance. Soon, when the sky totally lost its beautiful colors and was covered with a black veil, everyone in the commune lit the candles in their hands. The time for night prayers had come. When everyone had finished asking their own gods for their own benefit, Mother Abella and the other elder witch sisters raised their hands with the candles above their heads.

"*Adanai ord-ara noi,*" whispered Mother Abella.

"*Adanai ord-ara noi,*" another whisper was heard in the crowd.

Small flames at the tip of the thousands of candles detached from the base and rose high into the sky, shining brightly. The sparkling flames illuminated the night sky and soared in the air for a long time. Amare raised her head and looked at the tiny sparkling lights in the sky with admiration. Her heart was filled with warmth. The beauty seen above her head was indescribable. It filled the emptiness that Amare felt due to her inability to cast a spell.

Amare closed her eyes and prayed. She prayed for the power that she craved. Amare wanted to believe that one day it would come to her. And when that day came, she would no longer be a useless and odd girl. On the contrary, she would become one of the most powerful witches on the earth, even more powerful than Mother Abella. This was her promise to a girl who dreamed of a miracle . . .

Chapter 11

Deal with a Traitor

The night sky over the beautiful city located in the north of France was as bright as day. Hundreds of thousands of lights soared in the sky, looking fairy and bewitching. The people were still celebrating Iggnos Odivar on the streets.

The sounds of merry songs could be heard in some corners of the buildings. More mugs with hot ale and beer clinked whenever jolly cheers and wishes were uttered. The air was filled with the festive mood of the celebrants. Standing on a balcony of a small wooden house on the shores of River Seine, Celia watched the blinking lights over her head. The night was cooling. Despite the long-lasting wars in the country and a declining population number, Rouen was a beautiful city. Hundreds of ships visited Rouen daily. It was one of the main port cities located on the River Seine.

"Raurun ma idonas," whispered Celia, looking at the sky. "All lights go out some day."

Then her gaze fell on the people who were still walking on the streets. Celia watched a dozen men in black wool cloaks who significantly differed from the inhabitants of Rouen. Although Celia couldn't see their faces, she knew those men came to the city not for the celebration. They came to make a deal, and Celia knew about it. She had been waiting for those men since morning. Watching how those strangers disappeared behind the wooden door of the building where Celia stayed, the witch smiled slyly.

In a while, after two knocks on the door, an old, skinny man appeared at her doorway.

"You have a visitor, my lady," announced the man.

When Celia went downstairs, one of the visitors was already waiting for her next to the fireplace. His wool cloak fully covered him from head to toe. The others were probably in another room.

"Do I have the honor?" asked Celia loudly.

The man turned at once to her voice.

"Your Grace!" said the witch, slightly bowing.

"My lady," Thaen said, looking straight at Celia with a smile on the corner of his lips. He pulled off his hood and nodded to her.

Celia noticed a long scar starting from his right chin and going down to his neck and further. His outfit was in dirt and blood. Celia indicated to the table in the corner and offered a seat to her guest.

"The path was difficult, I see," she said.

"I am not complaining." Thaen gave a wide smile to the witch.

Of course, he had to fight for his life against his own men on the island. Thaen had planned to bring the Arsandars of the Skin Island to Perle de la Mer. He had planned to open the gates and let the people select between those who would follow him and those who would be left behind. Even though Thaen had known perfectly well that the task would not be easy and he was prepared for any unexpected outcome, he didn't expect that he would have to go into the battle long before the arrival of the savages. His men were the minority.

"I had heard you are beautiful," said Thaen, watching the woman in front of him. He sat crossing his legs and leaning backward, as if welcoming a guest into his house. "Great lies!"

Celia watched him with her one eyebrow lifted. She couldn't help but notice that the youngest son of King Arawn was self-confident.

"You are extremely beautiful," added Thaen, giving strong intonations to his every word, his smile even wider. Yes, the prince was too self-confident and flattering.

"I am aware of that," Celia said coldly.

At that moment, the door opened, and the old man brought in something to drink with some bread and butter to eat. He also left a bowl of fruits on the table. When the man was about to leave, Thaen stopped him and indicated to the wooden cup. He was a prince and wanted to be served, even if he had to stay in a common place for the poor.

"I expected a better welcome," Thaen complained, his face grimacing while tasting the ale.

"My apologies, Your Highness. Remind me if we are here to please you," said Celia. Her words sounded rude. Celia never hid her distasteful feelings toward mortals, be they a king or a commoner.

"Wow, why so rude?" Thaen tried to laugh aloud to hide his offense. The witch's words insulted him. "I am not an overly particular person. Maybe a little . . . But I go easy with my friends, and I kindly ask you to choose your words wisely."

"My dear prince!" Celia approached Thaen and leaned over him. "I don't want to seem rude, but please don't forget who is who in this room, who's the servant and whom to serve."

"I am a prince of Rhodareen—"

Thaen tried to object, but upon looking into the icy-cold eyes of the witch, he understood. His position didn't mean anything to the one standing in front of him. He had heard a lot of tales about the night witch.

Some said she came to you at night—she always did—and the surroundings sank into deep darkness. The moonlight faded away. She brought trouble; she always did. Some said she could make people disappear and turn her enemies into ash. Rumors were spread about the night witch. No one on earth had seen such power. Evil power. Some said she took her power from the moon. Some said she was a sister of the moon: the cursed one, the one who destroyed her own sisters—the moon sisters! People spoke about the night witch with fear. Maybe Thaen also feared. A little, somewhere deep in his heart, he knew, he was scared of her.

He straightened up and added with a murmur, "I am not forgetting."

Celia didn't pay attention to his darkened facial expressions.

"Good!" she nodded. She slowly walked toward the open window in the corner of the room. "You can stay for the night in this house," Celia added.

Thaen thanked the witch for her hospitality, trying hard to hide the bitterness in his tone.

"I admire your generosity. Surely, you could find a better place as your shelter rather than this old, cracking house," Thaen remembered that it would be better not to complain to the witch. "But it is much better than sleeping under the open sky."

"This house is good," said Celia, still watching the outside. "It's cheap, unnoticeable, with a good view of the river."

Thaen took a sip from his cup. "Well, it's old, dark, and cold . . ."—he glanced over his head—"and dusty . . . I like it." He looked at Celia, showing his teeth in a broad smile.

"Liar!" Celia said laughing. "Surely, you prefer big houses, bright and fancy. Would be even better if it were a castle or a palace."

"Big, bright, and fancy. Kings live in big castles," Thaen admitted.

"Yes!" said Celia. She went to the middle of the room. "And you are not a king!"

"I am born to be a king." Again his temper was failing him.

"No, you are not," seemed Celia was trying to tease him. "You are born to live and fade away under the shadow of your father, born to fade away under the shadow of your brothers . . ." Celia approached Thaen. She was very close. She stood high over him as Thaen felt himself shrinking very small sitting on his tiny chair. "And their children. Born to disappear . . ."

"No, I am not," refused Thaen loudly. "I won't! I am going to change this fate, and you will help me!" Thaen stood up with a shout, throwing aside his chair. "You will give me the throne, and you will give me eternity!"

"You do claim eternity like you are equal to centenarians! Shame! I won't give you anything." Celia laughed out loud.

"Then why did you agree to help me? Why did you call for me?" wondered Thaen. Wasn't it she who set their meeting? Wasn't it she who started all this plot?

Almost a year ago, before the last leaf fell, he had gone to the palace. On the way, he'd met a man—skinny, tall, and with gray skin covered in black blisters. When the man had seen the royal guardsmen, he had thrown himself to the road, shouting out loud, "My king! My king!"

He had tried to reach Thaen, but the guardsmen had thrown him away with threats.

"Out of the way of the prince, or I'll cut your throat!" the man in armor had yelled.

The man wouldn't give up. "King Thaen! King Thaen! Eternity is yours!" he'd kept screaming. "Prophecy will come to life, the world will never be the same!"

The man had known his name, and he had called him "king." Thaen wasn't "the king." He was a prince, but the man had called him differently. He had been waiting for him. Thaen had wanted to talk with the man, but his guardsman had refused as they had feared for his life.

The man had been mad, but Thaen had met with him. He had talked to him. Under the roof of his house, when the guards had been unaware. The man had appeared in his room from nowhere. Had it been magic, stubbornness, or hard work of the madman? But he had come to see Thaen. He had told him about his fate, about all his capabilities and chances. He had told him about the witch and the eternal life that she had promised in exchange for his help.

"Want to be a king? Then you must serve, and you must deserve it." Celia's voice brought him back to the present.

"So you want proof. The throne is mine, and I'll do whatever it takes to get it into my hands." Thaen looked at Celia, reassuring her, "Trust me!"

Celia burst into laughter, a very loud one. "Trust you?" she asked with irony. "A man who betrayed his own blood? Never!"

"Then what should I do?" Thaen didn't want to be rejected.

On one hand, he hated the witch. How could a woman make fun of him and laugh at his words? How could she, the fool, ignore his position? However, he needed her help. He needed this woman's support. Thaen had already taken a step—a big step toward his fate, the first step of a traitor, the step of a murderer. He had destroyed everything he left behind. From now on, he had no way back. He had no choice but to only step forward.

"Mess up the world so that Leon Ulyses couldn't do anything but disappear in the chaos that you created," said the witch at last.

Thaen laughed. The witch was mighty, but surely, she was powerless in front of the centenarian king. If she started her game without having prepared well, Leon Ulyses would destroy her effortlessly.

"I'll create such chaos. Look, even you can disappear," Thaen said with a cunning smile.

The answer of the traitor satisfied her. "Good!" said Celia.

It was all she needed. A mess. The world was in wars among countries. It had been in wars for centuries but without centenarians involved. All Celia needed was the centenarian king to be involved in the war that would destroy himself in the end. Totally sunk into the cycle of endless wars and bloodshed, Leon Ulyses wouldn't be aware of what Celia was planning in reality. He couldn't find out and prevent the chaos that she was about to unleash on the world. Leon had to be kept busy until the right time came. She was hopeful that Thaen could manage what he planned to do.

She approached the table and poured ale into the cup. "For your dream," said Celia, "and my revenge!" She drank the ale.

Thaen also raised his cup and repeated her words. "For my dream and your revenge!"

The witch nodded. She took her road cloak and directed toward the main door, stopping at the threshold.

"Don't fail me!" she said to the prince.

"I won't!" the prince assured her. "Trust me!"

Celia laughed at his words. "I won't!" she said and left, leaving behind the open door.

Thaen laughed too. He didn't know that Celia really did mean what she meant. The witch never trusted people, and she never would.

She went down by the road. On the shores of the river, she took a handful of Kaia dust from her Muscovy belt bag and poured it into the water.

"*Roien ag' Selestat,*" whispered the witch, and then she took a step into the water, walking further until she disappeared fully from the surface.

Chapter 12

The Escape

The evening was cold and windy. The woman's steps were slow. She walked east, passing by the old trees of the Illwald Forest. When she reached the hill, she looked down to the valley. At the center was a small commune: Selestat. Celia smiled with satisfaction.

"Hello, Selestat!"

The time had come, and she was the one to make the first move. Celia was standing so high and so far that no one in the city could see or feel her. She was invisible. The people, unaware of the unexpected arrival, were still celebrating the holiday. Their mood was uplifting.

Amare and Charlotte were so enjoying their time celebrating Iggnos Odivar that none of them noticed how the time quickly passed. Only when hunger started torturing the girls did they remember to return to the abbot. However, when they reached the gates of the abbot, some noise grabbed their attention. The girls quickened their steps to see what was going on at the main gates of the abbot.

Several witches were gathered around the gates. In front of the main gates, two guardians were trying to keep a person away. A man the age of thirty was trying to enter the abbot. The man looked very awful. His face and hands were with scars, his clothes half torn. The poor man stood in front of their gates barefoot. He was begging the guardians to let him in.

Soon, Mother Abella appeared at the gates. She looked at the guardians. "What is happening? Why did you let him enter the yard?"

"Mother Abella, he is requesting for a safe stay. We tried to stop him, but he doesn't want to leave," answered one of the guards to the witch.

"Who are you?" Mother Abella asked the stranger.

"Erhardt. I am Nicolaus Erhardt. I beg you, let me stay in your abbot, ma'am! I beg you." He tried to reach Mother Abella, but the guards pulled him away.

"We can't let you enter the abbot, young man," refused Mother Abella.

"I need a sanctuary. I need a safe house." The man didn't want to give up.

"This is a house of centenarians. Humans are not allowed to enter. You better seek a sanctuary in another place," advised the head of the witches.

"I can't," the man said, shaking his head.

"Go to the church. They will give you a safe place to spend the night. They'll feed you. They will take care of you," said Mother Abella. Even though she was giving advice to the man, her words sounded like an order.

"My lady, I can't go to church. If you don't let me in, I will not live till morning. I won't survive," begged the stranger with tears in his eyes.

The others said nothing but watched the man. They could not intervene as only Mother Abella had the right to decide what to do.

"Go to the church! The doors of the light house are closed for you," repeated Mother Abella.

"I can't enter the church!" cried the man, lifting his shirt up.

What was on his body scared everyone around.

"Everyone, step back!" shouted Mother Abella to the other witches around. "All, step back. He is cursed!"

The other guards of the abbot put their spears against the man.

The man knelt and started crying to the old witch, "Please help me, or I am dead. You need to help me!"

Amare could not understand what was happening. The man had a strange symbol on his stomach, close to his navel. The symbol looked like a snake circling a flipped-over moon. The snake's mouth was wide open, as if it was ready to swallow the moon. The symbol was carved with something sharp on the man's body. Amare could easily see traces of blood.

Mother Abella took two steps toward the man. "Where did you get the mark?" Mother Abella asked the man, her voice sounding menacing.

"In the Forest of Illwald, the other side of the river," answered the man in tears.

"Who gave it to you?" asked Mother Abella again.

"I don't know," said the man.

"I am asking again, who gave it to you? And don't dare to lie!" threatened the old witch.

"I swear, I really don't know," the man put his head to the ground. "I really don't know," he cried.

Mother Abella looked at him for a while then told the guards to take him to the roof of the abbot and lock him there. The guards took the man and started pulling him inside. Their act scared the man, and he tried to get away from the guards.

"Please don't kill me. I only wanted a safe house. I'll leave in the morning. I promise. Don't hurt me . . . please," cried the man.

No matter how hard the man resisted, the guards didn't release him. They were strong enough to restrain him. When the guards took the man inside, one of the elder witches protested against Mother Abella's decision.

"Mother Abella, you can't let a human enter the light house," said the witch.

"He doesn't belong to the world of the mortals anymore."

"But he is cursed!" objected the witch.

Mother Abella pushed the witch aside and whispered to her with anger in her voice. All who were around watching them could hardly hear what Mother Abella was telling the other witch.

"That is why he must stay with us. Did you see the mark?"

The elder witch nodded.

"It is not just a mark of a curse. It is forbidden magic."

"Dark magic?" asked the witch with astonishment.

Mother Abella nodded in approval. "Very powerful. There is no witch left living on earth who has such power to do this, but if there is one . . ."

"What will happen then?"

"Pray for my thoughts to be a mistake." When the old witch finished her words, she looked at the others. "Go and do your work. No need to stay here."

The others did not know what to do or how to react to what they had seen and heard at the gates of the abbot. They obeyed the old witch and went to the common hall to join the other witches for dinner. Mother Abella ordered her assistant witch, Andreanna, to deliver the man's evening meal and afterward light the candles around the room he was given for the night's stay. The guards had to watch him the whole night.

At dinnertime, everyone sat still. Even when some of the girls dared to talk to each other, they only spoke in whispers. For the first time, a human was staying within the walls of the abbot. No mortal had ever dared to enter the witches' house till that evening. Amare listened to the conversation of some girls sitting next to their dining table. They also were talking about the new guest at Saint Daman Abbot.

"The elder witches are saying that the man is cursed," said one of the girls.

"No one is saying that, Marie. Stop scaring everyone around," said another girl.

"She is not lying. I heard, the elders were talking about the curse," the third one said to them.

"I heard it too," confirmed the other girl sitting opposite the others.

Amare looked at her friend Charlotte sitting next to her. Charlotte also gave a look at Amare, but she did not say anything. She just continued eating. When dinner was over, all the members of Saint Daman Abbot were sent to their rooms. No one was allowed to leave their rooms late in the evening.

That night Amare tried to fall asleep in her bed, but all her efforts were in vain. It was already midnight. How many hours were left till sunrise? She didn't know. She was staring at the ceiling of her room. Everything was still. Her fingers were playing with her friend's red ribbon on her hair.

Charlotte had started watching sweet dreams a couple of hours ago. She had always been very good at sleeping. However, Amare had always had a problem. At last, she closed her eyes. Her mind became misty. Amare started falling asleep, but a sudden sound made Amare open her eyes again. It was like a whisper, like someone was talking in the dark.

Amare rose. She sat on her bed and looked at the door. She concentrated her thoughts. With all her body, she tried to catch any noise. And then again . . . a whisper . . . She looked at her friend.

"Charlotte . . . are you really sleeping?" Amare asked in a low voice.

Charlotte did not say anything.

"Charlotte, is it you? I am a bit scared. Please stop it if it is really you."

Amare approached her friend's bed. Charlotte was sleeping.

"Charlotte! Wake up!" Amare tried to wake her friend up, but the girl turned to another side of her bed and continued sleeping.

Amare heard the whisper again. Who was whispering? And what were they talking about? Amare did not know. She could not understand the words. She went to open the door but saw no one in the dark corridor. Although she was very scared, Amare decided to go outside. With one hand holding the walls, Amare directed toward the staircase.

Amare went upstairs, and on the last level, she turned to the right. She didn't know how she came to the place where the guards kept the human. His room was supposed to be at the end of the long corridor. Taking small steps toward the end of the corridor, Amare's hands felt water on the walls. Then she stepped on a puddle. The floor was full of water. While walking, Amare could hear splashes of water. She wondered whether the roof was leaking. Suddenly someone held her shoulders and pulled her back.

Amare wanted to scream, but that someone covered her mouth with cold hands and whispered, "Why aren't you in your room?"

"Mother Abella? I am sorry . . . I heard—" Amare tried to talk but was silenced by the eldest witch.

"You better keep quiet." The woman did not let Amare finish her words. She dragged her and directed her toward the staircases.

"Mother Abella—"

"I said, keep quiet. We need to hurry," Mother Abella almost yelled at Amare.

The old woman held the girl's hand tightly and led her to the very bottom level of the abbot. She was walking very fast she was almost running. Amare could not understand why the old witch wasn't returning her back to bed. As they were crossing the long corridor toward the dungeon stairs, Amare heard some noise from the passway leading to the main gates.

At the very bottom level of the abbot, when the two of them approached a big, black wooden door, Mother Abella took a big golden key and opened the door. After they entered, Mother Abella closed the door with the key.

"*Noi!*" whispered the woman, and the lights in the room lit on.

Amare looked at her hands and screamed. Only under the lights did she see that her hands and feet were all covered in red. What Amare had believed to be leaking water was, in fact, blood.

"Dear God, what is it?" Amare cried.

Mother Abella said nothing. She went up to the old fireplace and put her hands on the wall. Afterward, Mother Abella closed her eyes and read a spell in a whisper. The wall of the fireplace started moving aside, and a small, long corridor appeared behind it. Mother Abella pushed Amare toward the corridor.

"*Roon eib!*" whispered Mother Abella. At the same time, a little light ball appeared behind them. The eldest witch looked at Amare. "Follow the light. It will show you the way out."

"Mother Abella, what is happening?"

Mother Abella took something out of her robe's pocket and handed it to Amare. It was a round silver locket with very strange symbols on top of it.

"Take this. Don't lose it! You must reach the end of this corridor, then you will go out. Go to the forest. Go to the south. Don't trust anyone. Find the Moon City," ordered the woman.

"I don't understand," Amare shook her head.

"I made a mistake. The curse didn't belong to the human. It was a spell for us, and I did let it in. Find the heart! It will save you, save you all!"

The old woman pushed Amare to the small corridor even harder.

"We have no time!" she shouted.

"Mother Abella, I can't leave. What about you? What about Charlotte?" screamed the girl, trying to get back inside.

Mother Abella held the girl's shoulders with both her hands. "I had lived a millennium to seek you. I promised to keep you safe when I found you. You must live. Whatever happens, stay alive. Do you hear me? Stay alive!"

What Mother Abella said made Amare shiver. The woman returned to the threshold of the corridor.

"Now go! Run!" she screamed, and after two knocks on the wall, she closed the way between Amare and herself.

"No! Mother Abella!" Amare said, throwing herself against the shut door.

She was all alone in a small corridor with a small light ball that helped her to see in the dark a little. She could not understand why Mother Abella wanted her to go—alone. If the witches of the abbot were in danger, why couldn't they all leave through the secret path?

Mother Abella sacrificed her life and all others in the abbot and saved only Amare. Why? She didn't know. The girl screamed at top of her voice, striking the door with her hands. Then she heard a noise like the sound of a thunderstorm from the other side of the door. The ground started shaking, and the frightened girl started running in the opposite direction.

The corridor seemed endless. She ran as fast as she could. It took maybe more than half an hour before Amare breathed fresh air again and smelled the ground after the rain.

Suddenly the brick road ended, and Amare fell to the wet ground. With her fingers, she felt cold grass around. It was very dark. The road brought Amare to the edge of the forest. It was very cold outside. All she was wearing was a sleeping robe sodden with blood and dirt. Shaking awfully, Amare looked to the east in terror.

Down the valley, she could see the fire bursting out of Saint Daman Abbot's high tower and the dark smoke rising into the night sky. She was far enough from the place where the fire was set to hear any scream or shout for help. Her consciousness couldn't accept the truth. Yet she knew that Saint Daman Abbot—where she found home, friends, and family—no longer existed. Everything she loved had turned into ash. What was left had gone into smoke.

Amare looked into the heart of the dark forest. It was very cold outside. The old and tall trees looked scary in the dark. Amare could hardly see what was three steps away from her. She kept staring for a while into the darkness with horror. She knew very well that she couldn't return to the abbot, and the only way ahead was through the Forest of Illwald. The scared girl tried to take a few steps into the forest. However, every step she took became even harder, even heavier. She closed her eyes to think of any other option. If she went into the forest, she might never come out.

Amare sighed deeply and whispered, "Mother Abella, forgive me!"

Amare opened her eyes, then she turned and ran down the valley toward the small town of her childhood. She ran, and she ran fast.

The closer Amare came to town, the better she could hear the screams of her sisters calling for help. The ones who survived the fire were put into iron cages. The whole town was in chaos. Every road, every corner of the town was guarded by soldiers. They were marching under the flag of their king, King Louis XIV of France, who inherited his father's throne a year ago at the age of four. Most of them directed toward Saint Daman Abbot. The others drove away the people who came out to see the reason for the commotion on the night of Iggnos Odivar. The ones too scared to go outside looked out through the windows of their houses. Because of the happenings, everyone was embarrassed. Staying in the shadow of an old eatery house, Amare looked at all those soldiers with anger.

"Rats! Traitors!" cried Amare. Tears washed down her face; she could not stop crying. She wished she had the power to stop all those betrayers and save her sisters. However, she was helpless!

Amare hit the wall of the old building several times to kill the pain somehow. Then she turned around and went south. Amare had to disappear in order to not be caught, and the only place she believed she could go at night was an old gardener's house on the other side of the Selestat commune.

Chapter 13

Song of the Sea

The surroundings were in deep silence. Only the uneasy waves of the sea dared to break the silence, being thrown to the ship's sides and scattering into splashes. Cael was lying on a wide bowsprit of the ship. He was watching the night sky full of stars that shone brightly in the expanses of heaven. The cold winter wind was howling, and the ocean was singing its song. Cael could feel a slight swing of the ship in the waves of the Mediterranean. He sighed. Then heavy footsteps grabbed his attention.

"Put aside your torch. I can't see the stars," Cael complained to his friend Belen.

"Why aren't you in the common cabin?" asked Belen, watching his friend. "Is it what I guess, the reason?"

"You know the reason, so why are you asking?" Cael was rude.

Belen fixed the torch at the stand and leaned on the handrail to look down. He watched how the big, white waves bubbled at the waterline of the ship.

"I can't sleep either," admitted Belen.

Cael closed his eyes. He knew his friend's thoughts. He himself had been drowning in the same thoughts since they left Valona. Cael loved the sea. It always seemed amazing and amusing for the son of the captain. The sea was luring . . . Cael loved the smell of the sea; he loved how it looked. Under the clear night sky, the sea had its reflection, as if millions of stars were shining under the dark water. For Cael, the sea was his home. It had always been . . . However, in the last few years spent on this ship, he had become tired of this home. When the next big wave struck the ship, Cael felt the water's spray under his feet.

"What do you think, what could have happened in the cave in Valona?" Belen interested. "Did you talk to your father?"

"He said he will let us know when the appropriate time comes," Cael answered lazily.

"The witch didn't free us from the oath," Belen stated. "How long is she planning to keep us under her command? Hate that witch . . ."

Cael said nothing but sighed to his friend's words.

"There is an additional thing that bothers me a lot these recent days . . ."

"What is it?"

"It's Sullivan. Something is not right with him," said Belen. "I noticed he has a lot of gatherings in the corners. People are restless because of the witch, and it seems he is going to use this opportunity."

"Sullivan is just a member of the crew. He is not even the first mate! He won't dare to go against his captain." Cael sat on the bowsprit. "But it would be better for him to be watched."

"The witch is making everything worse. I wish I could kill that witch." Belen clenched his fist.

"If someone had to kill that witch, it would be me. It must be me!" Cael dared to say to his friend.

Belen knew that Cael's hatred toward the witch was stronger than his own. He didn't just want to gain freedom; he wanted his vengeance. As well as Belen, Cael was tired of the prisoner's life on the ship.

Their life in *Incombusto* was hard. It was restless, full of danger. There was no way to escape. There was nowhere to go. Since the tragedy, they had to wander the seas performing the orders of the witch. Both Cael and Belen knew very well that no matter what was destined for them, they could never become other people anymore. They would never be who they used to be in the past. However, despite all difficulties, Cael never complained. The years had hardened him. He became who he had become. What he had faced changed him; it changed his whole world.

"We will do it together!" Belen offered.

Cael laughed at their transparent dreams. Would they ever be able to go against the witch? No matter how many times they talked about it, the witch couldn't be defeated easily. Even though they dreamed about the day of their revenge all the time, no one could deny the fact that they were helpless.

Cael rose to his feet and jumped onto the deck. He looked at his friend. "Sure, we will. And where could I go without you?"

Cael put his hand over Belen's shoulder, giving him a brotherly hug. They stood in silence for a while, letting the sea carry their thoughts away.

"How long could he keep everything a secret?" Cael asked thoughtfully at last.

Belen closed his eyes to take a deep sea breath and enjoy the night. "Still thinking about their meeting in Valona, aren't you?"

"I just can't understand why he is as silent as the dead! He could share with me his thoughts at least." Cael shook his head.

Several times he had tried to talk to his father, but the result was the same as always. Aquila refused to talk. He was quiet.

"I fail to see the thoughts of the captain," Cael admitted. "He had to use his sword when he had the chance . . ."

"It is always too easy to make the judgment." Belen tapped his friend's shoulder. "The captain is not a coward. He is the bravest man I have ever seen. There must be some significant reason for all his steps and decisions."

"Must be," Cael agreed.

Belen was right. Aquila would never walk the path of a coward or a traitor. If needed, he would die for his men. Yet he wished he knew the reason for their never-ending imprisonment in *Incombusto*.

"The one who is to be blamed is the witch . . ."

Again, silence fell on the surroundings.

"Have you decided on what to do after we gain our freedom?" Cael asked as he wanted to disturb the silence.

"Probably return to Crete. Home is waiting for us."

"I, too, am dreaming about home for a long time," Cael confessed. "The possibility of ending our lives in the dark waters of the sea bothers me a lot."

"No way!" Belen gave Cael a stern look. "I made a promise to Carissa not to live as my father did. I can't disappear in the seas, and I won't let you sink down with the ship. Promise!"

Cael said nothing but nodded. He was there when Carissa took the word of his son, the day Cael lost the woman who had become his second mother. He felt the pain equal to that of his friend. He didn't cry that day, but Belen did.

"I don't think I will ever be able to leave the ship," Cael said after a pause. "Father never will. So won't I . . ."

"You must be kidding. If you stay on the ship, so must I," said Belen. "But I can't . . . I must return home. I have my own plans for life."

Cael laughed loudly. "Haven't you ever thought of being separated from me? What about my plans?"

"I know you don't have any."

Cael looked at his friend surprised.

"You let the waves take the course of your path. Always!" continued Belen.

Cael smirked. "And what are your plans for after the ship?" Cael inquired.

"The life of a commoner. No blood, no fight, so simple."

"You are not like that," Cael tried to contradict his friend's words. "You can't tolerate the odd life."

"Really? Don't talk like you know me," Belen answered half smiling.

"I warned you." Cael slightly pushed his friend aside as if he wished to tease him.

"Let's go in," Belen proposed. "We have been outdoors for so long. It's too late, and I am sleepy as a bear."

Cael wanted to spend more time on the deck. He loved how the breeze cooled his body, but he was tired and couldn't stay awake longer. He followed his friend. Cael had almost reached the door when he heard a voice.

Help me! Uttered the voice.

Cael turned around, his abrupt action startling Belen.

"What happened?" Belen asked in surprise.

Cael rushed to the edge of the deck and looked down. He looked around, desperately waiting for another sound. He was wondering whether he had really heard a voice, but he wasn't sure.

"Cael, what's wrong?" asked Belen impatiently.

Cael once again heard the voice, so low that it could hardly be heard. The distant voice called for help.

"Did you hear that?" asked Cael from Belen.

Belen looked down. From all around, they were surrounded by the noise of the raging sea.

"You mean the howl of the wind?" asked Belen.

Cael said nothing.

"Cael, what is it?" His friend shook his head.

"Nothing! Just . . . It isn't worth your attention." Cael leaned on the handrail. He exhaled a deep sigh.

I am slipping down . . . Again, Cael heard the voice in his head.

He had already forgotten his dream. He couldn't explain the reason for such a meaningless dream. Why did it bother him in reality? He wasn't dreaming at all, but he could still hear the voice. The premonition that he had made his heart uneasy. He worried about his sister. Was something wrong? Had something happened? And was it really Hester who needed the help? In his dream, she was falling. She slipped down, and a shadow got her. Cael had lost her in his dream . . .

Suddenly he felt the thunder's hit on his palm from his dream. His memory reminded him of that pain. Cael removed his hand from the handrail, very abruptly, as if the thunder was going to hit that place at that very moment.

"You are acting weird," said Belen, still watching him.

"Am I?" asked Cael in a low voice.

Belen said nothing. He waited for his friend's response. Cael hesitated. Nevertheless, he decided to say what was bothering him.

"I am not sure, but I think I am hearing something."

"Something?" wondered Belen.

"Someone needs help. She is calling me . . . ," answered Cael thoughtfully. "It sounds crazy. It doesn't make sense, yet it bothers me. I don't know what exactly I must do."

"Is it a song of the sea?" asked Belen. "I heard sometimes sailors can hear the song of the sea, there are some sayings . . ."

"What sayings?" wondered Cael, his heart beating fast. His thoughts frightened him.

"Warnings . . . That sign is not good," said Belen. "The bad-luck messengers." Belen watched his friend attentively. "Do you hear that song?"

Cael shook his head. "No . . . I don't know!" he answered. "I am not sure . . . It's about Hester."

Belen's facial expression changed at once. "What did you hear?"

"Not what I heard, but . . ." Cael hesitated to answer.

"Cael, don't make me ask repeatedly. What did you hear? What happened? Why Hester?" Belen grabbed his shoulders.

Cael could feel how tense his friend was. His eyes were full of fear.

"I am not sure," Cael said, staring at his friend.

As well as Cael, Belen, too, was concerned about Hester. Cael had noticed that his best friend had feelings for his sister long ago. He knew that his feelings toward her were as pure as water. Belen admired the girl, but he had never thought, even for a moment, that there could be a basis for their relationship. He was almost twice her age, and surely, the girl loved him like her brother, no more. Cael knew it. Belen was a pirate but a man with dignity. He would never dare to ask the hand of the captain's daughter, especially when he was aware that the girl was special. Her fate had been written long ago.

"I saw her in my dreams," continued Cael. "There was something, a shadow. Could it be what Rhea had predicted?"

"Only a dream?"

Cael nodded to his friend's question.

"How long have you been dreaming? How many times did you have it?"

"It started recently. I had it twice."

"I believe . . . ," Belen started slowly, "Hester is fine. She must be! She is in Crete." Belen exhaled a deep sigh. "But if your dreams foreshadow the future, then I assure you, we'll find a way out to protect her. If it is required, I'll protect Hester with my life. You know me . . ."

"I know." Cael gave a nod. He knew Belen would rather die than let Hester suffer. He was a man of his word.

"You definitely must rest," Belen said, looking at his friend. Cael looked poorly. Especially after his behavior, Belen started worrying about him. "Let's go inside. It's really too late." He led Cael to the common cabin.

It took quite a long time for Belen to fall asleep. He was thinking about his friend's words. His worry didn't let him rest. However, soon fatigue made itself clear. Belen closed his eyes to welcome new dreams. The snores in the cabin were loud.

Cael didn't close his eyes however. He knew, even if he tried hard, he wouldn't be able to fall asleep till morning. His thoughts were far from the ship. They were about Crete, about his sister. He believed that everything had a reason. And whatever the reason was for his strange dream or these signs, Cael had to remember it and be ready for any obstacles to protect the one he loved.

Chapter 14

Leaving Home

Mr. Bastien was looking at the abbot's roof on fire through the window of his attic. His wife, Mrs. Bastien, was standing beside him, holding his hand tightly. She was stunned with terror to see what had happened to the abbot. She and her husband had known the habitants of the abbot for many decades, almost all their life. And in one night, everything was destroyed.

A sudden knock on the front door scared the old man and his wife. Mr. Bastien ran downstairs. When he took his robe and approached the door, he asked who was outside the door, but the man did not receive an answer. The unknown guest again knocked on the door, this time even harder.

When Mr. Bastien opened the door, he saw a young witch at the doorstep. He did not say anything but pulled her inside and closed the door, locking it behind him. Mrs. Bastien, who was standing on a staircase, covered her mouth with her palms.

"Oh, my dear goodness!" she exclaimed.

Amare looked pale, and all her clothes were soaked in blood. She was breathless, shaking because of the cold. The old man looked at the girl attentively. He tried to check her condition to know whether she was wounded.

"Amare, are you hurt?"

The girl just shook her head.

"Any pain?"

"They attacked us!" screamed Amare with tears. "Mr. Bastien, they attacked us. All are dead! They are dead!"

Amare lost her last strength and fell to her knees. She started crying in pain. The old man looked at her wife. Mrs. Bastien understood what her husband wanted and ran to the kitchen to bring water. Mr. Bastien hugged Amare tightly, saying nothing.

What he could do? Words would not help; they couldn't change the past. A person with a broken soul would not listen. Words couldn't heal . . . He knew it well, so he said nothing. He just let the girl splash out all her pain, at least what she could get rid of.

Soon, Mrs. Bastien came out of the kitchen bearing a wooden cup with water in one hand and a warm cloth in the other. She handed the water to the girl and covered her shoulders with the cloth. Amare tried to take a sip but couldn't. Again tears came down, and she hugged her knees. The more she acknowledged the safety of the surroundings, the more pain she felt in her chest.

Mrs. Bastien talked to her husband. "Help me with the oven. I need to prepare herbal tea for her," said the woman.

When Mr. Bastien left for the kitchen, Mrs. Bastien sat beside Amare. She lifted her face and gave her a kiss on her forehead.

"Take a deep breath," said the woman. "You need to take a deep breath. We'll do it together. I am here with you."

Amare felt the warmth of Mrs. Bastien's hands. She obeyed the old woman and started breathing at one pace with her . . . first breath, second, third . . .

Mrs. Bastien's words helped Amare to calm down in an inexplicable way. Soon, despite the strong pain and sorrow, all her tears disappeared. Her emotions became stable. However, Mrs. Bastien and her husband did not leave her alone. They took her to the living room. Even though everyone sitting in the room was still, Amare could feel their support and understanding. She was very grateful to have these two people in such a time.

Amare decided to break the silence first. "When I knocked on your door, I had no idea I was endangering you with my presence. I didn't think. I just came to you. I don't know why . . . Please forgive me."

"You shouldn't worry about this, kid," said Mr. Bastien. He bent over to hold Amare's hand as a sign of support.

"Even now, you are in great danger because of me. Soldiers are everywhere." Again tears appeared in Amare's eyes, and she made a strong effort to stay calm.

"I don't understand why this has happened. The previous king, God rest his soul in peace, supported the light house. The sole regent of France couldn't give such an order." Mr. Bastien rubbed his eyes. "Unbelievable."

"The abbot is always believed to be a sacred place for the centenarians, and they dared to attack! How could they take it so easily without any resistance?" Mrs. Bastien said.

"We were betrayed," said Amare, interrupting the old woman's thoughts. "They used a curse to destroy us from inside. A traitor opened the gates to the men of the king."

"Traitor among the witches?" asked Mrs. Bastien with astonishment.

"No! A mortal. We gave him a safe place. And he—" Amare covered her face with both hands and sighed deeply, trying hard to stop herself from crying again.

"It's too much for today, Jacques. Let the kid have a rest," said Mrs. Bastien to her husband.

Mr. Bastien nodded. Mrs. Bastien took Amare's hand and told her to come with her. Amare followed Mrs. Bastien to the attic. In the corner of the attic, a narrow bed was prepared for her with fresh clothes on it. Nearby was a small table with a chair. Mr. Bastien's house wasn't rich in furniture. The old man and his wife lived a very odd life. All they owned was a small house with a backyard where he had a small garden of different herbs.

"This was the room of my husband's brother. I prepared clean beddings for you," said Mrs. Bastien. "Sorry, they are not new, but this is all we have."

"Thank you very much, Mrs. Bastien," said Amare to the old woman, feeling grateful.

"Change your clothes and sleep well, my dear," said Mrs. Bastien, holding Amare's face in her palm. Then she pointed to the cup on the table. "Drink the potion before going to bed so your thoughts will not bother you."

The woman gave Amare a warm hug before leaving the attic. Both Mr. and Mrs. Bastien were very kind to Amare. She knew that the only safe place she could go on this terrible night was the old gardener's house. Only next to them could she feel herself protected at the very moment. Amare had known them since her childhood. It was only a few days ago when Amare and Charlotte visited the small garden in Mr. Bastien's backyard asking for different herbs. Amare couldn't believe that only a few hours ago, she had been enjoying Mrs. Bastien's stories under the bridge with her best friend, who wasn't alive anymore. How happy they were . . . Who could have known that their happy childhood would end so soon?

Yet Amare was lucky to have the support of these two people. Mr. and Mrs. Bastien didn't have children. They had never had a chance to have them. For many years they had lived in an old house together with Mr. Bastien's brother, who had died four years ago because of a disease. The lonely old people loved the children very much. They loved Amare and her sisters.

After emptying the potion into the cup, Amare lay down on the bed and closed her eyes. She tried to think about what had happened in the abbot. She tried to recollect the image of Mother Abella in her mind. She tried to imagine Charlotte's face; she wanted to recreate the sound of her voice. She tried hard, but the power of the potion was very effective, and soon, Amare fell asleep with tears in her eyes.

Amare! The girl heard her own name from far.

Amare! Once again the voice called her name.

Mother Abella, is that you? said Amare in her mind.

Amare!

Amare felt a touch on her forehead. The hand was cold with calluses, but a sweet and soft voice again said her name.

"Amare, wake up, dear!"

Amare opened her eyes with difficulty. The sun had already risen high above. Its rays were shining brightly and giving light to the room. She raised her palm in front of her face, trying to hide her eyes from the rays. She tried to get up from the bed but was too weak to do it alone. With great effort and the help of the woman next to her, she was able to sit on the bed.

Amare felt very dizzy. Her mouth was dry. She looked at the woman.

Mother Abella . . .

She was looking at Amare. Her lips were smiling, and her eyes were full of tears. But gradually, the image of the old woman disappeared. Amare saw Mrs. Bastien beside her. Amare could hardly hold her tears when she remembered where she was at the moment and what had happened the previous night.

Mrs. Bastien tapped her shoulders and handed the girl a cup of water. "Drink this," said the woman. "How are you, dear?"

"Much better," answered Amare after taking a few sips.

"Then good! Dear, it is already daytime. I prepared breakfast for you. It is on the table in the kitchen. Me and Jacques will go to the main square to observe the surroundings. Maybe there is something we can do . . . Also, some work is waiting for us in the greenhouse for later. I wish I could stay here with you, but work never ends. It would be safe for you to stay at home. Also, you may have a little giddiness. It is all because of the potion you drank last night. Wait a little, then you can go downstairs. After breakfast, have some rest, agreed?"

Amare nodded to the old woman. "Mrs. Bastien, I don't know how to express my gratitude to you."

"You owe us nothing," said Mrs. Bastien and wiped the girl's face. "Stop worrying, dear."

"Mrs. Bastien, thank you!" Amare took the old woman's hand between her palms. "I don't know what would happen to me if it wasn't for you."

"Shush! Let's hope all this will be left behind. And let's hope that you can stay with us in safety. Agreed?" Mrs. Bastien released her hands from the girl's grasp and tapped Amare on the shoulder. "Well, I have to go." The woman stood up and directed toward the door.

"Mrs. Bastien," Amare called for the old woman.

"Yes?"

"It would be better if I leave you." Even though Amare was scared, she didn't want to be a threat to Mrs. Bastien and her husband.

"What are you talking about?" Mrs. Bastien interrupted the girl. "Do you think we will let you leave? Where will you go?"

"I don't know, as far as I can," Amare said, shaking her shoulders.

"You should stay, girl. It might be dangerous." Mrs. Bastien was too concerned about Amare.

"Staying here is dangerous," Amare stated sadly.

"We will keep you safe. You won't be in danger." Mrs. Bastien could understand the girl's fears, but she couldn't let her leave. Amare was just a kid. She wouldn't survive out there in the world.

"It is not me who's in danger. You are!" Amare objected.

"Oh dear," Mrs. Bastien said, coming back and sitting close to Amare on the edge of the bed. "What can happen to two old people? You can't leave. Do you want us to die because of worry? Stay with us. We will be happy to help you."

"You can't help me. You can't do anything but hide me . . . and this can't last forever." Amare tried hard to hold back her tears. "I am a threat. I don't know the reason. I don't know why those people attacked and destroyed our house. But one thing is clear. They are against witches, not against mortals."

"Kid," Mrs. Bastien said, sighing deeply and pausing a little, "you have had a very tough night. I understand your situation. At the moment, you have no destination point. You have no friends or relatives to go to. Let's wait a little, at least for one day. One more day. We will think together with Jacques what to do further."

"Mrs. Bastien—"

Amare tried to object, but the woman shushed her.

"Give us just one more day. We will talk about it in the evening." Mrs. Bastien looked at Amare with hope.

The girl gave a sad smile and nodded a sign of approval.

"Good, we will talk in the evening. I promise, we'll figure something out."

After their agreement, Mrs. Bastien left the house. Amare was on the second floor and watched the old woman till she disappeared from her sight behind the gates. She kept watching the gates for a while.

"Please forgive me for everything, for God's sake," Amare whispered.

She went toward the bed. Under the pillow, she took a wrapped handkerchief. She looked into it to check whether the hidden things were still in their place. All she had was the small silver locket that Mother Abella had given her and Charlotte's red hair ribbon.

After checking them, Amare again wrapped her belongings with the handkerchief. Then she went downstairs and started inspecting the old furniture in the kitchen. She looked into the shelves hung on the wall, where she found a white cloth bag. She put her wrapped handkerchief inside it. Amare then took a hand towel. She wrapped the bread and boiled egg that Mrs. Bastien had left on the table with the hand towel and also put them inside the cloth bag. Then she took the cup of herbal tea and sipped it fast.

Afterward, Amare went to the dining hall and looked into the drawers of a wardrobe. Inside the second drawer, Amare found a small box with a few coins. She took the coins. She wanted to count them, but a very strange feeling prevented her from doing so. The girl knew it very well. Without resources, she would not reach her destination. She looked at the coins with hesitation for a long time, then Amare closed her eyes and let go of a deep sigh.

There is always a choice. They don't deserve this kind of treatment.

With this thought, she returned the coins to the box and put them back inside the drawer. Amare took one of Mrs. Bastien's winter scarves and covered her head. Before going out, the girl checked the street through the kitchen window. She didn't see any of the king's men. When she was assured that it was safe outside, she opened the door and took the first step toward her new future, toward the unknown new world. The only thing the girl knew was that she had to go south.

While walking the streets of the Selestat commune, Amare was very careful. Every time she faced the king's men, she was scared to be recognized and, even worse, to be caught. She had to leave the town as soon as possible and decided to walk by the main road of the town. She believed her decision would raise less suspicion.

When she reached the border of the town, the meadow leading to the forest, Amare got off the main road and ran into the forest. She ran very fast and didn't look back. Not even once.

Terrified, Amare ran away from Selestat, leaving her hometown, leaving her sisters. Amare didn't know what was waiting for her ahead. She didn't know whether she would ever be safe away from home. But at least for now, she knew, she was able to escape . . .

Chapter 15

Everyone Has a Right to Live, but There Is a Cost to Pay

The first days of winter were cold and severe. The days grew very shorter, and it seemed that the night god decided to establish his own reign over time itself. Strong winds whistled outside as the high waves rocked the old ship mercilessly. Raindrops mixed with snow were hitting the windows of the captain's cabin. Inside, it was quite cold. Aquila sat on his sofa and listened to the sound of the rain. His thoughts took him afar, to his homeland.

Aquila was walking on a reeds field on a sunny spring day. He was in the right place—at home, where he could find peace of mind. Home was where he was safe, where he was happy, where his family once had been. A sudden knock on his door distracted his thoughts. He didn't answer. The visitor opened the door.

"Captain," called the young pirate boy.

It was Cael, Aquila's son. He entered the cabin with the permission of his father.

"You wanted to talk?" asked Cael, closing the door from inside.

Aquila said nothing.

The boy rubbed his hands together. "Father?"

"You are late," Aquila said indifferently. After a little pause, he continued, "You know that we couldn't breach the oath, don't you? We still must serve that witch."

Cael nodded in confirmation. Aquila sighed and buried his face in his palms. He was thinking of what words to choose. Aquila knew very well that all crew members were hopefully waiting for freedom, but instead they got a new order. Everyone tried to guess what could make the captain change his mind. These people didn't know why they were not able to gain their freedom. Aquila blamed himself as he believed that he failed his own men, but he couldn't let the crew know about his thoughts. They were living the hardest times. They didn't need to see the weak side of their captain.

"We must sail to the western seas. I sent a message to the black market in Maguelone. Our men will prepare the needed reserves and weapons. We will have more guests on the ship. When I go to talk to the crew, you must be on my side . . ."

"What is the order?" Cael asked his father. He had so many questions to ask, but the only thing he could mention was the witch's order.

Aquila put the map on the table. "The witch wants us to go to the Mahv land and bring the silver leaf of Vu Ula."

"This is impossible. How could she send us to the gates of the lost world? No one had ever returned from the dead land. No one even knows whether it really exists. If we go, we'll die . . ."

"We won't!" Aquila objected. "The witch knows something that we don't know. She said we will make it. Seems impossible, but we'll make it."

"How?" Cael couldn't understand Aquila. Could it be possible that his father had lost his mind?

"There is still hope."

"There can't be any hope. Those who go to Mahv are doomed. And you . . ." Cael stared at his father, his eyes full of regret and disappointment. "Why didn't you kill that witch in that damned cave?"

"It's not that easy. You don't understand . . ."

"If I were you, I would have beheaded her without hesitation. You are a coward—"

The moment Cael uttered these words, Aquila slapped his son's face. His words hurt the old captain. All his life, Aquila tried to protect his children and his crew. He became all that he could be: a warrior, a murderer, a thief. He had become a slave, but he had never become a coward in his life. The strength of the slap made Cael step backward. He covered his cheek with his hand and didn't dare to look at the captain.

"We were burning in that cave." At last, Aquila decided to break the silence. "She returned us to the night where the whole city was in flames. I was in hell. I was burning alive. I felt the agony with every inch of my body, my skin melting . . ."

Speechless, Cael stared at his father.

"I even tasted the smell of my burned bones. If she doesn't get what she needs, we all will return to hell, forever. Death will not be the end," Aquila finished with a deep sigh.

"No one will ever agree to go to Mahv willingly." Cael disturbed the silence that reigned in the air.

"And I won't force any of them." Aquila leaned over the table, arms outstretched in front. "When we reach the mainland, I'll let them choose to stay or to leave."

"And what about you?" Cael asked his father.

"I can't leave the ship. It is my home. Even if I must die within the next few months, I don't care. I am confident in one thing," said Aquila. "If I die, it won't be the witch who kills me."

Cael said nothing and watched his father. Somehow he could understand Aquila's decision, and he could understand his father's fear. They had a mission to "do the impossible." There were only two ways ahead. Disobeying the witch meant dying continuously, forever. Their souls were cursed. On the other hand, going to the land of Mahv promised death to all who found the courage to make such a foolish decision. Mahv belonged to the demon of the underworld, and all who crossed the borders of the dead land died. There was no return. The only question left to ask was, which type of death would the man who was leaving life behind pick?

Cael knew his father was not ready to accept reality. He was not ready to die. Even though their destination point was marked with a spot of black ink on the map, both Aquila and Cael wanted to believe that the end would not reach them that soon. At least they could prolong their life for two miserable months.

Cael approached the window and looked outside. The rain became stronger. The howl of the wind was louder. The waves were very high this evening.

After sending Cael to the captain's cabin an hour ago, Cosimo decided to stay on the main deck. He swiped left his long, wet hair soaked in the rain under his hood. The deck was slippery in the rain. He held one of the lower shrouds and looked down at the waves.

"Don't like this! Don't like this! No good!" said the old pirate.

The next whistle of the rain was even stronger than the previous one. It seemed like nature was trying to show its anger. In seconds, very bright lightning hit the water, connecting the sky and the sea with a fat, long thunder line.

"Oh, God!" murmured the scared Cosimo.

Suddenly strong hands grabbed him from behind.

"What happened? What is going on?" screamed Cosimo. He couldn't see the one holding him from behind. "What did I do to you? Let go!" he screamed. "Let me go, you bastards! What is going on?"

The third pirate put a rug inside Cosimo's mouth. The other two forcibly took him to the orlop deck. When they arrived downstairs, Cosimo saw about twenty other pirates waiting for them in the farthest corner of the orlop deck.

"Why are you doing this?" Cosimo asked his fellows when the pirate named Sullivan approached him and took the rug out of his mouth.

Cosimo felt nothing good was going to come from this summon. The other pirates looked at each other.

"We want you to talk." Said Sullivan coldly.

"What? What 'to talk'?" asked Cosimo as if he didn't know what Sullivan meant.

"Tell us the truth!"

"What truth? I don't understand," said Cosimo. His heartbeat quickened.

"Do you think all on this ship are fools? You know what happened in that cave. You were with the captain," said Sullivan.

Cosimo shook his head. He knew his fellows would not leave him alone. After all, they had spent more than enough time in hell trying to get rid of the debt. The cost they had paid all these years had been very high. Patience couldn't be the best friend of those who went to the world's end with the last droplet of hope and lost it at the very last moment. They were angry.

"Maybe he will talk when he starts losing his fingers?" asked another pirate. He pulled out a small knife from his waist belt.

Cosimo felt the cold creep over his skin.

"Speak!" ordered Sullivan.

"I can't speak."

"You will speak of what Aquila is hiding, or I will kill you," said Sullivan.

"Don't be a fool, Sullivan. Only the captain will give answers to your questions. You must step back. We are one crew—"

Cosimo had tried to sound calm, but he wasn't able to finish his words when Sullivan put the rug back into his mouth again and struck his right thigh with the knife. Cosimo grimaced and tried to scream because of the pain, but he could make no sound. He bit the rug between his teeth. Tears appeared in his eyes. Sullivan turned the knife in Cosimo's thigh, trying to worsen the pain.

"Look," whispered Sullivan to Cosimo, "I sacrificed six years of my life to correct his mistake. Six years, I lived the life of the dead, and when at last I had a chance to get rid of this miserable life, again he is drowning us. I don't care what Aquila wants or what he orders. Either you are telling me the truth, or I am killing you and giving a new chance to Orrin."

Cosimo knew very well that if he didn't talk, Sullivan would kill him. There was another one who also knew the truth about the cave. After finishing with Cosimo, Sullivan would probably switch to Orrin, the other witness, and torture him too. Cosimo tried to make a sound with the rug in his mouth.

"Do you want to talk?" Sullivan asked.

Cosimo nodded. Sullivan took off the rug, and Cosimo groaned with pain.

"I'll talk," said Cosimo. "We gave the chest to the witch, but she wants us to do more work. She is sending us to the land of Mahv. We'll bring her the leaf of Vu Ula and get freedom. Otherwise she will kill us."

"The dead land? Why did the captain agree with that witch?" asked one of the pirates.

Cosimo told the other pirates what had happened in the cave, from the beginning till the end, with all details. Some pirates got scared while others got even angrier. Some couldn't accept reality. What they heard from Cosimo seemed impossible. They believed that the land of Mahv was just a legend, a created story, and nothing more.

Cosimo's words irritated Sullivan. He blamed Aquila for all their ill luck. He didn't know how to cope with his anger. He hit Cosimo with his fist.

"Coward! And you are on his side, aren't you? He betrayed us!" Sullivan turned to the other pirates and shouted, "Aquila betrayed us! Six years, we worked for him devotedly, and he betrayed us all. He made a new deal and didn't even bother himself to tell us the truth!"

"We can't go to the land of Mahv," said another pirate. "Why didn't he say where we were going?"

"We had the right to know the truth," said the other one.

"He is taking us to a death mission."

"Aquila lied to us!"

"All our troubles are because of Aquila," said Sullivan. "We are paying the cost of his mistakes. Think! We were cursed because he decided to be under the protection of the Ottomans. Whose decision was it to go to Valona? Who did it to us?" shouted Sullivan with anger.

"Aquila!" shouted the other pirates.

"We paid his debt. And now he is selling us out, once again," continued Sullivan. His every word caused more spite from others. "Aquila is not our captain. He is our curse!"

"Yeah!" shouted the other pirates.

"We overthrow him, we'll get our freedom!" shouted Sullivan loudly.

"Yeah!" the pirates shouted again. Most of them took out their swords from their scabbards with a fighting yell.

Sullivan continued his speech. No one noticed a shadow watching them in the dark. Belen was standing behind all the other pirates, witnessing all the happenings. When he saw the others getting ready to raise a riot on the ship, his anger couldn't meet its border. The people got mad. They wanted to overthrow the captain. What they planned to do would definitely bring death to his captain, Aquila, and his best friend, Cael.

Belen took a few steps back, trying not to catch the attention of his fellows. Then he turned around and directed toward the exit stairs. However, at the very last moment before he could make a turn, Sullivan saw him.

When Belen got to the main deck, he ran toward the quarterdeck, to the captain's cabin. The rain was pouring as if from a bucket. The wind's howl was louder than even the thunder. Crossing the deck, Belen tried hard to stay on his feet. Waves as high as mountains raged within the deck of the ship as if they were controlling the sea, and the surroundings were covered with a black veil.

Belen ran further. He had to warn his captain. However, when he had reached halfway to the main deck, he felt a strong pain in his left waist area. Sullivan's sharp knife had reached its aim. Belen turned around to look at his opponent.

"Where do you think you are going?" asked Sullivan.

Belen noticed several pirates on the forecastle deck behind Sullivan. The traitor didn't see them. Due to the bad weather, those who were on the forecastle deck didn't notice that Belen was injured. However, Belen knew it could be his last chance to prevent the chaos and save his captain.

Belen prepared himself, then his loud and sonorous yell echoed across the deck.

"Treason!"

Orrin was the first to react to his yell. Cursing, Sullivan attacked Belen. More followers of Sullivan joined the fight. Their opponents were the minority. Belen and Orrin would have lost the fight if the young pirate who had taken Cael's place in the crow's nest had not rung the bell as a warning.

Cael was arguing with his father when they first heard the bell ring. He ran outside. Aquila followed his son. When they reached the quarterdeck, one of the crew members attacked Cael on the stairs. Cael stopped the enemy's strike with the claymore in his right hand and raised his flintlock pistol to shoot. The pirate fell aside.

The shooting as well as the bell ringing attracted the attention of everyone on the lower decks. The pirates who went up to the main deck to face the enemy's ship were numbed in surprise. They didn't expect to see their own brothers raising their weapons against each other. They couldn't understand the reason for the fight and didn't know on whose side they had to fight.

With the sudden attack on Belen, Sullivan tried to get the advantage over his opponents who were yet unaware. However, luck was not in his hands. Belen, too, didn't give him the opportunity to start the riot later, when all the other pirates would be on his side.

Cael shot another pirate who dared to attack him. Then he saw Belen. His friend, injured, was fighting in the middle of the bloodshed. When he saw who was fighting his friend, he turned red with anger.

"Sullivan!" Cael squeezed the hilt of his claymore.

Aquila had already reached the middle of the fight field. About five dozen people were fighting against each other. Cael headed toward Sullivan. No one else but only he, the son of the captain, had to kill the traitor.

The deck was slippery, and fighting was hard. The people didn't look aside. No one cared about who was killing who. The pirates were ruthless. Their eyes had been blinded with blood.

Clearing his way from the others, soon Cael reached Sullivan. Cael was a good fighter. He had spent half of his life on the ship. He had been taught to fight by Orrin, the most ruthless and most loyal pirate in *Incombusto.*

When Cael approached Sullivan, he was busy fighting Belen. Sullivan didn't notice Cael in the mess. Cael acted quickly, running toward Sullivan. He bent over and stretched his claymore. He cut his enemy's calf muscles. Sullivan knelt, screaming in pain. He tried to strike back, but Cael's elbow hit the back of Sullivan's neck with all his strength. Afterward, Cael took Sullivan's hand and disarmed him by turning his hand to the side and shooting his shoulder. Sullivan started choking. When a pirate fighting next to Sullivan saw him dying, he raised both his hands in the air.

"I surrender! I surrender!" the pirate shouted very loudly in order for the opponents to hear him clearly. He was among the pirates who followed Sullivan. Sullivan's death meant the end of their plans.

Cael wasn't surprised to see the pirate's actions. Life was always interesting. Cael knew, a man always needed someone to believe in, someone to follow. Encouraged by others' speech, he could be ready to change his fate; he wouldn't be afraid. He could fight for the one he trusted, whether he was promised a better life or salvation. He would be ready to sacrifice his own life. He would always be ready to sacrifice for others, for their ideology. But when he had to fight on his own, for his own benefits, the hero would turn into a coward.

The pirate who believed that following Sullivan was the right decision couldn't continue the fight when he saw that Sullivan had been defeated. He gave up his fight for revenge when he lost the leader for whom he chose to fight. The pirate followed the wrong man, and he understood his mistake too late. The others, who noticed what was happening, also started putting down their weapons. Soon, the fight was over.

Aquila approached the dying man. Sullivan was still sitting on his knees. His head down, he could barely breathe. Aquila raised his sword and struck Sullivan's heart. The pirate's dead body fell onto the deck. All the pirates who participated in the riot against their captain were sent to the jail on the bottom deck of the ship.

After the riot was suppressed, accompanied by Orrin, Aquila directed to the infirmary. The screams of the people were heard from the very beginning of the long corridor. Aquila tried to control himself even though he was very angry. On the bench near the entrance, one of the pirates was wrapping Cosimo's wound on his thigh. The other pirates who also got serious injuries during the revolt were receiving treatment. At the very end of the infirmary, the main physician was taking care of Belen's injury. Cael was next to them. Aquila watched the men from the side.

"Tough night," said Aquila.

The physician nodded.

"How many dead?"

"Twelve," said the physician, rubbing his hands to his blood-soaked shirt. "Dozen wounded."

"What about the boy?" Aquila made a signal toward Belen.

"His wound is not that serious," answered the physician. "What are you going to do with the others? How are you going to punish them? Execution?"

Aquila exhaled a deep sigh. He didn't know exactly what to do. He looked at Cael. The boy noticed his father's gaze and looked back at him. Aquila turned to Orrin.

"We have to talk," Aquila said before leaving the infirmary.

Orrin obeyed his captain. For a while, Cael looked after his father and Orrin in hesitation. He rubbed his forehead and followed after them. When the three men entered the captain's cabin, they locked the door from inside. Aquila went directly to his armchair and sank into it. He closed his eyes and frowned, his eyebrows looking as if he was fighting his own thoughts. Cael and Orrin waited for their captain to say something. However, Aquila didn't bother himself to talk, as if he was alone in the cabin. Cael became impatient.

"Father?" Cael first broke the silence.

"Riot on my own ship. Unbelievable," said Aquila. "Should I punish these ungrateful beasts?"

"Captain, the decision must be made. These bastards deserve execution!" Orrin said with anger.

"Everyone has to pay for their sins. Wish I could look at their faces when their dead bodies are hanging over the shrouds of my ship."

"Do you think it is necessary? Will the punishment be enough?" Cael asked his father. He knew punishment couldn't change anything but just worsen the situation. "Are you sure there won't be another riot? It may have consequences."

"Fear is the best weapon," added Orrin.

"We could hold the whole crew with fear and threat," said Aquila. "But our situation is more serious. Now they got to know the truth before I managed to tell them." Aquila stood up and went toward the wooden table. He threw everything on it to the floor in anger. "Damn it!" shouted the captain.

"What will we do then?" asked Orrin.

"Cael, gather everyone on the main deck in an hour. I need everyone to be there. Orrin, you will come with me," Aquila said and took the keys from his shelf.

Cael looked at his father with a questioning expression. He knew they were in great trouble, but he couldn't fathom what was in Aquila's mind. What was the old man thinking about? Was it good, what he planned to do? He didn't know. Aquila didn't bother to share his plan.

"Father?" wondered Cael.

"You received your task," said Aquila.

Cael nodded and left the cabin together. He received the order. Cael knew, whatever it was, his father had made a decision, and the decision was irrefutable.

Aquila went to the bottom deck of his ship. When he got downstairs, all the pirates on the ship jail stood up. They were waiting for the captain's sentence. Orrin opened the jail's iron door, threw a bag full of weapons inside, and closed the door, locking it again. Aquila's look was frightening. The prisoners could already guess the decision their captain had made to punish the ones who committed a crime.

"I am giving you an hour. At its end, only one of you will cross the door alive. Who that one will be, you will decide. Don't make me wait. Otherwise, I'll bury everyone in this cage with my own hands," Aquila concluded and made a turn to leave.

"Captain, please forgive us!" shouted one of the pirates.

But Aquila didn't bother himself to stop and listen. He went upstairs.

The pirates stood still, looking at each other. One of the pirates who stood behind hit his fellow and rushed to take the weapon. His action brought the other prisoners into consciousness.

Aquila waited a little on the upper level of the ship, listening to the sound of striking swords, shootings, and people's screaming. Then he went to his own cabin to spend an additional hour resting. He opened his eyes when Cael came to inform his father about the summon. In an hour, everyone had gathered on the main deck. Aquila went up to the forecastle of the ship.

In the middle of the main deck, a dozen dead bodies were piled together. A severely injured pirate, who could hardly make a step, pulled the last body to the pile. With his last strength, he screamed and laid the body on top of the others and fell to the side. He swiped his forehead and looked at his captain. He did what he had to do. He survived. He took lives to keep his own.

"All, see! This is the cost you pay for unfaithfulness! This is the fate of everyone who will raise a weapon against the captain!" shouted Aquila to all who were standing below. "No sin will be forgiven!"

Aquila went down. He approached the pirate who survived the fight in the cage and took his sword.

"Pray to your gods!" ordered Aquila.

"My captain," said the pirate with a trembling voice. His hope for forgiveness withered as soon as it appeared.

Aquila raised his sword high.

"Captain, please! You promised I could cross the door alive!"

"And you did!" said Aquila.

He made a swing, and the sharp blade of his sword cut the throat of the pirate. The unmoving body of the pirate fell on top of the pile. Aquila swiped the blood off his sword and went to the forecastle deck. He looked at the others. Everyone still waited for their captain to talk.

When Aquila spoke to his people, he chose his words carefully.

"Fellows! I gathered you all to talk about a very important thing."

Everyone on the ship was listening to him attentively.

"The witch from the cave ordered us to bring her a precious thing located in a very dangerous land. The road is long. Not everyone can reach the destination safely. Maybe not all of you will be able to return alive." Aquila sighed. "I can't return from this way. Rejection means death."

The crew members started whispering to each other.

"Everyone has the right to live. In a few days, we'll reach the mainland. We'll make a stop to collect food, weapons, and other necessary stuff. If you are on my side till the end, I will appreciate it. If anyone wishes to leave the ship forever, the decision is yours!"

Aquila looked at his people for a while, then he went down. He crossed the main deck and directed toward his own cabin. The people said nothing. Everyone silently watched how their captain went away, stepping aside to open his way.

Cael said nothing. Even though he was against the cruelty and execution, he couldn't object to the decision of his father. Aquila was a smart man. He was a brave, honorable man. But at the same time, he was ruthless and wild. Cael knew his father very well; that was why he couldn't believe that the captain could ever let others leave the ship. He knew what the ship meant to his father—his people . . . The ship was his home; the people were his family. Aquila had lost everything. Looking after his father, Cael saw a man no longer fearless and strong but old, tired, and with blood on his hands.

Chapter 16

Darkness Is Where He Belongs!

The evening was mildly cool and pleasantly silent. Sanders loved walking on the streets of Incitydoor. At such a late hour, when the sun had hidden behind the great mountain walls long ago, nobody could recognize one with royal blood under the lights of twinkling stars.

The fourth pearl of the royal family and the rightful heir to the throne dressed in ordinary attire could walk among the commoners without a special escort of guards. He loved being thrown into the flow and drowning in the city bustle. Here, among thousands of people, being unknown and unnoticed, Sanders could be treated as an ordinary passerby without special honors. In these times he wasn't a distant star whom people couldn't dare to look at. Instead, he belonged to the place. He belonged to the people who could openly accept him into their modest community without any fear or formalities.

Pushing the reins of his horse, Sanders came to the southwest tributary of the Duur River. The white marble stones bordering the river from two sides sparkled in the moonlight. On the opposite coast of the river, a group of street music bands played a melody on their traditional instruments. First, a man with a long flute in his hands came forward and blew on his instrument. Another man with timpani drums joined him, and together they performed an unnaturally beautiful melody. They played melody so affectionately that it worked like a spell for those who came to listen.

Sanders closed his eyes, acknowledging the musicians' ability to create a masterpiece with odd instruments in their hands. The way the musicians performed the melody was both amazing and amusing. It could deeply penetrate one's heart and awaken both the happiest and saddest memories.

Sanders felt uplifting in his mood and uneasiness at the same time. The melody sounded like a whisper of the rain on a late autumn night and reminded him of cherry blossoms falling in the springtime.

The musicians stopped playing their instruments when the third player came to the scene with his lute. He started playing the same melody, but in comparison to his companions, his melody was faster and livelier. In a while, the first two musicians joined the one who played the lute. Their play became faster, the sound louder.

The performance was mesmerizing. Everyone around was enjoying the melody. The surroundings became lively. Not far from the place where the performance was being held, a group of people gathered at the coast of the river tributary: night prayers.

Sanders watched their religious ceremony with interest. People dressed in long, white dresses down to their toes prayed while looking at the river, over which the reflection of the full moon's silver light laid colors. The golden threads sewed onto their vests glittered under the lights of the streets. They worshipped the moon goddess and dedicated their life to serving their goddess. Sanders wasn't closely familiar with the origin of the religion. However, he had to admit that this religious movement's supporters had increased in number over the last decade. After the prayer, the people went to the edge of the border and threw a silver coin into the river.

Incitydoor was not only the capital city of their kingdom; it also was a center of different religious institutions. It was common to meet a person belonging to this or that religious cult while walking on the streets: believers, nonbelievers, those who cherished one god, those who named hundreds of them in their prayers, those who sacrificed goods in their gods' names, and those who sacrificed lives for their belief . . . The world was divided by those people who would never be tired of fighting for their beliefs and were undeniably confident in the righteousness of their way of worship.

Once his teacher taught him: "People quarrel and fight with each other for the name of their gods, unaware that, in fact, they worship the same god. They don't know that the Lord just speaks to its children in different languages . . . in the languages that they can comprehend."

Sanders had his own views regarding celestial faith however. He had stopped being committed to any of the religions many years ago. Sanders never dared to tell his relatives about his attitude. For him, there was no purity and sincerity in these people's oath, no faithfulness under their faith. It was just a game played by the ones in power to control the ignorant ones. As well as the games played by kings, the games of gods were also played under two main rules: power might be obtained by giving hope or by killing it. At his young age, Sanders had already faced these fierce rules of the games, and he had already played by both rules.

Soon, raising their torchlights up high, the night prayers went out of sight. Sanders stayed to listen to the music at the coast. When he returned to the palace, it was very late. He decided to go straight to bed and rest. But on the way to his chamber, a maid in a rush accidentally collided with him.

"Your Highness, please forgive me!" begged the maid, falling on her knees.

"What happened?" Sanders asked the maid. He was a little surprised to see a maid rushing inside the palace. "Where are you hurrying at such a late time?"

"We can't find the junior crown prince, Your Highness!" the maid answered trembling.

Sanders nodded understandably. His nephew, Prince Xander, who was the next heir to the throne after his father, the crown prince Asael, was always distinguished from his peers for his smartness, upbringing, and obedience. Naturally, the maids and servants were at a loss when they couldn't find the junior crown prince in his chamber, especially considering the strict rules of his mother, Calanthe.

"I'll look for him," said Sanders after a moment of thought. "Don't tell anyone. If someone finds out, tell them he is with me!"

The maid nodded. Sanders went downstairs and directed toward the backyard of the palace. Slowly passing through the persimmon grove and leaving behind the sky-colored gazebo near the inner lake, Sanders crossed the short stone bridge. Through the arched gate carved in the stone, he entered the late queen's garden of roses and headed north. Under the high walls of the garden, Sanders found an old weeping cherry tree. With a little effort, he climbed up the tree and reached the top of the wall. On the other side of the wall, Sanders followed the path that led into the wildings. The moon stood at its highest point. The air was cooling, and the surroundings were in a deep sleep. Soon, he heard the clanging sound of metal drowned out by the noise of the waterfall. He was close.

"You lose!" Sanders heard a voice.

Passing the tall hedges, Sanders came up to the open area. He saw his nephew running toward his cousin Keon with a sword in his hands.

"I demand revenge!" shouted the crown prince's son.

"Then prepare for another loss!" Keon laughed out loud, making fun of Xander.

But Xander didn't want to give up, so he raised his sword and dodged the strikes with dignity. He also managed to attack his uncle, forcing him to step back. For an eleven-year-old boy, he was very skillful in sword games. But Keon was older and stronger, and with a strong wave of Keon's sword, Xander knelt and dropped his own weapon.

"You lost! Again!" shouted Keon.

Sanders, who was watching them from the side, clapped loudly, praising the fight.

"Uncle!" shouted Xander. A smile appeared on his lips as he was happy to see Sanders at the waterfall. "What are you doing here?"

"You still keep training here at night," Sanders said calmly.

"What can I do? Mother is against sword games and fighting. I had no choice but to train in secret. Besides, I have a great master," the young prince looked at Keon. He loved his uncles. Next to them, he always felt protected.

"Are you aware that everyone in the palace is looking for you?" asked Sanders.

Xander got pale at the moment.

"The servants can get into trouble because of you . . ."

Sanders's concerns were reasonable. The duchess, Lady Calanthe Layland, was someone with traditional views who adhered to strict rules. She could punish the servants severely if something should happen to the prince.

"Yes," nodded Xander and added with a sad voice. "Let's return to the palace . . ."

Seeing the gloomy face of his nephew, Sanders felt pity and laughed, giving him a warm hug. "Relax! You may stay. I told them that your absence is my responsibility. They are informed!"

Xander jumped up out of happiness. "Uncle, you are the best!" he exclaimed joyfully.

"What about a fight of three?" suggested Keon. "It would be good practice, especially for you," he said to his nephew.

They all accepted the idea in one vote. Soon, the three of them started training. Equal to his uncles, Xander had to both attack his opponents and defend himself from them simultaneously. He knew that both of them would never treat him as a child. They never spared his age or status. They always forced him to fight as hard as a real man, equal to them both in strength and skills. Xander loved the way his uncles treated him. He never wanted to be a boy. Next to them, he always wanted to be stronger, wilder. He could be fearless, uncontrollable. Next to them, he could become a man, a man that one day could become a king . . . a real king.

It was very late when they finished their sword fight at last. It was Sanders who decided to end the training and take everyone back to the palace. They all were melting in sweat. When Sanders, his cousin, and his nephew entered the palace backyard, an unusual noise grabbed their attention. Everyone in the palace was in turmoil.

Keon bent over his nephew. "You better go to your chamber."

Xander looked with big, surprised eyes at Keon and nodded. On the way, Sanders stopped one of the servants and asked him for an explanation.

The servant looked alarmed. "Your Highness!" said the servant with a bow. "A rider came from Westbridge Tower. He brought an urgent message to the king. They are in the silver hall now. The king called a summit. All the counselors must arrive soon."

After shortly informing the princes about the night visitor, the servant bowed and asked for permission to leave. Sanders and Keon hurried to the silver hall located next to the king's chamber. Westbridge was a watchers' tower located in the northwest part of Incitydoor. The rider must have galloped for more than a day to reach the palace at this time. Sanders and Keon feared the worst. Both of them couldn't guess what kind of urgency the rider could bring that he dared to bother the king at night.

The king's eldest son, Prince Asael, and the king's brother, Lord Tomaso Layland, were already in the silver hall when Keon and Sanders entered. Under the fading torchlights, the hall was slowly sinking into darkness. The shadows around rose high, performing their unnaturally odd dance under the soundless melody of the twinkling flame.

Keon first approached the people in the silver hall. Together with the king, his brother and uncle were gathered at the round table in the middle of the hall and seemed to be discussing something important. The rider standing next to them bent his knees to greet the newly arrived princes, showing them his respect. Keon made a signal to the rider, letting him stand.

"Father!" Keon looked at the king. Sanders, next to him, gave his king the honors. "What is the matter?"

The king's face was gloomy. Keon shivered. Not knowing what kind of news brought the night visitor, he already knew, whatever it was, there was nothing good in it and it would affect all of them.

"Perle de la Mer was attacked by the Arsandars," informed Asael, handing out the scrap of paper to him.

Sanders came closer to look at what was in Keon's hands.

Arsandars attacked the fortress.

We cannot hold the siege for long.

We need help! They are not alone.

"When did they send the message?" asked Keon. His voice trembled.

"We don't know," answered Asael. "Maybe six days ago or more . . . Seems the one who wrote was in a big rush."

Keon also noticed that the writing was hardly readable.

"How fast can we get prepared for the ships to sail?" Sanders inquired.

"Tomorrow afternoon is the fastest," answered Tomaso coldly. "Lord Calhoun promised three hundred men. Additional one hundred men from Westbridge will follow them. Lord Aegeus, the second chief commander of the Rhodareen Armed Forces, will lead the army under the command of Prince Asael."

Hearing his uncle's words, Keon wanted to object, but Tomaso cut him.

"It is already decided."

Keon loved his brothers, especially Thaen. He imagined his brother Thaen defending the fortress under his command against the savages of the north. He would eagerly go to the fortress and fight for his brother. However, seeing his father and uncle, he said nothing. He didn't want to annoy them as their thoughts were already drowning them to the bottom of Perle de la Mer.

After counseling, Princes Asael and Keon stayed in the king's chambers to support their father in such a hard time. Sanders said nothing but followed his father. When they reached a secluded place where no one could hear them, Sanders stopped Tomaso.

"Father, you should talk to the king! Make him change his decision!" he said, grabbing his father's hand.

"What decision? Change what?" Tomaso got angry at once. He was very upset with the news brought by the rider.

"Don't send Asael to the island," Sanders said calmly, his words sounding like a command.

"I can't do this. It is already decided," Tomaso refused his son. "We can't delay anything. It is all about the king's son. Prince Thaen may be in danger."

"That's what I am talking about. It is too dangerous. Asael must stay," Sanders insisted.

Tomaso's expression suddenly changed. "Don't even dare to say that." Knowing his son very well, Tomaso already guessed what his son might say. He refused to listen to his useless words.

"He is the crown prince. He is our future," continued Sanders. "Instead, send me!" Sanders bordered his father's way.

"Don't be mad!" shouted Tomaso. Then he looked around quickly. Afraid of being heard or noticed, Tomaso whispered fiercely, "How dare you oppose the king's will!"

"Because I know the savages. Asael doesn't know. I can fight them back. I did once. I have already seen the enemy. I have lived with the enemy. I have fought the enemy. It must be me! The one who goes to Perle de la Mer . . . is me!"

"Impossible!" refused Tomaso angrily. "Asael will go! And you . . . boy, don't mess under my feet."

"You are not listening!" Sanders shouted bewildered.

However, his father interrupted him, "No! You don't want to understand! I love my brother. I love my nephews. But you are my treasure," said Tomaso with cold eyes. "I won't send you wherever it is."

"Asael might die! He is our feature king . . ." Sanders's eyes were full of pity. He couldn't understand his own father. "He has never faced the Arsandars."

"We have enough future kings in line." Tomaso took Sanders's hand into his palm and squeezed hard. "Don't make any mess."

Sanders said nothing. He had his own thoughts. He apologized to his father for taking his time and left. Sanders knew Tomaso would never listen to him. On one hand, he would only waste his time and efforts trying to persuade his father in vain; on the other hand, he couldn't let his brother go alone to the island. He knew that it was too dangerous.

They are not alone . . .

The last words in the message surfaced in his memories. Whatever could it mean? The Arsandars, wild and ruthless, never had allies, and Sanders knew it. They had never gone to war without proper preparations. Even the Arsandars' failure meant a great loss for the opponents still. They would lose equally.

Sanders went directly to his room and took his road bag. In an hour, he was ready to go. It was already dawn. He planned to hide in one of the ships sailing to Perle de la Mer. He couldn't leave Asael alone. He had to be next to Asael and protect both his brothers.

With a knock on the door, a maid appeared with his morning breakfast and tea. Sanders used to have breakfast early in the morning and go to training. He allowed the maid to put the things on the table. This time he didn't have time to eat. He only took several sips from the cup and went out. He already reached the backyard when a strong headache bothered him. Something was wrong. Mist blinded his eyes, and he fell.

Bells were ringing in the distance. Sanders still had a headache, so strong that he grimaced while opening his eyes. He shivered . . . The room was cold. He wished he could get a blanket . . . Trying to move, he just realized that his hands were tied. He was tied to the wooden chair in the attic of the west tower. His body was in pain all over. Sanders looked around and shouted out loud. Soon, the door of the attic opened, and a servant appeared at the threshold.

"What is going on?" yelled Sanders at the servant. "What are you doing? Release me! Now!"

"Your Highness, forgive me." The servant bowed to his master, but he didn't make any further attempt to release Sanders. His lack of movement angered Sanders.

"What are you waiting for? I gave you the order to release me! Untie my hands!" Sanders blushed with anger.

The light of the sundown reflected in reddish colors on the ceiling of the attic. The day was coming to its end. He still could hear the ringing sound of the bells. Incitydoor was saying goodbye to the royal ships sailing the long way. He had planned to get onto the ship before daylight, but tied up to the chair, he could do nothing but yell with anger.

"I can't release you, Your Highness," the servant admitted coldly. "Your father, the first hand of the king, will arrive soon," he added.

How could Sanders not have foreseen that his father would try to prevent him from going to the island? He was sure that he didn't raise any suspicion. How could he fail his brothers? When Tomaso entered the attic, Sanders couldn't hold his anger.

"Coward! Why are you doing this? How can you treat your son like this?" Sanders shouted.

"I hope you had a good sleep?" Tomaso asked coldly. It seemed he wasn't so bothered by his son's condition.

"Release me! Order them to release me!" Sanders shouted impatiently. He tried hard to tear the ropes around his wrists.

"You know that it is impossible!" His father's calmness and indifference pained him.

"How can you be so ruthless, Father?" Sanders was helpless. He begged Tomaso. However, his father didn't seem to hear him at all.

"Don't make me a fool! It is all your fault. I told you not to mess up with the island issue." Tomaso's words were sharp, his gaze icy cold. He looked at his son with resentful eyes.

"I didn't do anything wrong!" Sanders tried to object, but what he said wasn't enough to make excuses.

"Then what is this?" Tomaso made a signal, and a servant took Sanders's road bag from the wooden trunk and put it beside him. "Did you really plan to escape in secret? How can you do this to your father?"

"And you?" Sanders cut his father's words. "How can you do this to your kingdom? To your king?" Sanders tried to read Tomaso's thoughts. "What are you hiding, Father?"

Tomaso sighed. He knew that his son would never understand the worries of a father unless he himself became a parent one day.

"You may not understand me right now, but one day you will definitely thank me."

"You are not leaving me a chance to understand you! Don't make me hate you, Father. Release me!" Sanders was desperate. He couldn't recognize his father.

"You will stay in the attic for today," stated Tomaso firmly. "I forbid you to leave Incitydoor with any excuse. Any person who dares to take you onto his vessel will be beheaded. Don't try to escape. Listen to my words, and stay within the palace. Otherwise . . ."

"Otherwise?" Sanders repeated after his father.

"He will be the first man to die in my hands," said Tomaso, threatening the servant who stood next to him.

"My lord!" The poor servant fell to his knees, crying. "Your Highness, I beg you, spare my life! I beg you! Please spare my life!"

Tomaso turned and left the room.

Sanders didn't know how to cope with his anger and yelled after his father, "Never! Listen, never will I ever forgive you if something happens to Asael or Thaen! I will never forgive you!"

Tomaso heard all the curses that his son sent his way. Sanders's words struck his heart like a sharp knife. He loved his son more than anything in this life. After his wife's death, Sanders and Isabelle were his only reason for living.

You may never forgive me, if you wish. I did it for you . . . You must live! Be alive, thought Tomaso. He directed to his chamber.

With closed curtains, the glittering candles couldn't illuminate the chamber brightly. A burden that lay like a heavy stone on his chest burned in him. He knelt beside his bed and took a scrap of fabric that he had hidden under his bed earlier. He took out a small piece of paper wrapped in that fabric.

> One wrong step may lead to death! And what will be your decision?

Tomaso read what was written on the paper again. Then he took out a handful of curly golden hair. It belonged to Isabelle, his beloved daughter . . . It was a warning to Tomaso. His mistake could harm his children. He didn't know why someone needed to threaten him with the life of his children. Isabelle was far away. No matter how desperate he was, he couldn't protect her. She had left Incitydoor with the centenarian king almost a week ago after her wedding. Could the one who wrote the message be related to the centenarian king?

His first suspicion fell on the king, Leon Ulyses. With Tomaso's daughter in his hands, only he could approach Isabelle. Who would ever dare to threaten the royal family without a direct order from the king? If Tomaso could, he would kill all his enemies to protect his children. If only he could get to know them . . . if only he could get them . . .

Tomaso squeezed the piece of paper and the cut hair in his palm as if he was squeezing his unseen enemy. A sudden knock scattered his thoughts. Tomaso threw into the fireplace what he held in his palm.

"Yes," he said out loud.

A servant entered the room and bowed to his lord. "Your Highness . . . His Majesty, the king, wants to see you," he informed his lord.

Tomaso nodded. He took a quick look at the burned paper in the fire. Being assured that no evidence was left in the fireplace, he hurried to the king's chamber. Soon, the last log in the fireplace totally burned out, leaving black dust behind. With the withered flame, the cold swam into the dark chamber.

After the visit to the king's chamber, Tomaso returned to his own place. Entering the cold and dark room, Tomaso felt satisfied. All in all, he felt guilty in front of his beloved brother. Today he made the first step of a traitor. Even though he was unsure regarding the warning, he kept it secret from his own brother. Tomaso was sure that he would have to choose again between his love for the king and his love for his children in the future, not just once. And in this torturing moment, he could hide his pain and wronged eyes under the darkness. He had to live in the shadow, as if the light could expose his deeds. From now on, it was the place he belonged.

Chapter 17

Last Chance to See

A splash of water. The boy lying under the old oak tree raised his head and looked at his friend. For almost an hour, his friend had been throwing stones into the lake.

How annoying, thought the boy, but he did not say anything. He wondered how long he could tolerate his friend's behavior. The boy wanted to have some rest. He closed his eyes again.

"Are you sleeping?" asked his friend. "Really, Garth, how can you sleep in the middle of the day?"

The boy turned to the other side. "I deserve this rest. Leave me alone."

The last couple of weeks had been real torture for the boys as they had to pass a special training inspection in the military camp on the foot of the Riphean Mountain ridge. The boys first met in the northern lands four years ago when they arrived at the camp. Since then their friendship had grown stronger.

"I am trying to kill time. Too bored! How dare you rest in such time and leave me alone in this field? It was you who offered to get out of the camp."

"You are the one who agreed. Can't remember that I forced you out . . ." Garth sighed, his eyes still closed. "Nevertheless, stop bothering the water."

"Mind your own business," mumbled his friend. "If sleep is your only wish, you could stay in the camp and lock yourself in the room."

"Lionel, because of you, I can't get my thoughts together," complained Garth.

"Really? Because of me? You have just broken my heart," Lionel joked and threw another stone into the water. "Still thinking about that girl?" asked Lionel.

Garth didn't answer.

"I thought you had a fiancée," Lionel said. "Shame on you."

"You think too much. Cecilia is the choice of my parents, not mine," Garth answered shortly.

"You can't be that serious. You are a jerk!" Lionel threw the other stone. "She is a dream girl. Beautiful, noble, gracious . . . not like your shepherd maiden."

"Lion!" Garth tried to reprimand his friend. His friend's words hurt him. "You don't know her. Shut your stupid mouth up."

Garth got to his feet and left his friend by the lake. He directed toward the meadow. In the distance, the lone tower of the Dolorem fortress could be seen. The fortress was located in the middle of the Dolorem Valley. The ruins of the old castle were turned into one of King Layland's main military forts in the northern lands.

The area was first resided by people in the third century BC. Gradually, the population increased. The people made a big city base in the place, and the city flourished. However, the consequences of the war greatly affected the welfare of the city. The city was totally destroyed. The massacre near Lake Itkul put the final dot in the city's history. Not one of the nine million inhabitants survived. Darkness took the light off every house, every person. It didn't spare even children. King Layland named the place Dolorem, "the Land of Pain and Grief."

Fort Dolorem became a symbol of loss and tragedy. Except for a few families, all the people moved away from the neighborhood. Only military personnel stayed in Dolorem. It had become a second home for Garth. The boy had dreamed of serving in the north troop of the royal military force from a very young age. He had dreamed about knights: fearless and valiant. The sons of Dolorem had fallen on the battlefield a thousand years ago, and Garth wanted to get their bravery; he wanted to get their valor. All the male members of Garth's family, as well as his father, had served in the kingdom's royal military force.

Garth was the only grandson of Lord Harvin Calhoun, the head of the royal arms. By following the steps of his father and grandfather, Garth had become one of the squad's best soldiers. He had been raised in a noble family. His family's position promised the boy a bright future both in his life and career, and he was proud to bear the family name. On the other hand, Garth knew that his position not only gave him the opportunity to realize his dreams but also built strong borders around his private life.

At the age of nine, Garth had been engaged to the daughter of one of the noblest and richest houses in his neighborhood. Cecilia had been seven years old at that moment. All their childhood had passed in Garth's grandparents' East Castle. Garth loved Cecilia, but not like as fiancée. He loved her as a sister, though he didn't want to disappoint the two families.

However, everything changed when Garth met Sienna during the first year of his service in Dolorem. She was a daughter of a shepherd who lived in a small village east of the fortress. Year after year, his feelings toward Sienna grew stronger, and now all his thoughts belonged to an ordinary girl from the village. He could neither blame nor hate himself. He didn't want to think about his family and the promise made by his father in the name of his son. Garth took a straw from the ground and put it between his teeth, sighing deeply. At that moment, a sudden scream of an eagle grabbed his attention. Garth ran ahead and climbed onto the big stones piled in the meadow. He extended his hand. Soon, the eagle lowered and sat on his arm.

"Hi, beauty!" Garth said to the bird and rubbed its neck. "Let's see what you have."

He untied the expanded piece of paper from the eagle's tarsus and let the bird enjoy the freedom of the sky. Garth ran toward the lake, calling his friend.

"Lionel, we are returning to the fortress!" he shouted.

Lionel was surprised by his friend's haste. "But you wanted to rest . . . What happened?" Lionel wondered.

"We got a message. Hurry up!" Garth urged his friend.

Garth and Lionel took the horses and galloped toward the fortress. When they reached the military fort, Garth found his chief commander, Roderick, and gave him the paper. The man in his late forties read the message carefully.

"Tom, call Johnathan! Gather everyone in the inner yard," shouted the commander.

The soldiers who already had received the orders obeyed and left the yard while the others looked at their commander with great surprise.

"What is in the message, Commander?" Garth asked Rodrick.

"The king orders to meet the centenarian troops at the northwestern foothills of the Riphean Mountain in two days," answered Roderick.

Soon, a man in his thirties approached the commander. He bowed to his commander in respect. Johnathan was the commander's most trusted person and best disciple. He had served under the commander's patronage for decades.

"Did you call for me?" asked the man.

"Yes, we have work to do," the commander answered.

Together they went to the inner yard. All the soldiers also quickly gathered in the inner yard. Garth and Lionel stood in a row with their peers. They all waited for the commander to announce the news. Roderick rose to the stairs beside the backyard gates and talked to everyone.

"We received an order from the king," said Roderick in a loud voice. "The Riphean Mountain is to be passed to the hands of the mortals."

When Roderick announced the news, all the soldiers rejoiced. Roderick raised his right hand to let the soldiers know that he had not finished the announcement and asked them to keep silent.

"We must go to the northwestern foothills and meet the centenarian troops. The centenarians will move the mountain's inhabitants. Our task is to control the process. The second and the third groups will escort me to the destination point," said Roderick. "Johnathan will be in charge in my absence. His orders are my orders."

Everyone listened to the commander attentively.

"Groups! Get ready by noon. We have two days left. Go!" ordered the commander.

The soldiers raised their swords and hit their own chests with their sword hilts three times, shouting loudly. Finally, they had arrived at the day the legendary Riphean Mountain, with all its treasure, would be passed to the hands of the mortals.

When everyone left the inner yard, Commander Roderick called another servant.

"Emmett," said Roderick, "prepare supplies for the road. Count two weeks. We may stay there longer than expected."

Emmett nodded and left the commander.

Roderick looked at Johnathan. He was still waiting for his commander.

"Now you are responsible for the fort. I trust you, Johnathan. You can bear this position."

"I am honored by your trust. You can completely rely on me," said Johnathan to his commander.

After the announcement, everyone went to do their tasks. However, not everyone was happy about the commander's words. The news about their leave made Garth sad. He served in the third group that had to go to the foothill. There was no time to delay their campaign. Garth directed toward the warehouse. Near the warehouse, he met a servant boy. Garth handed the boy a message that he had written with a sharpened lump of coal on leather.

He was supposed to meet the girl from the village in the morning of the next day. Knowing that the girl would be waiting for him, Garth had to inform Sienna about their task. Garth had to break the promise he had given to the girl and leave the fortress that afternoon. Together with the message, the servant boy took a silver coin and promised to deliver the message to Sienna.

After sending the servant boy to the shepherd's house, Garth returned to the soldiers' common room and started preparing the necessary gear for the road. Once the groups got ready to leave the fortress, it had already started getting dark. Each group consisted of twenty-five people. Additionally, they were accompanied by ten armor-bearers and a military physician.

Garth looked at the fortress's main towers. Johnathan was looking at the leaving soldiers from up high. How Garth dreamed to stay at the fortress instead of Johnathan. Garth knew Commander Roderick wanted to go to the Riphean Mountain himself. He was thirsty for more power. He couldn't send anyone else to the foothill. The first group of soldiers was under Johnathan's commandment while Emmett was responsible for the second and third groups. Choosing the first group meant choosing Johnathan for the campaign. However, Roderick needed his eyes and ears in the fortress.

Roderick raised his hand high to say farewell to the one staying in the fortress. Johnathan also raised his hand high, as if he wished a fair trip to his commander and other comrades. Then Roderick gave a command to his horse.

The Riphean Mountain was located on the northeast side of the Dolorem fortress. The trip promised to be difficult, and on a cold December evening, the military groups under the commandment of Roderick marched to their new destination point. The soldiers following their commander were in a lifted mood—except one. Garth kept looking behind. He didn't want to go. He had a feeling that today was his last chance to see Sienna, and he just lost that chance.

Chapter 18

Doors of Adahhar

Leon was watching Isabelle from the sterncastle deck of his royal ship. The queen was walking with Leonor on the shores of Nur-adamantas. Her two maids were walking a few steps behind the queen, in case of any need. The servants were loading the royal family's belongings onto the ship at the bay. All the royal family members were waiting to sail. Soon, Lady Devora joined Leon at the sterncastle. She stood beside the king in silence and watched those who were enjoying the morning on the shore.

"How good that Leonor got a friend again. She needed a female companion," admitted Lady Devora while watching the two women.

"I am happy that my sister and the queen found a common language. They had gotten close the last few days," Leon supported the conversation.

"What about you, Your Highness? Have you become close to the queen?" inquired Lady Devora.

Leon didn't answer. He kept watching the queen. Soon, Estevan approached the ladies and bowed to them. Leonor took Estevan's hand, and they walked aside. Lady Devora watched the king. Leon acted like he didn't notice her gaze.

Lady Devora looked away and after a small pause, she continued, "I heard rumors . . . It says, 'The mortal queen is rejecting the mighty king.'"

"Rumors? Or your spies?" Leon inquired.

"You know what will happen if the world starts talking. You are not family yet. You are not united. The House of Ulyses needs an heir. The world is unstable."

"I don't want to force Isabelle into anything." He kept watching his wife, who was standing alone and looking at how the low waves were striking the shore. "She needs time, and I am giving it to her," the king concluded.

His words were cold. He didn't like to have a conversation about his private life, especially with Lady Devora. Lady Devora was the eldest of their family, and Leon respected her very much. She was a strong woman who had devoted her years to protecting her family. But from time to time, her curiosity was irritating.

"How long?" asked Lady Devora, not wanting to give up.

"As long as it takes." Leon was rude.

Lady Devora wanted to object to the king's words, but a servant that appeared at sterncastle disturbed their conversation.

"Forgive me, Your Grace. Everything had been prepared. We are ready to sail."

"Good," said Leon. He nodded to Lady Devora, showing his respect. Leon left the ship and directed toward the shore, where Isabelle still was.

From time to time, Isabelle would turn around to look at Leonor. Not far from where Isabelle was standing, Leonor and Estevan were having a conversation. Leonor was a little upset since the morning of that day. They all were returning to Adahhar except Estevan. He had to go south, to the land of the Ifrans. It would take several months to call the army for the mortal king's service. He had to choose and train a special squad and hand over the command under the control of Arawn Layland. He possibly would miss the expected birth of his child.

Estevan was holding his wife's hands. He said something to Leonor, and she looked down. Estevan gently pressed her palms into his face. For the last few days, Isabelle noticed that the two of them could hardly be separated. How strong was their love? She also felt sorry for their temporary separation. When Isabelle once again turned around to look at the sweet royal couple, she noticed the king approaching. Estevan and Leonor also noticed him.

On the shore, Leonor met Leon warmly. "Brother! Are we already leaving?"

"Yes!" confirmed the king. "The ship is ready to sail."

Estevan helped his wife to walk toward the ship. These last few days, Leonor was getting tired so easily. Even if the expected delivery date was far to come, bearing a child was becoming harder for the king's sister.

Leon made a signal to Isabelle, letting her go toward the bay first. He walked a few steps behind the queen. He liked watching her walk. Her steps were less clumsy when he was far. When they approached the ship, two maids came down and took Leonor's both hands. They helped her to get onto the ship. Leon held Isabelle's hand and helped the queen pass the wooden passage connecting the ground with the ship.

"Raise the anchor! Set the sails!" shouted the first mate to the sailors.

Several handymen untied the knots. Estevan waved to those on the ship for the last time, and the ship left the berth. When the ship sailed from the coast for a significant distance, the first mate ordered the others to take off the sails.

"Get ready!" he shouted.

Isabelle wanted to stay on the main deck, but Leon asked her to come with him to the nautical bridge on the upper sterncastle.

"You'd better stay inside, my queen."

Isabelle obeyed, and together they went up. She never dared to object and always looked at her feet during their conversation. The queen was still avoiding Leon.

The ship's nautical bridge was a small, half-round room with big, thick windows all around and a wooden door at one side. When they went inside, Isabelle approached the front window to look at what the sailors were doing.

"Whatever happens, don't be afraid," Leon warned her.

His words surprised Isabelle. Even though she tried to act indifferently, unwilling to reveal her true feelings, for a moment her eyes fixated on the floor again.

"I am not. Should I be?"

Leon didn't answer.

Soon, one of the sailors shouted, "Ready!"

Several other sailors repeated after him. All who were on the main deck rushed inside the ship. The helmsman entered the bridge, closed the door, and locked it.

"We are ready to dive, Your Highness!" informed the helmsman approaching the ship cockpit.

Leon nodded. "You may start!" Then he slightly bowed toward Isabelle. "We are going to have a little adventure," said Leon.

Isabelle noticed an easy push under her feet. The ship sped up. The water level around the ship started rising quickly.

"What is happening?" wondered Isabelle.

She couldn't hide her fear anymore. Her worries had no borders. The ship was sinking into the sea. Soon, the ship's nose part fully disappeared underwater. Isabelle took two steps back. When the sea struck the windows of the nautical bridge, the queen screamed and hid behind Leon.

She dared to open her eyes, and the surroundings were pitch-black. Only the few lit candles inside the room gave some light. Isabelle could feel how massive the pressure underwater was. Her heart beat faster. She could hear her own breath buzzing under her ears. The darkness around was pressing. Then she noticed a white shadow ahead. When the ship came closer to the shadow, Isabelle saw a white veil. The ship was swimming under the water toward a veil of a billion boiling bubbles. When the bubbles covered the nose of the ship, Isabelle held her breath. She was afraid to make a sound. Then the bubbles reached the windows of the bridge.

When the ship passed through the bubbles, water struck the windows from above, like a downpour. Isabelle saw light behind the wet windows. The strong downpour noise could still be heard with an echo. Isabelle got confused. In a hurry, Isabelle ran toward the door and threw herself outside. She grabbed the handrail of the right-side sterncastle and bent down to see what they had left behind.

Isabelle was left speechless upon seeing a high sea rock arch with water falling down from its top. The ship's poop deck was still behind the waterfall. The rock arch was so high it seemed its top would touch the sky.

"Unbelievable," uttered Isabelle.

Leon approached the queen and took her hand. He bowed and kissed the back of her palm. "Welcome to Adahhar!" announced Leon.

He led Isabelle to the front of the sterncastle. The northern peninsula of the great centenarian kingdom appeared in front of them. Adahhar was located in the North Sea. Its borders were connected with South Norway. Despite the fact that it was already winter, the peninsula was covered with reddish autumn colors. In the middle of the peninsula, a lone mountain rose high to the sky. White houses with red roofs were located all along the moon-shaped bay. They were located all over the slope that went up to the mountain foothill. The bay's crystal water reflected the houses and the raised mountain behind covered in red leaves. Golden, fluffy clouds were gathered over the mountain. Behind all the buildings, at the very foothill of the mountain, the big, white palace of Adahhar could be seen. The sea wind brought the scent of late autumn mixed with the first snow.

"This place is unconditionally beautiful," said Isabelle.

"I am glad you like our home," answered Leon. He really hoped that Isabelle would accept his home like her own. She was born and raised in a warm continent where most of the year it was hot; the north was cold.

Soon, all the sailors appeared on the main deck. The first mate started giving orders. The sailors pulled the ropes and released the sails. The ship moved toward the land and stopped at the bay's deepest pier. When the passage was set between the ship and the berth, the queen and the king took the first steps onto the land.

All the inhabitants of Adahhar gathered on the streets to joyfully greet their king and queen. In front of the row, the children were waiting for the newly arrived royal family with flowers. Isabelle marveled to see the centenarians surrounding them from all sides. There was no army from both sides of the row to keep the people behind the border. The inhabitants were free to cross the way, approaching their king and throwing flower branches with laughter.

One of the little girls in the row ran to Isabelle and handed the queen a branch of crocus. Isabelle bent down to take the flowers. The smile the queen gave to the girl made her happy, and she ran back to her parents. According to the traditions of Rhodareen, common people were not allowed to walk beside the royal members. On special occasions, when the king or queen had to visit public places, they were surrounded by guards.

Isabelle had always believed the centenarians to be evil, but standing in front of them at the moment, she couldn't see any difference between people and centenarians. They were all similar in appearance. She felt like she was surrounded by people who were happy to see her, and looking at the little girl who gave her flowers, she was happy too.

Accompanied by the centenarians, the king and his family headed to the palace. At the beginning of the main road, a carriage was waiting for them. Through the carriage's open windows, Isabelle watched the centenarians who were celebrating their arrival. The carriage stopped at the long stairs leading to the palace's main gates. The white marble stairs were covered with rose petals from the middle and with reddish autumn leaves from two sides.

At the palace hall doorway, a group of king's men met them. All of them bowed together.

"Hope your trip was peaceful," said one of the men.

"Tertius!" The king widely opened his arms to hug his friend.

After greeting his king, the man knelt to Isabelle. "Your Grace."

The other men repeated what he did. Isabelle nodded, accepting their respectful gesture.

"The servants will show you to your royal chamber," said Leon, looking at Isabelle. "You should rest." Then he turned toward his sister. "Leonor . . ."

"I should probably go straight to my room too," Leonor informed him.

"I'll take her to the room," said Lady Devora.

One by one, the ladies of the House of Ulyses went upstairs. Leon watched them leave.

"You have been missing for a long time." The way Tertius spoke reflected his displeasure regarding their long absence.

"We stayed at Nur-adamantas for a little while," responded the king shortly.

"Why did you ever go there?" wondered Tertius.

"It was a sudden decision. Unplanned stay."

"Unplanned stay?" Tertius repeated the king's words with a raised tone. His surprise grew. "Rush decision from your side? Really?" Tertius knew his king very well. He would never dare to do things without careful thought. Leon always was careful, always alert.

"We haven't been there for eternity. We had a good time at the place of our childhood."

"I am glad for you, my lord. But it is not the right time to sink into your memories of the past."

"Did something happen?"

Tertius nodded. "Would be better if you arrived earlier. We received a message from King Arawn," said Tertius.

"What is it?" Leon asked his man in service.

Tertius's behavior made the king worry. He said nothing but moved aside and with a gesture let the king know that they needed some privacy to talk. Behind him appeared a long corridor that led to the meeting hall of the king's men. The king hurried to the room. Tertius followed him. They had to talk, and their talk probably was going to be a long one.

The king's steps on the marble floor echoed all over the empty hall. He went directly to the throne and sank into it.

"Now you can speak," ordered Leon.

"We got news that the north fortress of Rhodareen was attacked by the Skin Island savages. The king wants support."

"When did this happen?" Leon inquired.

"Approximately two weeks," Tertius sighed. "King Arawn wants us to send him his promised army!"

"Estevan can't reach the north in time, the braafs are too far in the south." Leon squinted his eyes, considering all the possibilities of support that he could provide Arawn with. "But," he said at last, "we can send him the north troop. The distance between our troops and their fortress is not far."

"They are the main and only armed force that we have in Adahhar. Don't you think it's too risky?" Tertius asked worriedly.

"No! You can send the Fourth and the Fifth Divisions. That will be enough," said Leon. "Send a letter to King Arawn. He will get help."

Leon stood up to leave. Tertius knew the king was tired, but he had no choice but to bother him with one more issue.

"Your Highness, I am afraid there is another thing you should know."

What Tertius said shocked Leon. He rushed down the stairs and directed to the east wing of the palace. When the room's doors were widely opened, Leon looked at the man sitting next to the fireplace.

Dalir stood up to greet the king.

"This is true then!" said Leon with astonishment. He approached a small cot in the other corner of the room. "This is truly him!"

said Leon, watching the tiny body of a sleeping child. "When did it happen?" he asked Dalir.

"About a month ago, Your Highness!" Dalir said and looked down, feeling guilty. "I didn't know what to do and where to go. Please accept my apologies for coming so late."

"Who else knows about the child?" asked Leon, still watching him.

"No one!"

"Good," nodded Leon. "He can't stay in Adahhar. Soon, everyone will know about his existence. We can't hide him forever." Leon turned at Tertius. "The child must be taken to the Moon City."

Tertius nodded. "When do we have to set off for the road, Your Highness?" he asked.

"Today! We are leaving today. Prepare everything in secret. No one must know about him until we reach the city," said Leon, his heart beating fast.

All his life, Leon had heard a lot about the child. He used to read books about the prophecy of the madman who sang a song of the fifth child and then threw himself into the old well on the lone mount only to meet death. His father used to tell him stories about the war and warned him about the future. Leon never thought that he would be the one to meet the child. Even when he dreamed of the meeting, he never believed in the possibility of this event. For the second time in his life, he was scared. His heart was inconsolable.

* * *

The big, white wooden doors opened, and four servants entered the room holding two big dower chests. Isabelle followed them. Her room was wide and bright. In comparison to the green palace where she had lived during their stay at Nur-adamantas, Adahhar palace was built of white marble. The rooms, even the furniture, were made of white materials. Tall windows, from the floor up to the ceiling, allowed the sunlight to fully enter the room.

Miray and Jael entered the room after the queen. They wanted to unpack the chests. However, the queen wanted privacy.

"Leave them in the corner. I want to have some rest at the moment."

Miray nodded to the queen. "Let us help with clothes," the old woman asked permission and looked at Jael.

Together the two maids helped the queen to take off the heavy travel clothes and pulled off her leather boots. While the two of them were helping Isabelle, another servant set a fire in the fireplace close to the bed.

"Do you wish for anything else?" asked Miray from the queen.

Isabelle shook her head.

"We will be on the other side of the door. If you need us, please ring the bell." Miray bowed to Isabelle and left the queen alone in her room.

Isabelle went directly to the bed and sank into her big, soft pillows.

What kind of world is this? thought Isabelle.

She couldn't forget what she had seen on the ship's bridge. She didn't know whether she was to be terrified or amazed. What kind of wonders was she yet to see? She tried to think about everything she had faced after her wedding and to understand the world that she had become part of. But the trip tired her, and Isabelle soon fell asleep.

* * *

"Isabelle! Isabelle!" shouted a man. "Where are you, Isabelle?" Tomaso Layland looked around. "Isabelle!" the man called for his daughter.

Then he heard the sound of laughter. Isabelle was sitting under the stairs leading to the captain's cabin in the royal ship. Three-year-old Isabelle covered her mouth with both palms, trying not to utter a word. She was hiding and didn't want to be noticed.

Tomaso approached from behind and grabbed his daughter's shoulders with a shout, "Found you!"

Isabelle screamed, then her scream turned to a shrill laugh. Tomaso lifted Isabelle up and with one hand started tickling her.

"Here you are! Here is my little naughty."

"Let go, please!" begged Isabelle.

She had fun with her father during their sea trip. They were returning home—to Akhrezoob, the main island of the New World—after spending the spring festival in the king's castle in

Incitydoor. The island was located in the northwest part of the North American continent.

"Papa, when will we get home?" asked Isabelle, putting her small hands around Tomaso's shoulders.

"Soon, my princess, soon." Tomaso gave a tight hug to his daughter.

"I miss Mama. When we're home, I'll hug her. I'll give her a lot of kisses and hugs." Isabelle widely stretched both hands in the air, showing how big a hug she wanted to give her mother.

At that moment a strong wind blew her hat away. Isabelle looked around to see in which direction her favorite floral hat went. The hat landed on the surface of the water not far from the ship.

"My hat!" exclaimed Isabelle.

The ocean became uneasy. Tomaso looked up. Dark clouds covered the sky. He put Isabelle down and looked to the east, to the island of Akhrezoob. The tall towers of the Ardoran castle could be seen from afar. What was ahead scared Tomaso.

He turned around and shouted, "Drums! Hit the drums! Call for the men! Warn the other ships!"

One of the sailors ran up to the forecastle and started ringing the bell. All the royal men went up onto the deck. Two of the men took up the long sticks and hit the drums hanging on the ship's nose several times. The drums were needed to alert other neighboring ships of any possible danger.

Isabelle covered her ears with both hands. Still, she heard the hits. The first hit was followed by the second . . .

* * *

Isabelle opened her eyes. She was in the white room of the marble palace. Someone hit the drums. Isabelle closed her eyes. Her thoughts were hazy. Was she still sleeping? Her dream from the past bothered her. When another drum sound was heard, Isabelle rose. She approached the glass door that led to the open balcony.

Isabelle shivered because of the evening chill. The sun was sinking into the ocean beneath the horizon. Little snowflakes were dancing in the wind under the reddish sky. She opened her right palm to catch the snowflake. The sound of drums could still be heard from far away.

With the appearance of the first snow—the messengers of winter—the guards went up to the hill west of the palace to inform everyone. Winter had already come. The sound of drums did not subside. Isabelle knew the guards would not stop throughout the night so everyone would know about the message. In every nation, in every country, playing drums with the first snowfall was the tradition.

Isabelle stood on the balcony, breathing the cool scent of the snow for a long time. Staying on the open balcony, she understood how much she had missed the winter. She went inside only when she heard a knock on her door. She had hardly given an answer to the person on the other side when the door opened and Leon entered inside. He was surprised to see his wife in the middle of the room, barefoot, pale as cotton, and with pink cheeks. The room was cold. The fire was almost out. Leon rushed to the bed and took a wool blanket. He approached Isabelle and covered her shoulders.

"You could catch a cold. What were you doing outside?" Leon inquired.

"Nothing," answered Isabelle shortly. "What happened?" Isabelle wanted to know the reason for his visit.

"I need you to come with me," answered Leon, still holding her shoulders.

"I'll get prepared," said Isabelle.

Leon nodded and informed her that he would be waiting at the door. When Isabelle went out, Leon led the way. Together they went toward the stairs. At the upper level, Leon turned to the left. On the other end of the way, Isabelle saw three big arches located next to each other, separated by fifteen-inch-wide walls between them. Following Leon, Isabelle entered the inner room through the middle arches.

The wide room with marble floors was lit by a lot of candles. In the right-side corner, Isabelle noticed a bookcase filled with books and different animal-shaped figures on top. Near the bookcase was a sofa with a round reading table. Another three arches on the opposite side led to the open veranda. In the other corner of the room, Isabelle saw a harp. She approached and touched it.

"I heard you like playing it," said Leon.

"I used to," answered Isabelle timidly.

Leon smiled. He noticed that every time he tried to do something valuable for her, the queen acted rudely instead of being grateful or supporting their conversation. It was her way of acting defensive. She was clumsy and shy.

"This room is yours. You can come here anytime," said Leon.

Isabelle looked at the king. "Thank you, Your Grace, for your generosity."

Isabelle always talked to Leon in a formal way. However, it didn't offend the king. As Arawn Layland had said during their conversation in the private room, Isabelle was too young. She was like a kid trying to look like an adult.

"I hope you'll enjoy your time here," Leon said. "In truth, I have two pieces of news to tell you. I apologize as I may upset you, they are not pleasant news."

"What news?" Isabelle felt his body become tense. She looked at the king with eyes wide open.

"We received a message from Rhodareen. It says the north fortress was attacked by the Arsandars. Your uncle asked for support."

"What about my brother? Is Thaen safe?" asked Isabelle with great worry.

"We don't know," Leon shook his head. "The second thing is, I have to leave too. We won't be able to see each other for a while."

"Are you leaving, really? To Rhodareen?" asked Isabelle with surprise. She was shocked to hear such news on their first day of arrival at Adahhar.

"No, I have to go to another place. I have already sent my people to Perle de la Mer. They have to reach the fortress soon."

"When are you leaving?" Isabelle inquired.

"Tonight," informed the king. It seemed he wasn't happy about his upcoming trip.

"Everything will be fine, right?" Isabelle asked with worry.

"Yes," said Leon.

Isabelle heard footsteps from outside. Soon, a man appeared at the arch crossing.

"Your Grace," he bowed. The man looked straight at the king with a firm gaze. He probably was much older than the king.

Leon turned to Isabelle and extended his hand, asking her to come closer.

"Isabelle," said the king, "I want to introduce to you Will Segar."

Isabelle nodded to the man's bow.

"He and his men are responsible for your safety," Leon finished his words.

The queen's surprise became even greater. Even though the centenarian king had a small group of military personnel at Alaasouad, the main army was kept in the south. As far as Isabelle knew, Alaasouad was always famous for its safety, and no guards were allowed in the palace territory. Isabelle couldn't understand the reason for these changes. Why now? Where exactly Leon was going? What could have ever happened?

"The other royal members will also be given protection."

Something is wrong, thought Isabelle. She wanted to know the truth, but she understood that the king had no intentions of sharing any information with her. Knowing that soon he would leave the palace, Isabelle decided not to bother the king with her meaningless questions.

"Sure," said Isabelle. "Thank you for your care. Fare you well, Your Grace!"

Leon smiled and nodded. "You too, take care." Leon turned to Segar. "You are responsible for my family."

The man bowed to his king, showing his gratitude for the trust. Leon looked at Isabelle as if he wanted to say something for farewell. However, the words didn't come. Leon leaned forward and gave her a slight kiss.

The queen's lips burned. She couldn't object. Trying to control her emotions, she didn't notice how Leon had left the room. Her heart was uneasy, her hands trembling.

Isabelle went to the veranda. Soon, she heard shouts below, then the gates' creaking sound. The king with a small group of people left the castle galloping on horseback. Isabelle watched the king going away. Leon and his people soon disappeared from sight.

Isabelle turned around to leave. She went out. Segar was waiting for her on the other side of the middle arch. Followed by the private guard, Isabelle directed to her own room. Isabelle was uncomfortable being followed around by a stranger. To her great disappointment, from that moment on, it had to be always like this.

When Isabelle reached downstairs, she hesitated, not knowing which way to turn. The palace was big, and Isabelle forgot the way that led to her room. The guard noticed what was bothering the queen. Segar cleared his throat and showed the queen the direction with a gesture.

"Your Grace," said the man.

Isabelle said nothing and went to the left side. The guard was here to protect her; however, his presence scared her more than his absence. When she reached her room, Isabelle locked the door from the inside. She didn't want to be disturbed.

Left alone in her room, she covered her lips with her fingers. She couldn't understand her own feelings at that moment. Then she remembered her dream. The attack on the northern lands by the Arsandars didn't promise anything good, and Leon was hiding something. The world was full of danger. Hiring a personal guard was a testament to it. Isabelle sighed. She sat on the floor next to the fireplace and embraced her knees. She knew she wouldn't be able to sleep that night . . . and probably the following nights too.

When footsteps were heard from the other side of the long hallway, Segar turned around. Seeing Tertius, Segar's vigilance weakened. Everyone knew that Tertius was the king's trusted friend.

Tertius said nothing and passed by the one who greeted him with a bow at the doorway of the queen's chamber. He went down to the meeting hall. Then he went to the narrow path between the sculptures room and the second dining hall. Tertius crossed library's double-arched gates and directed to the back door at the very end of the book rows. Behind the royal library's heavy back door appeared a long staircase leading to the dungeons. The circular staircase was lit with flaming torches from the right side. At the very bottom of the stairs, Tertius turned left. With the two guards who had met him at the arched gates of the dungeons' bottom level, Tertius went toward the oubliettes chamber, at the very end of which he bent over the iron bars of an oubliette built into the ground.

"Hello, my dear friend!" said Tertius, crouching down.

Under the flickering light of the flame torch, he could barely see the prisoner's bloody face.

"Did you miss me?" asked Tertius with a jest. "I have great news! Leon wants to help your fool king!" He giggled, and it echoed within the dungeons' cold stone walls. Then he ordered his men to get the prisoner out.

The prisoner's cry filled the surroundings.

"Shush . . . Why do you cry? I need you to serve me well!"

The prisoner cried louder, baring the mutilated part of his mouth where once there was a tongue. The bloodstains on his face had turned black long ago.

"Smile, my friend. You are going home!" said Tertius with an evil laugh, tapping the prisoner's cheek. "First, I'll prepare you for the mortal king."

Tertius stood up, took a knife from his waist belt, and went toward the big, rectangle stone in the corner of the chamber. The two guards dragged the prisoner to the stone. The prisoner's dumb screams slowly died down. When everything was finished, Tertius took an envelope sealed with the royal mark and put it on top of the dead body.

"Let's send a tiny gift to the king. Make sure Leon doesn't get to know!" ordered Tertius. His evil smile showed his satisfaction with what he had done.

The future had to be changed. Tertius believed that from that very moment, nothing would remain the same. He knew well that his king was in a sinking ship. The traitor preferred to be on the side of those who would write the future rather than those who were abandoned to their fate and had no other choice but to accept what was destined.

Sometimes life could be merciless. It could throw poor souls into its ordeals. And it didn't matter whether one was doing the right or wrong thing in his or her battle against the difficulties. All that mattered was victory.

Tertius betrayed his king. But it was his choice—his right! It was his step made toward an expected victory. Tertius didn't see anything wrong in his deeds. He decided to let the stream take over his vessel of life. For Tertius, his betrayal was a blessing to his king. Sometimes a long fight could break the person harder. A quick death could be less painful. Tertius knew that the future had already been written long ago. The song was sung. What was supposed to happen had to happen. And war was inevitable.

Chapter 19

Abandoned

"Stay safe," whispered the woman sinking into the arms of her husband. The golden armor perfectly laid on his vast chest was icy cold. The woman shivered. Her heart was breaking apart because of their separation. Their short privacy was disturbed when their ten-year-old daughter entered the room.

"Father!" the girl shouted and rushed toward her parents.

"Eireen!" Asael carried the girl and wrapped her in a hug. "My princess!" He smelled sweet apples mixed with mint in her hair. "I am going to miss you a lot!"

"I will miss too," cried Prince Noah with his thin voice, running toward them. The seven-year-old prince was half as tall as his father and could reach Asael's waist with his head. Asael put Eireen down then knelt to give a farewell hug to his son.

"I can't see Xander," Asael said wondering when he didn't see his eldest son.

"I guess he is still mad at us," replied the duchess. Calanthe took Asael's hand in support. "He is still a kid."

Asael shook his head.

"Life is complicated. He can't see it yet."

He squeezed Calanthe's hand in response. "Tell Xander I love him! I love all of you," said Asael with warmth.

He hugged them tightly once again before leaving. He had to say goodbye to his family many times. As the heir of the throne, he had participated in many world treaties and ceremonies. However, this time was different. He never felt pain until this morning. He never dropped a tear. How could this day be so different? So painful . . . so heartbreaking . . .

"We love you too," said Calanthe.

Asael took his horse and left the palace, leaving behind his home, leaving behind his family. The long row of the royal armed forces marched through the streets of Incitydoor. The people gathered outdoors to watch the parade and wish good luck to those who might not return ever. They watched the armored men with excitement, totally assured that the force would bring only victory to their kingdom.

Life was interesting . . . confusing. Its wheels of ordeal might lead mankind from one edge to another in a ruthless manner. Life expectations might be as promising as it was devastating. Watching the marching armed force, these people believed, without any hesitation, in undoubted victory. Would they be as undoubtful, as confident when they were broken . . . were demolished? Hope was dangerous. Its presence gave people strength, but its absence destroyed everything, leaving behind holes of fear and emptiness. Yet the people needed it. Despair sometimes was a bridge to salvation, and sometimes it was a loop on the gallows.

Would a desperate man fight for his life, or would he choose to end his life with a knife? The four hundred men marching the streets of the capital city listened to the hails of the people. Cheers, songs, wishes, flowers being thrown into the air . . . These men knew— it was their day: the day of becoming a hero, the day when names would be written on the pages of a new history. With great hope, these men dreamed to be safe and return home in a while. But not any of them could foresee that life had other plans. It planned to fill the pages of history with blood, pain, despair . . . Most of them would never return home, but they didn't know it.

They marched toward the main port. Most of them were happy. They tried hard to hide their joy and look decent. Their selection was an honor to their family. Most of them didn't know that so soon they would be praying for salvation at the other end of the world. They would find it on their last given breath . . .

Riding his horse, Asael entered the main area of the port to sail. Three giant royal ships were floating at the berth. They looked truly majestic. Leaving behind the hailing crowd, Asael slowly went onto the deck. Behind the golden sails, the view of the azure sea glittering under the light of the sinking sun appeared. The sea breath was cooling and ticklish. The first bright star twinkled up above in the scarlet sky. Asael loved the sea. He took a deep breath. He didn't notice how the surroundings had become still . . . The cold covered the ground, and then he heard a whisper.

"Run!"

Asael turned back toward the port to see the army and the crowd staring back at him in silence. Their faces were gloomy, their gazes cloudy . . .

"Run!" a whisper echoed again. Then Asael saw Xander. "Run!" repeated his son.

For a second the sea became motionless, waveless. Then it went up. The water rose high from the ground level. Asael looked around in terror, but the people didn't move. No one tried to run away. The water went up to their toes, their knees . . . It went up and slowly covered the entire surroundings. Then it reached the deck. Asael ran back and forth, but he had no way to escape. The water quickly covered the ship. Asael tried to swim to the surface, but all his efforts were useless. He went down like a heavy stone. At the bottom, the people were still looking at him, sinking in silence . . .

* * *

A hard knock on the door woke Asael up. With a cold sweat, he opened his eyes. The prince sat on his bed and buried his face in his palms, cursing his strange dream under his nose. An officer's voice followed another knock. He came to inform the prince about their arrival at Perle de la Mer.

"Your Highness, we have reached the destination point. Soon, we'll enter the bay," reported the soldier to the prince.

Asael hurried out. They had been traveling on the ship for about ten days. The sun had already painted the sky into the scarlet color of dawn. Big, pink clouds floated above their heads. On the main deck, the ship's captain and other royal guardsmen were waiting readily for their prince.

"Your Highness!" The second chief commander of the royal armed forces met the prince on the main deck.

"Lord Aegeus!" Asael showed his respect to the man. His gaze stopped at the black rocks of the fortress. The island was close.

"You need to see something!" Lord Aegeus's words sounded like a warning.

They went up to the forecastle deck. Asael took a small monocular telescope. It had five extending tubes springing from a golden base and sapphire borders. The fortress stood still on the rocks as if in a deep sleep. Asael didn't notice the sign of royal forces or the enemies.

"Seems the fortress is abandoned," Asael uttered in surprise.

"The gates are open. No guards at the battlements of both east and west towers. It is too suspicious," murmured Lord Aegeus.

"Sail closer!" ordered Asael. "We'll wait a little then send men to check. It might be an ambush!" said Asael.

Lord Aegeus nodded. The ship's first mate hastened to carry out the order. In a while, a boat with ten armed men inside lowered down. Soon, simultaneously rowing the oars, the men reached the island's shores. Everyone was waiting for the signal with bated breath. Then they saw . . . On the battlement of the west tower, a guardsman waved the kingdom's royal flag above his head. There was no one to fight for or against.

When the three dozen boats approached the shore, Asael was first to step onto the stone ground. Two of his men were already waiting for him at the gates. One of the guardsmen approached the prince.

"Your Highness!" The man looked pale. "We searched the fortress."

"Did you find anything?"

The guardsman lowered his head, trying his best to find the right words to answer his prince. "You should see it yourself, my prince," he murmured at last.

Asael looked at the half-opened gates. Swallowing became hard and painful. His first thought was about his brother Thaen.

This was no place to pray for a miracle. They were late. The help was late. When Asael first sailed from the Incitydoor port, he had hoped to reach the island in the middle of the sea battle. The fortress's walls were high, the soldiers well prepared. They could stand a siege well. Asael was thinking up strategies almost the whole time they were traveling. He imagined many times how he and his force would attack the enemy's ships from the rear, but the guardsman's words melted away his last hope.

With a heavy stone on his heart, Asael went inside. Crossing the fortress's iron gates, Asael clenched his fist. Despite the trembling all over his body and the horror that gripped his heart, Asael didn't dare stop. He didn't dare fall. He didn't dare fail the men—his men—who were looking at him terrified . . .

The fortress's stone ground was covered in blood that had turned black long ago. Dead bodies were everywhere. The air was saturated with the stench of blood and decomposition. The dead silence and freezing cold gave an even more terrible feel to the fortress. On the wall of the main tower, five bodies were crucified. For a second the prince turned his gaze away. How cruel of a death had the men faced? Asael had never seen such horror in his life. Ordinary men couldn't do such things.

"They are not alone . . ." Asael remembered the sentence from the message. What had that man tried to say in his message? What did he see? Asael was scared even to imagine what it could be.

Lord Aegeus put his hand on Asael's shoulder supportively and approached the wall first. He was an aged but experienced warrior. Asael stood next to Lord Aegeus.

On the wall, they saw two bodies hanging on top and two at the bottom, creating a square shape. Another one was in the middle. One of the bodies on top was burned, and the other one got arrows on his chest. The two bodies hanging below were turned upside down, one buried with his head under the ground and the other one drowned in a wooden basin with water. The fifth body was terribly mutilated.

"Seems those beasts performed some kind of ritual and killed them as an offering," Lord Aegeus voiced his thoughts.

"Take them down!" Asael gave the order at last. His gaze was still fixated on the bodies on the wall. "Call all the men. We can't leave the bodies. Their souls must get peace. Send a boat to the main ship, and bring the priest."

"Yes, my prince!" Lord Aegeus obeyed and turned to leave, but the prince's strong hands stopped him.

Lord Aegeus looked at Asael. He felt how the prince's grab eased up gradually. His face started changing, becoming paler. At last, the prince spoke in a very low voice, and the aged warrior felt the tremble in his voice, as if he was about to cry.

"Find him . . . please . . ."

Lord Aegeus gave one nod. He himself became speechless. He understood what was hurting his prince. Asael was thinking about his brother. A tear on the prince's face didn't escape the gaze of Lord Aegeus. He once again turned at the bodies on the wall, following the prince's look. Another wave of terror gripped him. At that moment, Lord Aegeus took a few steps backward, as if he wanted to escape the place if he could. He understood why Asael was staring at the bodies. As if he just read Asael's thoughts, Lord Aegeus once again carefully observed the bodies. He prayed that none of the bodies belonged to Thaen.

"I'll find him, my prince!" said Lord Aegeus, trying to sound convincing, then he left.

The sun was already setting down when Asael's men pulled all the bodies into the yard. Asael ordered the men to burn all of them. The smoke rose high, merging with the dark clouds in the evening sky. Soon, the weather grew even worse. In addition to raindrops, snow particles followed the wind. The waves grew stronger and higher. Asael and Lord Aegeus were giving orders in the yard, and the men hurried to the shore to pull the boats higher. After several lightning strikes, a strong, deafening thunder sound echoed. Everyone ran to the tower, bringing whatever they could carry inside. The men gathered in the main hall.

"Highness! Highness!" one of the watchers on the battlement shouted, running toward Asael. "Highness! We have a problem!" he said panting.

"Speak!" ordered Asael, not knowing what else to expect.

Noticing the others' gaze, the watcher felt depressed and lowered his voice, "The ships have lost their anchors. The storm is taking them away."

When Asael went up to the tower, the second watcher—totally soaked in the rain—stepped aside, opening a space for his prince. The surroundings were in darkness. It was raining heavily. Only the noise of the raging sea destroyed the silence. Asael couldn't see anything. Only through the illumination of occasional lightning could he see the ships' shadows appearing here and there, embraced in the waves' curves. When the last lightning appeared in the sky, Asael saw the top of the royal ships' main masts disappearing in the dark . . .

At dawn, the fortress was in deep silence. The exhausted men slept in the tower's main hall after the hard night. Asael watched the waves striking the stone island from the battlement. From a distance, he could see the ruins of the royal ships being thrown all over the rocky reefs. Asael looked gloomy. He was tired and haggard. Lord Aegeus, Assistant Commander Pearce, and a watcher were standing next to him. Asael was listening to Lord Aegeus's report.

"In total, we count two hundred and fifty men within the fortress," said Lord Aegeus. Sorrow was noticeable in his voice. The ruthless waters of the sea didn't spare anyone who stayed on the ships. "We were able to load only half of the goods from the ships. All our strength was spent collecting and burning the bodies. No one expected that strong storm to come."

"What about the fortress reserves?" asked Asael. He knew that the fortress was always provided with goods. Its reserves were enough and could withstand any siege for years.

"Everything was destroyed," answered Lord Aegeus. "All the goods and water reserves were emptied. The Arsandars burned the garden and poisoned the ground. They left nothing . . ." Lord Aegeus paused a little and then added, "They killed all the messenger birds. We can't inform the capital."

Asael lowered his head. His mind was blown. No matter how hard he tried, he couldn't foresee any solution to their situation. Both his hands and legs were tied tightly in a deathly chain. All that his consciousness accepted was the fact that he had failed everyone.

At that very moment, standing in the fortress's battlement, Asael was desperately thinking about any possibility of his survival and that of his two hundred and fifty men. Asael closed his eyes. It all happened because of his inattentiveness, his incompetence. It was his mistake. They couldn't survive the winter. Without food and water, wood and heat, and any ability to inform the others, they were all doomed.

Chapter 20

Massacre in the Riphean

It had been raining heavily for almost two days. The black clouds seemed to have no desire to open the veil so the sun could look down at the ground. At the troop's vanguard, Commander Rodrick and Sir Emmett rode their horses while four other horses carried the cargo for the road. They had been marching for so long. During the past two days, they stopped only to sleep for the night and to have a meal twice a day.

"Dear goodness, I had never thought that I would get a chance to see the mountain's inhabitants from the north," said Lionel to his friend marching next to him. "And what about you?"

"Me neither," answered Garth.

"What a freak must this nation be, having only one eye on their forehead . . ."

Garth didn't want to answer, feeling the disgust in his friend's tone.

"I've heard so much about them," continued Lionel. "I would commit suicide if I were them, honestly."

"You can't judge the poor 'them' with what nature rewarded them."

"Now you are playing the noble?" asked Lionel to irritate his friend.

"Shut up!" said Garth coldly.

His mood was as bleak as the weather. He was very tired. When they'd left the Fort Dolorem, Garth had a last hope: he had been eager to see Sienna on the way to the Riphean Mountain. When the troops had passed the meadow near Sienna's father's house, the old shepherd and his wife had watched them at their gates, but Garth hadn't seen Sienna. The girl hadn't been out in the yard, and the house's windows had also been closed. What if she hadn't received the message? What if she'd come to meet him the next day in the morning? That day Garth had been very hopeful to see her for once, even from a distance.

Rodrick's troop's way to the northwest foothill lay through the valley surrounded by a low mountain ridge. When they had almost reached the destination point, Rodrick met up with the centenarian king's people. About ten dozens of armored centenarians were waiting for the mortals at the foothill.

A tall and well-built man went up to meet Rodrick. He looked like the man in charge of the troop. Like all the other centenarians, he was on foot. Not one of the centenarian king's army rode a horse. All the soldiers wore long, black cloaks. They had cone-shaped helmets on their heads and long, black leather boots starting from the bottom of the black trousers. The red-colored shirts were covered by leather breastplates, wherein the shape of a griffin was engraved in the chest area. Their long swords hung in leather sheaths.

Rodrick moved toward the man, and he got off his horse as a sign of respect when the man approached him.

"Sir Waldo Ward," the man introduced himself, extending his hand to Rodrick, "chief of the northern troops of His Majesty the king."

"Commander Rodrick Burton," said Rodrick and shook Waldo Ward's hand.

"Hope the journey didn't create any troubles?" asked Waldo Ward.

"No trouble indeed." Rodrick watched the host's soldiers and said, "I believe that our countries support peaceful relations. Why call so many for the service?"

"The king's intentions are righteous. The north men can't be curbed," said Waldo Ward in a calm voice. "No harm from caution. We are here to make sure that all rights will pass to the hands of King Layland properly."

"Good. Then shall we begin the process?" asked Rodrick, observing the location.

"We'll start as soon as the chief of the Arimaspians arrives. He is late. He must lead us to the main gates of the mount cave Roghg."

"How long do we have to wait?" Rodrick inquired, becoming very impatient.

The day got even colder, and the cold was getting to his bones. At this time, the commander wouldn't say no to a bottle of ale and a hot bath. He dreamed about his cozy sofa in the corner of his room in the fort. At that moment, he wished for all this process to end as quickly as possible.

"I am afraid we'll be waiting for a couple of hours. My people checked the surroundings. No shadow on the horizon." Waldo Ward gave a sigh, spreading white smoke into the air. "He is being too late. My people are setting up a camp. Join us with your men."

"Well, no good conditions for outside camping. We need bonfires indeed. Anyway, thank you for the invitation." Rodrick nodded to Waldo Ward and then returned to his people, with one hand pulling the reins of his horse.

His men waited for their commander to talk, seeing his gloomy face.

"There will be no movements ahead until the Arimaspians' arrival. Set up camp! We have to wait a little while," announced Rodrick.

He didn't want to join the centenarian group; however, he wished to stay close in order to keep an eye on the opposite group settling down nearby. They took a spot not far from the centenarian camp.

"Why do we have to wait for these beasts in this cold weather?" Lionel murmured to his friend angrily. "It's damn cold out here."

"Pray they won't be late," said Garth to Lionel, pushing his hood closer to his face.

Rodrick's men took off the horses' cargo and tied the reins around a log's branches on the ground. The rain became heavier, and the day was dark as night. Because of the rain, starting a fire was impossible. The troops had to wait for two more hours, and Rodrick's people were starting to lose their vigilance. The cold made them weak.

The watcher looking after the opponents' camp became sleepy, his gaze becoming transparent. Most of the soldiers sat on whatever they could find: bigger-sized stones, broken logs, leather-wrapped traveling trunks.

Waldo Ward, on the opposite side, was watching Rodrick's people when one of his men approached Waldo Ward.

"The mortals are becoming impatient," said the man.

"They are always impatient. Fool of them," said Waldo Ward. "Let's do them a favor." Waldo Ward took the leather water flask and handed it to the man. "Take it to their commander."

The man took the water flask and directed toward the place where Rodrick and his people were sitting on logs. The soldiers from Rodrick's group watched the approaching man with suspicion.

"My greetings, Commander! Accept a token from my chief as a sign of his respect," said the man, handing the water flask with a slight bow upon reaching the mortals' camp.

"Thank you. I appreciate the attention of your chief. What is inside the flask?"

"It is *qymyz*, Commander. Sour horse milk," explained the man.

Rodrick looked at the opposite side, where Waldo Ward was still watching him. Emmet bent over his commander, trying to let Rodrick know about his suspicions.

"Commander, do you think you can trust the centenarians?" Emmet whispered to Rodrick.

Although the centenarians were always reliable, the way Leon Ulyses didn't dispute any points in the two-way agreement signed between him and King Layland had surprised everyone.

Leon had everything while Arawn Layland had nothing to give to the centenarian king in exchange. Yet he had been daredevil to request for the Riphean Mountain treasure. Was the centenarian king foolish or generous? Or had he another plan in his mind regarding the mortals? No one knew, and everyone could only suspect. But what was unknown to mankind always scared them the most.

"We are here as guests, and they are hosts. It won't be nice to refuse," answered Rodrick. He raised the water flask high and, after a nod he made to Waldo Ward, took a sip.

Waldo Ward nodded back to Rodrick and raised his own cup with qymyz to drink. Both troops kept watching the opposite group, each trying to look sincere and hide their mistrust, trying to look less suspicious. However, both sides had forgotten that they were not the only ones invited to the gathering at the foothill of the age-old mountain chain.

No one noticed the man climbing up the hill over their heads. In spite of the stones and the rain making the ground very slippery, the man in a long, hooded cape was climbing up so skillfully. On the contrary, he used the rain for cover. His every step was made with confidence, and he knew very well every inch of the ground under his feet. He was a son of the Riphean Mountain. He belonged to this land.

Occasionally, he stopped to look around with the only eye on his forehead to check whether he was still unnoticed by his enemies. Once again, the man looked around when he got to the very top of the hill. He waited for the signal. On the opposite side of the valley, two other Arimaspians on the hill raised their fisted hands, readily waiting for the command. Ten feet away from those men, another group of a dozen was hiding behind the rocks.

The man closed his eye and prayed. He knew his other brothers-in-arms were also waiting not far from him. It was time to begin. After a minute of praying, he took off his hood and approached a big horn built on the ground at the top of the hill. He took a deep breath, filling his chest with air, and blew into the horn. The horn's deep and resonant sound echoed all around.

Commander Rodrick got up on his feet from hearing an unexpected, strange sound. The sudden interruption scared him. The first thing he did was look around and check for the threat, subconsciously extending his hand to his sword. He looked to the chief of the centenarian army.

It seemed Waldo Ward was confused as was Rodrick. Their eyes met. Both of them were surprised and partially scared; they didn't fully realize what was happening. Seconds later, another sound grabbed the attention of those in the valley. But it wasn't the sound of a horn anymore. It was a scream, very loud and sonorous, a fierce and bellowing sound of an unknown creature coming from the north, behind the mountain range.

The weather was becoming even colder, the wind becoming faster and the rain heavier. It started snowing heavily seconds after the first scream. Snow covered the ground quickly, and the surroundings turned white as if enclosed by a veil. Soon, a second scream spread all over the valley. A white shadow, like a cloud, appeared behind the north hill. The shadow moved fast, flying back and forth.

With great terror, the people in the valley looked up at the thing flying so high in the skies, not believing their own eyes. It was a big bird with a wingspan of thirty-two feet. It belonged to the Accipitridae family of birds, with a shorter neck and longer tarsus and tail. Its plumage was crystal white, and its coverts sparkled like they were covered by a thousand dendrite snowflakes. The bird's flight feathers were made of crystal ice, and even its long beak was as white as snow. The mysterious bird, with dark-blue eyes and very strong vision, was one of the most dangerous creatures of the north. *Ater boreas*, "the dark north wind," the people of the north called it. The boreas was the messenger of the winter. It was believed to be the symbol of darkness and cold.

"What the hell?" murmured Waldo Ward. He couldn't understand why the creature had left its nest.

The boreas lived very high, under the rooftop of heaven. Its nest was located at the top of the mountain, where winter never ended and the ground was always buried under the snow. The boreas was never allowed to go down to the valley as the bird's free flight was banned by the great king of the centenarians.

Waldo Ward wondered, *Could it be a coincidence? Could have someone released the bird from his icy cave, and what could be their motive? Would the Arimaspians be the ones to blame?*

Even assuming that the Arimaspians had enough reason to rise against the king's will because of the land and treasure, they would never dare! Even for the Arimaspians, inviting the boreas to an open feast in the valley could bring a tragic end. The boreas would never stop. After the first massacre, it would just continue spreading its darkness and cold further to the inhabitants of the Riphean Mountain.

The boreas, flying high in the sky, directed toward the place where the groups of mortals and centenarians were gathered. Everyone in the valley stood still in terror, not knowing what to do and falling under the spell of fear.

The centenarian soldier who brought the qymyz to the commander was two steps away from Rodrick. He was watching the other side of the camp—not the bird, but his own people. At the very end of the camp of centenarians, behind everyone, a dozen centenarians took off their cloaks. They turned their cloaks inside out and put them on again. A white leather sewn to the inside part of their cloaks glittered as snow particles, and the white color made the centenarians less noticeable in the snow.

When the soldier saw that his people were ready, he took a knife from his waist belt and, in rapid movements, cut Rodrick's throat. Rodrick didn't notice the attack. The first thing he felt was a grab from his shoulders, then a sharp pain in his throat. Still unaware of what had happened to him, with both hands he tried to reach his throat in vain. Hot blood filled his mouth. He tried to swallow, but instead a huge amount of blood burst out. He felt the blood washing down his body. He could hardly move his hands, but he tried to take out what seemed to be stuck in his throat. He only grasped air, and then he felt cold, his body becoming numb. No matter how deep he tried to breathe, he could get no air into his lungs. He could no longer feel his legs, and staggering around, Rodrick fell to his knees. His eyes darkened, but before he was fully immersed in the eclipse, he saw for the last time a shadow flying toward him. Then he fell.

The centenarian soldier was quick. After attacking Rodrick, he took out his sword and hit another mortal standing beside him. After killing his victim immediately, he turned to another one. However, the second soldier had enough time to notice the enemy and was able to dodge the strike. The soldier repelled the hit with his sword. The third soldier standing close to them also attacked the centenarian from behind and severely injured him. When the other mortal soldiers and centenarians noticed the developing fight of the three, the centenarian was already almost defeated and Rodrick was already dead.

Everything had taken place in seconds. Unsure on whose side first betrayed the other, both groups pulled out their swords from their sheaths and rushed into battle. The mortals were both angry and terrified; they had lost their commander and been betrayed by their comrades. The peace promised by the great kings was a lie, and all of them were abandoned to be torn in the valley between the boreas monster and the centenarians.

On the other side, Waldo Ward tried to stop his soldiers.

"No! Don't fight! Don't fight! Pull back!" he shouted.

He knew well enough that they had come to the valley with the right intentions. They were not supposed to fight but to make peace.

However, something had gone wrong. Rodrick shouldn't have died! The army of two groups shouldn't have raised their weapons against each other.

But Waldo Ward was late. He couldn't prevent what had already happened. And worse, Waldo Ward was right: nothing could be a coincidence. The mortals were not the enemies he had to fear. The enemies were among his followers. He turned around when he heard a clink of blades behind the camp and saw a dozen centenarians attacking their own brothers-in-arms.

Waldo Ward had expected anything, but not the betrayal of his own soldiers. The braafs were the bravest soldiers of the centenarians. They were men of honor. Dignity was their greatest gift from nature, and they would never betray their own men, even their enemies. They showed valiance and mercy in battles. Waldo Ward wondered what price could have been paid to the braafs to make them betray their own brothers. What could be worth more than their pride, their honor, and their lives?

Terrifying thoughts bothered Waldo Ward. He wasn't just betrayed by his own men; he was led into an ambush. With a loud yell, Waldo Ward raised his sword to defend himself from the mortals. Soon, the valley turned into a battlefield where everyone slaughtered all others. Waldo Ward and his loyal men not only had to fight against the two groups but they were also being hunted by the boreas.

Waldo Ward stuck his sword into one of the traitors and then swung it in the air to hit another one, but suddenly the traitor turned away and jumped aside into the snow, hiding behind the white leather cloak barely indistinguishable in the snow. Waldo Ward stepped toward where the traitor jumped, but he had hardly made another step when a strong hit knocked him down.

Snow fell around him, burying Waldo Ward. Then a very loud scream of the boreas bellowed over their heads. Plummeting down, the boreas rose again into the sky, victims clasped in its claws. Every flap of its wings created a strong wind that froze the people underneath. Each time the boreas landed on the ground, it captured new victims, lifted them high into the sky, and tore them apart. Afterward, it threw them down. As the snow fell, so did the bodies of the dead.

The soldiers tried to flee from the battlefield by the path they'd come from. However, upon reaching there, they were trapped by another ambush. Hundreds of arrows fell from the top of the hill like rain. The Arimaspians waiting for the command decided to intervene to finish what they had started. It was time to put the final dot.

The terrified soldiers didn't know what to do. There was no way out from the chopping field. They were trapped between rocks, where from one side the Arimaspians attacked and on the other side the centenarians chased them, and the sky belonged to the boreas— the messenger of death.

Garth was running to the south after his friend, Lionel. He held his bronze shield high in one hand, trying to escape the rain of arrows. With his other hand, he held his sword. Garth didn't feel cold anymore. He was very hot inside. His chest was burning; his armor was scorching his skin. His palm was wet because of fear, and his sword became heavier and its grip slippery. It was more and more difficult to dodge the attacks of the enemies. Teary eyes made his vision worse. At any second, he was ready to scream, believing he would be the boreas's next victim. He could hear his own heartbeat, so loud that the other people's screams became distant noise.

At that moment, he couldn't think about valiance. He couldn't see any of the honor or bravery he had dreamt of once. All that he represented was just a boy who was crying, who was running away with a sword in his hands. He was a boy who wanted to live, who was sure that the day would never end, and that when it ended, it would be his end too.

Suddenly his friend, who was a few steps ahead of him, got hit by an arrow and fell. Garth stepped back, trying to hide behind his shield. He took two deep breaths before approaching his friend's dead body. Lionel was lying in a pool of his own blood, his eyes wide open. Garth could hardly get a moment to feel sorry for his friend's loss when another centenarian attacked him from behind. The hit was so strong that Garth dropped his sword.

At that moment, an arrow hit his right shoulder. With pain in his shoulders and chest area, Garth tried to dodge the enemy's sword, but he was not fast enough to avoid another strong injury. Garth knelt and crawled back with all his efforts, leaving a red line of blood on the snow. The centenarian raised his sword high to end Garth's life with a final hit, and Garth, his gaze fixed on the point of the sword, started praying to his own god.

But at the last moment, instead of giving the final strike, the centenarian bent over to the side breathlessly. Waldo Ward looked at the wounded mortal on the ground. Throwing aside the traitor's body, he rushed to another centenarian with a yell.

"Traitors! I'll destroy you! I'll smash you all, bastards!" Waldo Ward shouted as he attacked the others.

Garth leaned back and put his head down, placing his hand on his wound. Snow was still falling from the sky. Then he saw wings.

White crystal wings approached the ground, flapping slowly, and the sweet voice of a girl said, "I am waiting for you, Garth! Where are you?"

Garth gave a painful smile and repeated, "Sienna is waiting for you, Garth!"

Then he felt himself being lifted. The sky was calling for him . . .

Chapter 21

On the Verge of the War

The stairs were long, and the narrow passage that led upstairs lay in circles. Flame torches were flickering here and there, yet the passage was only light enough to barely see. A servant was slowly walking toward the attic with a wooden tray filled with a morning meal. He received a strict order from the first adviser of the king that no one must bother the prince. The servant didn't know what kind of a sin the father was punishing his son for.

More than ten days had passed ever since the first prince, Asael, had sailed away in three royal ships. Tomaso Layland had chained his son, Sanders, in the attic of the highest tower of the palace that day and hadn't visited him ever since. The servant brought a meal for him three times a day and put it in front of the prince. He was worried because every time he returned to take the tray, he found the meal untouched. However, he couldn't share his worries with the others as the prince's capture was kept secret from everyone.

If Prince Sanders continues refusing to eat, his health will be damaged, thought the servant.

At the very top level of the tower, the servant took the key out of his pocket and unlocked the door. With an unpleasant squeaking sound, the door opened, and he entered.

"Your Highness!" the servant hurried toward the prince with a scream. The prince lay unconscious next to the burnt-out fireplace. "Your Highness! Open your eyes!"

He first checked the prince's breath. Taking the glass, he washed the prince's face. He was still unconscious. The scared servant hastily unchained Sanders's hand with a prayer on his lips and tried to raise Sanders up. But suddenly Sanders opened his eyes and tackled the servant, and the servant gradually lost his consciousness.

When he woke up, it was late. He looked around and found out that he was beyond the walls of the palace. He was leaning on a tree in the forest. The servant tried to remember what had happened before his oblivion.

"You're awake!" said Sanders, observing him.

"Your Highness?" the man said, looking pale.

His consciousness brought back what had happened in the attic. Probably Sanders had been acting to deceive him. Despite it being the order of the king's brother, he imprisoned the prince in the attic for days, but now Sanders was free. What was worse—the servant's life was in Sanders's hands now. Even if Sanders decided to behead the servant, it was well within his right to do that.

"Highness! Forgive me! I made a sin! I beg for your forgiveness!" shouted the servant, throwing himself onto the cold ground.

Sanders chuckled. He approached the man and ordered him to rise on his feet.

"How is your head?" Sanders asked the servant.

"Good! My head is good, Your Highness!" the servant hurried to answer.

Sanders nodded.

"Thomas Walkers!" Sanders said in a calm but at the same time warning voice. "Listen carefully. From now on, you will serve me, undeniably! Not my father . . . This is the order!"

"I will, Your Highness! I will! I will serve you well!" Thomas merely cried. "I'll do whatever you'll say! I'll die for you . . . I—"

"There is no need to die," Sanders interrupted the servant's words. "Because if you die, your family will follow after you!"

The servant's face turned pale. Sanders told the servant that his family members were moved to another place and that the prince's trusted people would take care of them.

Suddenly the sound of galloping horses disturbed the silence in the forest. Thomas noticed four approaching riders in the twilight. The first rider who jumped off his horse and bowed to his prince was Ryland Lander, the eldest son of Clive Lander. He was a future brother-in-law to Prince Keon. His sister, Ada Lander, was engaged to the second son of the king. Next to him stood Ethan Magus and Arran Cassell, sons of the noble families of Rhodareen. Jayden Henderson was the last one to jump off his horse.

"Everything is ready, Your Highness!" said Ryland. "The Mesman brothers will be waiting for us at Westbridge."

"Did you send a message to the Trandale tower?" Sanders asked.

The riders nodded.

"Good! We are leaving now!" Sanders said, taking the reins of his horse.

The six horses galloped fast, passing by the old trees of the thin forest. They were rushing to reach the watchers' tower at Westbridge. Sanders's horse took the lead. A long trip was waiting for them ahead.

Sanders knew full well that his father had a great influence in the city, so he couldn't sail from the main port of Incitydoor. In addition, his father would send people to catch him and return him back to the palace. Sanders couldn't use the main road, but he could make a big detour to get to the destination point. He had to reach the closest port city to Incitydoor as soon as possible. He knew his time was limited. Sanders always trusted his father. He admired him and loved him . . . Tomaso was a man of honor and devoted to his family, to the king.

Until that day.

Sanders couldn't stop thinking about his father's words. He knew that his father tried to protect Sanders. But why? Something had happened. Something that no one else knew but his father. Tomaso sent Asael to the island while he imprisoned his own son in the attic to prevent his leave. Sanders hoped that his father's behavior was reasonable and that he wasn't involved in any kind of treason. Maybe he was forced to silence.

However, Sanders was sure of one thing: Asael was in great danger. Maybe it was already late to pray for Thaen being alive, but he had to try to save Asael. Asael, who had never faced the Arsandars of the Skin Islands, might have been ambushed. No one ever knew what to expect from these wild beasts. Even after facing them many times, there was a great chance of losing. They could easily deceive people, and Sanders hoped that Asael would not rush to make a mistake.

On the way, Sanders and his men made only four stops to rest. When they reached the Westbridge tower in about three days, the sundown was coloring the sky into different shades of rose. With his hood deeply pulled down, Sanders hid his face from the people. He met with his two other friends in the agreed-upon place.

Cole and Calix Mesmans were the eldest children of Lord Mesman of Deighton. Their family had distant relations to the English throne from their mother's side. The old tavern was crowded, so after a short conversation, all seven friends decided to leave the place, with Thomas following them.

The street was illuminated with fire torches. Despite the cold weather, outside the tavern was lively. People here and there were gathered in groups and chatting together, some of them laughing and some cursing during their conversation.

A sudden appearance of riders scared the people around. About two dozen riders on horses galloped to the northeast. Their way lay through the main square of the small town. The riders belonged to the royal armed forces and bore royal flags. The first two riders held the royal banner and the flag of the royal ambassador. Next to them rode a man in a golden vest. Despite his face being covered by his golden helmet, Sanders recognized the man leading the cavalry.

Nehorai Magus was one of the best warlords of the kingdom and the best negotiator. He was the most favorable adviser of the king and one who played a special role in the kingdom's foreign relations.

Sanders climbed on his horse and chased after the royal cavalry without thinking. Ryland Lander and the other men also followed their prince without hesitation. Sanders turned his horse to the parallel path to the main street. Using the shortcut, Sanders was able to reach those riding in front of the cavalry. When Sanders cut the road of the royal ambassador's escort, the horses in front jumped in fear. One of the riders pulled his sword out in response to the stranger who suddenly appeared from nowhere.

"Stop!" shouted Nehorai to his man. He raised his right hand to let his men know that there was no danger at all. He pulled the reins of his horse and moved forward toward Sanders. "My prince!"

Nehorai welcomed Sanders in a brotherly fashion and reached out his hand. He had known Prince Sanders from his childhood.

"Sir Magus!" Sanders accepted his hand.

The others showed their respect to their prince. Soon, Ryland Lander and his other companions caught up with Sanders. Nehorai's gaze didn't miss the young man standing behind Ryland Lander: his nephew, Ethan Magus. Then he looked at Sanders.

"You are not supposed to be here right now!" Nehorai stated to Sanders in a low voice. "The palace is in great turmoil! The king is mad."

"What happened? Where are you headed, Sir Magus?" Sanders asked, trying to understand the situation.

"The day before yesterday, at night a mass of night prayers from the red shrine brought a body to the palace," Nehorai said. "They found him on the way to the shrine."

"Who is it?" Sanders asked impatiently.

"The mutilated body belonged to the messenger sent to Adahhar to request for help in the conflict with the Skin Island savages. He had gone to see the centenarian king."

"What nonsense! King Leon has no reason to kill the messenger of Rhodareen." Sanders's thoughts were confused.

"There was a letter found next to the body. The last lines of the prophecy were written in the letter, and it was sealed with the royal sign of the centenarians. Rumors are spreading quickly, Your Highness," continued Nehorai. "They say the fifth child was reborn and is waiting for his revenge."

"Madman's prophecy!" Arran added angrily.

However, Sanders quickly raised his hand to silence his fellow.

"What is the king saying?" asked Sanders.

"The king called for the summoning of all the counselors. Everyone is alerted. They are preparing for war!" Nehorai said. "Whatever is your business out there, you'd better return back to the palace." Once again, Nehorai's gaze met his nephew's.

"What about you?" asked Sanders.

"I'll go to the north, then to the east! If we go to war, we need allies. The others are sent to the south and the southeast."

"May your trip be favorable and safe!" said Sanders.

"You too. Be safe, my prince!" Nehorai said goodbye to Sanders. He also waved his hands toward the prince's other fellows and ordered his men to continue on their way.

Staring back after Nehorai, Sanders shook his head. He tried to hide his deep shock and confusion. What had seemed impossible could soon destroy his peace and all his world. After somehow putting his thoughts in order, Sanders at last turned to his fellows.

"Arran will return to the palace with me," said Sanders in a strict voice.

Everyone listened to his words in silence.

"The others will go to the north. Ryland will lead the team. You must reach Asael as soon as possible."

"Your Highness . . ." Ethan wanted to speak about his opinion, but Sanders cut him.

"If the king decides to start a war, my father will need me. I can't leave. I have to protect my family. Moreover, Isabelle is in the hands of the centenarians. I must find out what dirty games these kings are playing." His gaze was cold as he said the words.

The others said nothing. They all knew that Sanders had already decided and his decision couldn't be changed.

"Your Highness, what about me?" Thomas, who was standing aside and watching the others all that time, said to Sanders.

"You'll stay with the others and help them to find Asael," Sanders stated coldly.

Thomas wanted to show his gratitude to Sanders, even though he didn't like the idea of leaving the country.

"Thank you very much for your trust, Your Highness! I must say—"

However, Sanders wasn't in the mood to listen to the servant's useless words. His mind was full of his own worries. He was mad . . . The way the servant disturbed him irritated Sanders, and he lashed out his anger at the servant.

"Who said I trusted you?" Sanders yelled at the man. "I never trust a servant whose life belongs to his master. When the master changes, the degree of the loyalty changes its direction like a wind vane. You chained me and kept me in the attic of the tower. Don't tell me you were doing your duty!"

"Your Highness!" Thomas was scared, and he took a few steps back. He had never seen Sanders being so threatening and fierce. No one ever had.

"I am letting you go only so you could pay me back your debt!" Sanders stated.

"Your Highness! Please forgive me!" cried Thomas.

But Sanders wasn't paying attention to Thomas's words anymore. He took a leather bag with coins and threw it to Ethan. Then he turned around and jumped on his horse. Arran quickly got on his horse and followed Sanders in the direction of Incitydoor in order not to fall behind his galloping horse.

In truth, Sanders didn't need Thomas's loyalty at all. A man without any skills in a fight would be useless in such a long and dangerous mission that he had sent his fellows to. At first, all Sanders wanted was to save the poor servant from his father's rage.

Thomas had served his father well; however, that couldn't save him from being penalized because of Sanders's escape. Sanders had planned to take care of him on the road and let Thomas help him and his friends with minor tasks on the road. But now the plans had changed. Sanders had to return back to the palace, so Thomas also could return to the palace safely. However, Sanders didn't let him. He ordered Thomas to stay with Ryland and the others. Sanders himself couldn't understand why he gave such an order. He was not in the mood of thinking about others. All he cared about at that very moment was his sister.

Isabelle . . . The centenarian king had taken her away. Now we are on the verge of war. Did my father foresee it? Was it the main reason he didn't allow me to sail away with Asael? Did he know? Then why did he send Isabelle away? Couldn't her marriage have been really prevented? Was there some way to save her from disaster?

Sanders couldn't find answers to many of his questions regarding his sister's safety. In what condition did the king keep Isabelle at Adahhar, and what were his motives for marrying her? Sanders didn't know, but he was angry. His heart was in turmoil.

"We are moving!" shouted Ryland at last. "Get on your horses. We had already lost enough time."

The others obeyed him as Sanders had left Ryland in charge of the rescue team of royal princes. All six men got on their horses and galloped away. Their journey was long and hard. They didn't know what was waiting for them ahead. All they had was the hope of not failing their lord and returning home safely.

Chapter 22

Life on the Edge

It had been snowing heavily for almost four days. The shepherd went to the sheep shed to check the animals. He had lived in Dolorem Valley with his family all his life. His father had lived and worked hard in this land, and after the death of his father and brother, his brother's family had moved away. The shepherd became the only man, with his wife and daughter, who stayed in the neighborhood. Their closest neighbors were the soldiers of the Dolorem fortress.

The man raised his hands over his face to protect his eyes from the falling snow. It was cold outside. Near the shed, the dog barked continuously. When the shepherd reached the shed, he shook the snow off his coat. Even his beard became totally white in the snow. The strong wind's howl could be heard from the shed holes, and the animals were uneasy. The shepherd tried to calm them down by covering the bigger holes with straws.

Afterward, he changed the oil for the hanging lamps in the corners. The shepherd raised the collar of his coat up to his face and went out. He closed and locked the door of the shed. Outside was dark, and going to his home not far from the shed, the man stopped near his dog and tried to pet it. But the dog reacted aggressively and jumped on the shepherd. Only its leash and collar stopped the dog halfway to the shepherd. It continued barking loudly. From time to time, the dog jumped toward the shepherd, wanting to get rid of its collar. When the shepherd moved aside, he noticed that the dog was not acting aggressively against its master; it was barking at the gates. The man approached the dog from its side, and the dog once again jumped high toward the gates with all its strength. The collar hurt its neck, and it howled. The shepherd bent over his dog to comfort it.

"Easy, girl, easy . . . ," he said and looked at the gates.

Earlier that day, he had forgotten to lock the iron gates. Because of the strong wind, the gates were now half open, but he couldn't see anything beyond the gates in the dark and the heavy snow.

"Who's there?" shouted the shepherd.

There was no other sound but the howling of the wind. The man was afraid to go to the gates as his dog growled at them. The shepherd didn't know what the darkness could hide out there. Taking the dog's collar, he released it, and the dog threw itself to the gates. In seconds, it disappeared out of sight. The man waited for a little while, looking into the darkness. He knew well that he had to free his dog. If there were wolves out there, the dog couldn't protect itself while tightly tied by the rope. For some time, he could hear his dog barking out there. Then it became still.

The man didn't hear any sound. No barking . . . No howling . . . He rushed to his house. As soon as he reached the doorway, the shepherd entered the house and locked the door from inside. He took his musket hidden in the closet under the stairs and stood by the window, watching the gates. The cold entered the house from a slightly opened window, and the wife of the shepherd appeared at the threshold of the kitchen. She got scared upon seeing her husband holding the musket.

"What happened? Why are you holding that thing?" asked the woman.

The shepherd said nothing, and the woman started worrying.

"Darling—" the woman started to ask, but her husband raised his hand.

His forefinger pointed upward, urging the woman to be quiet. He saw something. A shadow in the dark. It was coming toward their house. When the shadow came closer, the shepherd saw his dog under the window lights. The dog ran to the door and barked. It started scratching the door with its paws. The man hurried to open it, and when he let the dog in, it jumped on its master. Then it jumped around the hall and approached the door. The dog wanted its master to follow. The man hesitated. He was scared, and he didn't want to go out. Something was wrong. But the dog didn't want to give up.

"Maya," the man said to his wife, "lock the door, and watch the gates. Don't open it no matter what happens."

His wife looked at him with terror. "What are you talking about?" she asked.

Then he took another musket from under the stairs and gave it to her.

"You know how to use it."

The woman took the musket from her husband's hands.

"You and Sienna must stay at home. If I don't come back, you should go to the fortress in the morning. Call for help."

"I don't understand," his wife said indignantly. "You shouldn't go anywhere so late!" she objected.

"I must check!" he said, sighing. "First, release the sheep for distraction. Then take a horse—no! Take horses," the shepherd corrected his words. "Don't leave Sienna alone."

The dog became impatient around its master. The shepherd took a tiki torch and lit it. His wife watched him disappear behind the gates with the animal.

When the shepherd crossed the gates, the weather seemed to get even colder. Strong winds made every step harder. The dog was running ahead. From time to time, it stopped and waited for its master and then continued on its way. The shepherd went far from his house. Twenty meters away from him, the dog stopped and started sniffing the ground. The shepherd raised the torch and looked around carefully. He tried to see anything on the ground until he noticed a slight movement next to his dog. There was something in the snow bump under the dog's feet. The shepherd came closer. With one hand, he raised his musket. The dog started digging up the snow, and the shepherd heard a low moan.

He bent over and started digging the snow together with his dog. Under the snow, he found a man, half dead and barely breathing.

"Dear goodness!" shouted the shepherd, pulling the man out of the snow. "Hold on, boy. Hold on! I'll help you!" He dropped his musket and put the man on his shoulders. "Just hold on. Don't die!" begged the shepherd.

The shepherd's wife was still standing at the window, aiming at the gates with the musket's point. Her daughter, Sienna, was waiting next to her. The women were praying in their whispers. Almost half an hour had passed since her husband left the house. Sienna turned away and wiped her tears. She was worried for her father.

"Please," whispered the woman.

Then she heard the bark of the dog. The woman dropped the musket and rushed to open the door.

"He is coming! He is coming!" shouted the woman as Sienna ran after her mother.

"Maya!" the man called when he saw his wife in the doorway. "Maya, help!"

The woman went to the other side of the stranger and grabbed his hands. Sienna held the door open while her parents brought the man inside. The dog ran in after them.

"He is barely breathing!" said the shepherd when he put the man on the floor. "He is frozen . . . and probably wounded. We must warm him up."

"Let's bring him into the kitchen. It is warm there," advised the woman.

"Help me then!"

The shepherd and his wife took the man from both of his arms and pulled him into the kitchen. Sienna hurried to bring a basin with hot boiled water. She also brought clean towels and a warm blanket. When Sienna entered the kitchen and approached the man, her parents were taking the wet clothes off the man. Sienna gasped when she saw the man's face. Her hands became shaky. She recognized the unconscious man in their kitchen.

Sienna tried hard not to reveal her worries in front of her parents. She did not say anything because her parents didn't know about her acquaintance with Garth Bevin of the House of Calhoun. Garth had broken his promise to her and hadn't come to see her six days ago. She had waited for him to come to their meeting place for so long, but Garth hadn't appeared. She didn't know that he had written her a message because she hadn't received it, and she had been feeling terrible all this time.

She didn't know how to act or what to do at that very moment, looking at the grimaced face of the soldier suffering from pain. Sienna tried to hide her tears.

Maya took the towel from her daughter's hands and soaked it in hot water. When the towel touched Garth's body, he moaned. On his lower abdomen was a trail of a long wound left by a sword. His whole body was in deep scars, and there were wound holes from sort of some animal attack. Some of them were very deep. On his right shoulder was a pointy end of a broken arrow.

"He belongs to the Dolorem fortress's royal army," said the shepherd, observing his torn clothes. "I saw them going northwest several days ago."

"What had happened out there?" asked the woman, looking at the soldier's body with terror.

The shepherd shook his head. He had no idea of any possibilities that the man could have faced in the north.

"Do you think he is the only survivor?" asked his wife.

"I don't know," the shepherd replied. "We must inform the others in the fortress. I will go to Fort Dolorem in the morning," said the shepherd.

But his wife objected, shouting, "No! You won't go anywhere!"

"Look at the man. He is dying," he said. "We can't keep him here."

"He is almost dead. We don't know how long he has left to breathe," said the woman. "What if the one that attacked him is still out there? Outside is not safe!"

"Maya, we have to do something."

"I can't lose you!" the woman begged her husband.

"Mother is right, Father. What if something happens to you? We can't bear the loss . . ." Sienna said, supporting her mother's side.

"I'll go in the morning. Besides, he was able to crawl to our gates. I hope what was in the north was left in the north," the shepherd tried to persuade his family.

Even though the woman was worrying a lot, she agreed with her husband. The family decided to leave Garth in the kitchen. His body temperature was very low as he had spent a long time in the cold and got frozen. Probably he was living the last moments of his life and wouldn't make it till morning.

Maya hoped that he wouldn't suffer for long. She prepared an herbal potion, and together with Sienna, Maya soaked the corner of the towel with the potion and patted the soldier's mouth with it at intervals.

Garth was unconscious, but he had to receive treatment. It was already very late when Sienna told her mother to have some rest.

She informed her mother that she would be watching the man and would wake the others if something happened. For the first time in all those years, the family decided to sleep with a locked door. Their dog stayed at the door.

When the woman went upstairs, Sienna sat near Garth. She put her hand on his forehead. Garth was burning. Occasionally, he gave a long, painful moan. Every time he breathed in and out, his face grimaced out of pain. Sienna hated herself for not being able to help him.

"Please come back!" she begged. "Come back from your dark world full of pain and sorrow. You must come back to me!" Sienna covered her mouth with both her palms to hold her cry.

The night was long, and she couldn't kill the time that stopped for her, full of despair and precariousness.

Chapter 23

When the Surroundings Became Quiet

The long corridor was cold and dark, and there was the smell of burnt wood and blood everywhere. The dampness in the air was suffocating. Walking between the thick tower walls, Celia covered her nose with a handkerchief. When she approached the room at the last level of the Saint Daman Abbot tower, the two guards opened the door, and she stepped inside unwillingly.

At the very end of the room, Mother Abella was manacled tied tightly to the wall. For almost two weeks, the old woman had been kept in the tower and tortured by the king's soldiers. All parts of her body were covered in bruises and scars. For a little while, Celia stood at the door and watched the old woman.

Then she took away the handkerchief and said, "Long time no see!"

Mother Abella raised her head to look at her visitor.

"How have you been doing, my old friend?"

Mother Abella was surprised to see the witch in the abbot. More than feeling surprised, Mother Abella was scared to see her.

"You?" the old woman barely whispered. "Impossible . . . No. It can't be you . . ."

Celia laughed out loud. "If you could see yourself from the side . . . What a shame! I thought you would be happy to see me."

"How is it possible? You can't be alive," said Mother Abella, hardly believing her eyes. But her words didn't offend the witch.

Celia came closer, saying, "And you still have not died . . . You are full of disappointments!"

"Impossible . . ." Mother Abella shook her head. "Impossible . . ."

Celia bent over and put her palm on the old woman's face covered with blood.

"Poor Abella," Celia said and sighed.

"It was you, wasn't it?" Mother Abella asked the witch. "You did this to us! Yes. Only you could do this to us!" Mother Abella looked down, shaking her head as if she wanted to deny the horrible truth she had tried to avoid for many years.

"I never thought I would see you in such a miserable condition one day," said Celia with pity.

On one hand, Celia felt sorry for the old woman. She and Mother Abella had known each other for a long time, actually for almost more than a thousand years now.

"Why did you come back? What do you want?" Mother Abella asked, puffing.

"You know the reason. I came for the child."

Mother Abella shook her head, her every movement done with great difficulty.

"No . . . There is no child in the abbot. There never was. This is the light house of the witches."

"Shush!" said Celia, putting her forefinger over Mother Abella's mouth. "You know, I don't like when others lie to me."

With gentle movements, Celia swiped Mother Abella's dirty hair aside and looked at her face. Mother Abella shook her head harder, crying soundlessly.

"Just tell me where she is, and save the others!"

"Please," begged Mother Abella.

"Show her to me!" ordered Celia. "I know that no one had left the abbot. She is here. All I need is a name."

Mother Abella looked away. Celia took her jaw and forced Mother Abella's face to turn to her.

"Don't turn away! Talk to me!"

Mother Abella closed her eyes. While holding the old woman's face in her palm, Celia pressed her finger against Mother Abella's right cheek, and the old woman screamed. When the witch took off her hand, the mark her finger had left turned dark black with reddish blood particles around. The smell of burnt flesh spread in the air.

"Talk!" ordered the witch. "*Te!*"

"*Mamte!*" Mother Abella refused to talk. "You will never find her!" said the old woman.

"Are you playing with my patience?" asked Celia. "This is a mistake you should never make!"

Celia took a few steps back.

"*Irg'o eib!*" Celia said the spell, looking at Mother Abella.

The two soldiers on the other side of the door clenched their fists as if it were them being tortured inside. Mother Abella's scream was piercing. When Celia left the room, Mother Abella was unconscious.

"Gather all the prisoners at the main hall!" ordered the witch to the soldiers.

They obeyed and went downstairs.

Soon, all the witches in the abbot were waiting for Celia in the hall. The abbot's hall was half destroyed and in a mess. Most of the corner monuments and wall ornaments were broken, and parts of the building, built of wood, were totally burnt out. Some relics were stolen during the night attack more than two weeks ago.

When the witch's footsteps were heard, no one dared to raise their heads to look at her. Celia's power was so strong that she blocked all the witches' abilities to spell inside the abbot. All the other witches became weak and helpless.

Celia made a circle in the middle of the hall, observing every attending witch as she went.

"Sisters!" said Celia at last. "My beautiful sisters . . . I hope everyone present knows who I am?" she asked.

All the witches nodded. Most of them hadn't seen her till that day, but everyone had heard about her.

"Do you know the reason for my visit then?"

The witches said nothing. Everyone was still.

"Don't you know?" Celia laughed. "Well then, I . . . ," Celia said, raising his voice, "am looking for a girl. I am looking for the liar hiding within these walls. This girl is among you. A girl who thinks she is equal to you. A girl who calls herself your sister. The girl that cannot spell."

Celia approached the youngest girl in the abbot and played with her hair.

"She is useless. The liar has no power, and I need you to tell me who that one is," Celia continued.

The witches of the abbot looked at each other, but none of them dared to talk.

"Give me the one you have been hiding all these years."

Charlotte's fists squeezed the corners of her apron as Celia passed by her. She knew the witch was looking for her best friend. Amare was the only one who couldn't spell among them, who was far from magic, the girl without any ability. Why did the witch want to find Amare? Charlotte didn't know the reason. All she knew was that Amare was not in the abbot.

The night of the attack, Charlotte had woken up from the noise. She had felt a strong quake and saw everything in her room shaking. Amare's bed had been empty. Charlotte had gone out to look for her friend, but when she'd reached the first level, all lights had gone down.

"*Noi*," Charlotte had whispered.

A small, round light the size of her palm had appeared in the air and lit her way. Charlotte had heard a noise from the side of the gates, so she'd decided to return to her room, hopefully to find Amare there. But when Charlotte had entered the room, she couldn't recognize it. Her room had been half empty of furniture, and all of Amare's belongings had disappeared, like they never had been there before, like Amare had never existed.

It had seemed like the room had been set up for only one person. At that moment, Charlotte had heard a piercing sound, like a howl, and her spell, the only source of light in her room, had gone out.

"*Noi!*" Charlotte had said hastily, but no light had appeared in the air. The surroundings had been covered by complete darkness. "*Noi!*" Charlotte had repeated with a scream.

But all her efforts had been in vain. Soon, Charlotte had started coughing. She had smelled the burning in the air, and soon it had become hard to breathe. Then she'd fallen unconscious. When she had opened her eyes, she had been manacled in the dungeon of the abbot with the other sisters.

Since then, Charlotte hadn't heard about Amare, nor had she seen her friend.

At this very moment, the witch was demanding the sisters of the light house to tell them the name of the sister who had been missing.

"I need that one to take a step ahead. Tell me the truth, and I'll forgive all the other girls. Otherwise, you all will be so sorry."

At that moment, a man in uniform entered the hall and called for the witch.

"My lady," said the man.

Celia didn't like to be disturbed, but she decided to give the man a chance to speak.

The man slightly bent toward the witch and said, "We checked everything. Names' lists, rooms, belongings . . . According to the data, no one has left the abbot. Everyone is here . . ."

"Good!" said Celia, satisfied with his report.

"But there is one thing," continued the man.

"What is it?"

"There is a name . . . It belongs to a person not included in the list."

The man took an expanded piece of paper and showed it to Celia. The witch opened the paper and read what was written. Celia then understood that she made a mistake in hoping that she could trick the abbot's witches. The old witch had an advantage over her and was able to mislead her.

Now Celia was late. The one she was looking for had already left the abbot before her arrival. Mother Abella had managed to convince Celia of the illusion that she'd created by erasing all the evidence that could point to the girl, that could prove her existence. Celia had been deceived by the count. She had lost a lot of time in searching for the person she wanted among the unwanted ones. Mother Abella was able to win some time that Amare needed to get away.

"Cunning witch!" said Celia with irritation. "How far did you hope she would run away?"

Celia clenched the paper in her fist, and it turned into ash. The witch threw away what was left of the paper and turned to the other girls.

"Who is Charlotte?"

All the witches raised their heads at once. They looked at each other, not knowing how to react to her question. Charlotte looked down. She wanted to go down into the ground . . . so much. She squeezed her hands harder in order to stop the trembling. Her heartbeat became faster. Some of the witches standing close to her looked at her, but only for a second, not wishing her to be discovered.

"I am not patient. I have lost quite enough time by giving you a chance for forgiveness," said Celia, turning around. "So I'll ask you for the last time . . . Who is Charlotte?"

Celia didn't receive any answer from those in the hall. So she approached a young witch, approximately the age of fourteen or fifteen. She took her into the middle of the room and started interrogating her.

"What is your name?" asked the witch.

"I am Annabelle . . ." answered the girl with a trembling voice.

Celia made a sign at the soldier standing next to her. All the witches in the hall screamed with terror as the man took their sister's last breath. Celia said nothing. She approached another girl, one the age of five this time. She led the girl to the middle of the hall as well.

"Melanie!" screamed another girl. "Please let my sister live! Please!" she begged the witch.

"So this is your sister?" asked Celia.

The girl nodded, her eyes full of tears.

"What is your name?"

"Beatrice. My name is Beatrice," cried the girl.

Charlotte was watching her from the side. She closed her eyes and started praying.

"Please, Beatrice! Please don't! Don't dare! I beg you. Don't do this to me."

Charlotte felt the cold creeping over her body, which was becoming numb. Charlotte didn't know what was written on that paper. She didn't know that it was a paper taken out from her own notebook that she had kept in her closet. She didn't know that the witch read her name and her best friend's name from the paper.

To a friend and sister of mine.

To my soul mate, with great love, I

give this present to Charlotte . . .

Sincerely yours, Amare.

For her fifteenth birthday, Charlotte had received a carving of roses in a vase made and painted by Amare. Amare had also left a message on the paper next to the birthday present. Charlotte had kept her friend's message inside her notebook. If Charlotte had known that the message she had received for her birthday would destroy her one day, she probably would've gotten rid of it long ago.

"Tell me, Beatrice . . . ," said Celia. She took the knife from the soldier's hand and continued, "Who is Charlotte?"

"She is over there!" Beatrice shouted, pointing with her finger toward Charlotte. "That is Charlotte! Please let my sister live!" the girl begged again.

Charlotte closed her eyes. That was her end. She didn't dare to look at the witch. All the other sisters of the abbot stepped back, avoiding Charlotte. They didn't want to infuriate the witch even more. Celia released the little girl, who then ran toward her sister. Beatrice embraced her sister with a cry, and Celia raised her hand, making a sign to the soldiers waiting at the side.

"Move! All out! Move, I said!" shouted the soldiers, pulling the girls away back to the dungeon.

Celia approached Charlotte, who was still standing with her eyes closed. She turned pale and shook with fright.

"You may open your eyes!" ordered the witch.

Charlotte could smell her scent. Celia was standing very close to her.

"Look at me, girl!" said Celia.

Charlotte obeyed.

"Listen to me carefully," continued the witch. "I want to know everything about your friend. What she looks like, how she smells, how she walks, how she stands . . . sits . . . talks . . . Everything! Where she went . . . Do you understand me?"

Charlotte nodded.

"Good!" Celia looked at one of the soldiers waiting at the door and ordered, "Take her downstairs!"

When the two men in uniform approached her and grabbed both her hands, Charlotte spoke in such a low voice, like a whisper, that none of the soldiers could hear or understand her.

"Mirnat nisu adnihonap arsa! Namarovlo inem ratuq!" whispered Charlotte.

Celia knew the girl had started her prayer. She was praying to her own gods for salvation.

"Irg'o ameib . . . Taiba ratuq!"

Celia said nothing. She watched the girl being taken downstairs. She could pray as much as she wanted, but her gods couldn't help her now. Charlotte was left all alone without any protection. Nothing could protect her from Celia. The gods she worshipped and prayed to had abandoned her. The gods abandoned everyone.

The man who brought Celia the paper earlier approached the witch again.

"Do what you need. You must find out everything about the girl!" Celia ordered the man.

"I understand," he said.

"And prepare your men . . . We are going hunting!"

"What should we do with the other witches?" asked the man. He knew full well that they couldn't be released.

Celia looked at the man and gave an answer without blinking an eye.

"On the twentieth day of the winter, all of them will be sacrificed in honor of the god of fire."

"But that is in six days," the man asked in surprise.

Celia raised her eyebrows.

"Yes, indeed," she said scornfully. "Send the message all over the country. The penalty will be held publicly, in front of everyone."

The man bowed and left the hall. He wanted to argue, to object to the witch's decision, but he didn't dare. He was afraid of her. Celia belonged to an ancient witch family. Nevertheless, she chose the worst way of execution for the witches of the light house.

Celia looked around when she was left all alone in the great hall.

"I'll give the world such a performance that no one will ever forget," uttered the witch. "The world will get all that it deserves." Then Celia left the hall.

The abbot's empty corridors looked like the ruins of an old building left uninhabited for centuries, full of dust and dirt. It was too early to see the first rays of the sun in the sky. From the broken roof of the hall, the snow particles fell down, dancing in the wind. They covered the naked floor with a white veil, and the surroundings became quiet.

Chapter 24

Sundown in Dolorem

The old shepherd bent over and checked the young soldier's pulse. The wounded man was icy cold and hardly breathing.

"He is losing his fight . . ." the shepherd said, sighing with pity.

His daughter took a wet towel soaked in warm water and put it on the soldier's forehead. No one in the shepherd's house could sleep the whole night. Garth's condition had worsened since his arrival, and the shepherd and his family looked after him in turns.

"He won't make it . . ." The shepherd's wife shook her head. "What will we do?"

The old woman really didn't know what to do. She was terrified. She wished she could ease the poor man's pain. He was very young to die, probably the same age as her daughter.

Maya sat beside her daughter. Sienna also looked terrible. Maya believed that her daughter was scared as she had never seen anyone in such awful condition. A young girl at her age, who was too sensitive to see injured animals, surely was not ready to see the deathly wounds of the man sinking in his own blood.

Fight, Garth. Please fight, begged Sienna in her thoughts. She was trying to hold her own tremble. She wanted to cry out loud. She wanted to hug Garth and never let him go. She wanted to scream with all her voice.

The shepherd took his coat from the hanger and directed toward the main door. He was holding his musket in one hand.

"You can't go now. It is too dark out there," the woman said in despair.

"Maya, you know that I have to go!" the shepherd said, his words cold and firm.

"It is almost morning. Wait a little . . . ," begged the woman.

The snowy storm worsened, and the woman didn't want her husband to go out. Leaving the house was dangerous. Her husband could get lost in the storm and never make it home.

The shepherd put his hand on his wife's shoulder encouragingly and said, "I'll be careful. It won't take long."

His wife nodded helplessly. "Be careful," she said.

The shepherd went out and jumped on his horse.

"I'll be back soon. Watch the gates. Keep it locked!" the shepherd said to his wife. Then he looked ahead. "Yah! Yah!" he shouted twice to his horse, waving his stick in the air.

He knew well that he had to reach the fortress as soon as possible. Time was valuable. The shepherd couldn't take the wounded man to the fortress as he would die on the road to Fort Dolorem. His horse galloped down the road that led southwest through the wide meadow. The snowfall was thick. The shepherd forced his horse to be faster, but the weather slowed its travel in the snow.

After more than two hours, the man reached the fortress and saw its stone walls standing high on the white veil. The shepherd pulled his horse's reins to direct the way. Two soldiers met him at the gates when he came close to the fortress. The newcomers at the fortress didn't recognize the old man and looked at him with mistrust.

"Stay!" shouted one of the guards. "Who are you, stranger?"

"I am Erden Khenbish, a shepherd. I need to talk to your commander!" said the shepherd to the soldiers. "It's urgent!"

The two guards said nothing and kept looking at the stranger without saying a word. They looked as if they were observing him to figure out the man's intentions, wondering what kind of business the shepherd had for their commander.

"What do you need, shepherd?" asked another soldier.

"I have a message about the troop from the north," said the shepherd.

"You have a message?" asked the soldier with both astonishment and mockery. "A shepherd has a message!" he shouted to his fellows.

The shepherd heard low chuckles from behind the gates.

"Go home! Being a messenger is not a matter for an old man," continued the soldier.

The shepherd didn't want to give up and turn away, so he said, "Kid, I need the one in charge of the fortress. Show me the way to your commander, or step aside!" He was losing his temper, and his words insulted the young but arrogant soldier.

"Who do you think you are to talk to me like that?" the soldier asked with irritation.

The shepherd clenched the reins of his horse and said, "I need to see the commander. I said it's urgent."

He couldn't tell the guard about what he'd seen the other night. The soldier might not believe him and make fun of him even more. He made a mistake by leaving the proof of his words in his home. He should have taken a part of the soldier's torn clothes with him. He could've shown the soldiers the blood in the uniform and easily cross the fortress's gates.

"Call me Emmett or someone else!"

"What is going on?" shouted a uniformed man from behind.

The guard turned and saw Officer Tom from the First Division of the Dolorem troops.

Tom observed the shepherd and said, "Emmett is not in the fortress. What do you need?"

"He said he has news for the commander," informed the soldier who made fun of the shepherd earlier.

Officer Tom noticed that the stranger was nervous and desperate to meet someone in charge. The man didn't hide his worry; something bothered him a lot. Officer Tom couldn't understand the reason for his arrival at the fortress, but looking at the man's sad eyes, he felt a very strange coldness in his chest.

"Then what are you waiting for?" Tom demanded from the soldier.

"Sir?" uttered the soldier with wonder.

He believed that the members of Commander Roderick Burton's troop from the north would never ask help from some shepherd but send their own man to deliver a message. He was sure that the stranger bothered them for an unknown but at the same time useless issue. He couldn't understand why the royal soldiers should listen to the stranger who dared to talk to them in an insulting manner.

"Follow the order, soldier!" said Tom loudly.

The soldier couldn't resist the officer's strict gaze and felt ashamed for his objection. The soldier apologized to Officer Tom and turned to the man.

"I'll show you the way," he said to the shepherd with a low voice.

The shepherd thanked the officer and followed the soldier, who led him toward the tower's middle gates. At the end of the long corridor, they turned to the left. Inside the tower, it looked darker in poor lighting. The wind howled between the holes of the old tower walls. It seemed like the inside of the Fort Dolorem tower was much colder than the outside. The stairs ended when they reached the third level, and the soldier knocked on the heavy doors of the officer's room twice.

Officer Johnathan's lowered voice was heard behind the doors, "Come in!"

The soldier opened the door and entered the room. Officer Johnathan was sitting in his old chair at the round table near the window, looking at some papers.

"Sir, there is a man who wants to see you," said the soldier to Johnathan. "He has a message from the north," he concluded.

Johnathan rose from his chair instantly. "Bring him in!" he ordered.

He didn't take his place back in his chair when the shepherd entered the room but kept standing. With both his hands on the table, Johnathan observed the man.

"Sir, I apologize for my disturbance—" the shepherd started to say, but Johnathan interrupted him.

"Speak!" he ordered. "What news?"

"I saw the troops going north several days ago," continued the shepherd. "I don't know what had happened out there . . . One survived . . ."

Johnathan immediately left the room, his steps fast and in a rush. The shepherd followed him. Johnathan was already giving an order to prepare the horses for riding. With a small group of five men, he left the fortress.

"One survived," said the shepherd to the officer. "But he could give away his last breath anytime."

Johnathan hurried his steps. He had to see him before it was too late. The shepherd rode ahead of the riders, showing the way for Johnathan's men. At the very end of the line, the soldier who had laughed at the shepherd's words rushed his horse in order to keep up. He felt very guilty for mocking the shepherd.

Why didn't I believe him? thought the soldier. *One of my friends is dying at the moment, my brother-in-arm . . . What if he had already passed away?* the soldier continued ruminating. His thoughts frightened him.

"No!" he said under his nose. "He is alive. He must be . . ."

Johnathan and his men had to get off their horses and pull their reins to move ahead. The snowy storm was fierce, and the horses were unwilling to take a step. The animals were scared, so Johnathan's group reached the shepherd's house with great difficulty.

Upon arrival, the shepherd probed the lock's handle at the top of the gates with his hand and then pushed them. His wife sighed with relief to see their arrival. Johnathan went directly to the kitchen to see the wounded man that the shepherd had described. He knelt beside Garth and observed him, carefully moving the cloth away that covered the soldier's wounds to see them.

"Tell the men to check the surroundings," Johnathan said to a soldier while studying Garth's wounds.

The soldier hurried to inform the others.

"Where did you find him?" asked Johnathan. "And when?"

"He was in the field," answered the shepherd. "It is close."

Johnathan slowly touched Garth's forehead.

"Can you help him?" asked the shepherd, despite having no faith in his own words. He didn't believe that even a miracle could save the poor boy.

Johnathan shook his head.

"Only ease his pain . . ." Johnathan said, sighing with difficulty. His eyebrows were up, his face gloomy. "Do you know anything about the others?" Johnathan asked the shepherd.

"No," the shepherd answered hastily.

"Does anyone else know about him?" asked Johnathan again.

"No," said the shepherd. "Only my family."

Johnathan rose and made a turn to leave the kitchen.

"Sir," the shepherd tried to stop Johnathan, "will you take him to the fortress?"

The shepherd looked at the officer for a while but didn't receive any answer. He didn't follow the officer but instead stayed in the kitchen. He couldn't leave the wounded soldier alone while the others were looking around. He couldn't read Johnathan's thoughts and wondered what kind of decision the officer would make.

The shepherd's wife and daughter were waiting on the house's second level. Sienna slightly moved the curtains and looked out. She wanted to believe that the soldiers' arrival from the fortress could bring a miracle to their small house. She wanted to believe that one day she could see the steps of her beloved again, to stay with him, to hug him. She didn't want to believe that a happy ending would never be written in her book of life. Sienna stayed behind the curtains for a long time. Soon, she saw the officer from the fortress getting out of the kitchen.

Johnathan stayed in the yard and watched the gates. He bowed his head and covered his face with his right hand. His left hand, he kept on his belly. He was angry at himself. He was angry at his people.

How could they have let it happen? his inner voice screamed. *This could be a failure. A very big failure. I have already sent the message to Rhodareen. No one should have survived! The king must not know the truth . . .*

Sinking in his own thoughts, Johnathan didn't notice the approach of one of his men.

"Sir," said the soldier.

"Did you check?" Johnathan asked the man.

He nodded and responded, "No one else. I think the boy is the only survivor that came down from the foothill."

But his words didn't satisfy Johnathan.

"You *think*? Do you think I am interested in your stupid opinion? I need the answer hundred-percent assured. You shouldn't think!" shouted Johnathan while putting his pointing finger on the man's head and pushing it hard. "You must know!"

The man stepped back and looked down.

"There are no other traces," murmured the man. "Moreover, the message from the mountain stated no one was left alive . . ."

"The message, then, lied." Johnathan's words were full of irritation. "Look who do we have in this damned land?" Johnathan raised his hand, pointing at the house. "No one had to come down from the foothill alive. No one had to know about the plot. Everyone had to be buried under the snow in the mountains."

He sighed. The man said nothing. He couldn't object to his officer. Johnathan and his men knew very well what kind of fate was waiting for those who went to the foothill that day. It had been planned for a long time. For years, those trying to change the world had been working on the plans that could affect the fate of many lives.

Johnathan served those who planted the seeds of treachery. He was a servant, one of millions, who had to take care of the plan's success. The Riphean Mountain tragedy was the beginning of the plan, and it had to be kept secret for some time. No one was supposed to find out about what had happened to the victims buried on the north foothill of the mountain until the right moment—especially the king of the centenarians.

"What will we do next?" the man asked Johnathan.

"He will die anyway . . ." Johnathan made a few steps toward the sheep shed, his gaze seemingly fixed at nothing and his thoughts bringing him to distant places.

The man waited for a little while for Johnathan to speak again, then getting impatient, he said, "The others . . . ?"

"You know what to do," Johnathan interrupted him. "Make sure there's no sign of their existence left."

The man nodded and turned to leave.

Johnathan gave the last order before the man went inside, "And the soldier . . . His mouth must be shut forever . . ."

The opened door of the shepherd's house brought cold wind inside. Snow particles flew inside and lay on the corridor's floor. The man approached the young soldier who had led the shepherd to Johnathan's room in the fortress earlier that day.

"Go to the yard to meet the others, and get the order from the officer," said the man.

The soldier nodded and went out, unaware that his brothers-in-arms would be waiting to kill him. After sending the young soldier to his death, the man found the shepherd in the kitchen.

The old man jumped on his legs when he saw the man. He was dying from waiting and not doing anything for the wounded soldier.

"Have you finished checking the surroundings?" asked the shepherd.

The man nodded, "Yes, we did." He looked at the man and put his hand around the shepherd's shoulder. "Thank you so much for helping our man. You are a very brave man, Uncle."

The man knew very well that this softhearted old man had to die.

Poor man, thought the man. *He had no sin. He was so unlucky to find the soldier in the snow. He just wanted to help. If I were found in the snow instead of Garth, this poor man would also rush to help me. He would definitely send the message to the fortress.*

However, his own men would also definitely send people to end his life and erase all traces that led to the Riphean Mountain.

The man sighed, thinking, *Garth did it. He cursed this man and his family. The night he crawled down from the foothill, he put the death mark on this man's door.*

"Where is your officer?" asked the shepherd.

"He is outside, giving orders to prepare," answered the man.

"Are you leaving?"

"Yes, we are. Don't worry about the soldier. We will take care of him," said the man.

The shepherd nodded approvingly.

"But before we leave, I have some more questions to ask you and your family. Then I'll meet with the neighbors. Are there any other families around?"

"No, we don't have any neighbors. You can't find anyone living around here but us," the shepherd said.

His response satisfied the man.

"Then would you please show me the way up? It would be great to finish our questionnaire as soon as possible."

The shepherd understood that the condition of the soldier could get worse anytime. Despite their rush, the shepherd admired the attentiveness of the man from the fortress. He pointed to the stairs with a gesture, inviting the man to go upstairs. When they reached the reading room on the second level, the shepherd knocked on the door and entered inside. His wife, Maya, and his daughter, Sienna, were waiting for them on the sofa next to the window.

"We have to answer some of this man's questions," informed the shepherd.

The man standing behind the shepherd entered the room and closed the door from inside. In seconds, the women's screams could be heard. The fight didn't last long. When the door opened, the man appeared at the threshold, his face was awash with blood . . . He did what he had to do.

When Johnathan and his men rode their horses down to the fortress, they left behind dark smoke rising high into the sky. The fire destroyed everything. No one would ever know the people who had lived there before; no one would ever know what had happened there that day. The history written in blood on the plains of the Dolorem Valley was erased from the earth's surface and would live only in the memory of those who created this history with their bloody hands.

Chapter 25

Red Hall Council

The horses galloped fast, scattering dirt under their hooves. It had been almost two days since Sanders had left the Westbridge. He was galloping next to Arran. Despite their horses getting tired, Sanders didn't want to stop to rest. He had lost so much time. He wished he had never left the palace. Sanders tried to chase away the scary thoughts from his mind, but his worries almost strangled him. All that time, he was thinking about his father and sister.

When the horses entered the open area, leaving the forest behind, Sanders hurried his horse. The high towers of the Incitydoor palace could be seen from over the trees. The city's huge gates were wide open as usual, and despite the bad weather, the capital city's streets were quite busy. Loudly hitting the stone roads with their hooves, the horses galloped along the River Duur.

Entering the palace's front yard, Sanders jumped off his horse and ran toward the main hall. Arran followed him. It seemed nothing had changed since his leave. The servants were busy with their duties as usual, and the palace looked quiet and empty after the tremendous wedding ceremony of the millennium. No laughter could be heard within the high walls of the palace, but there were the occasional whispers of those who served their masters loyally.

Sanders hurried to the silver hall, next to the king's chamber, hoping to meet his father next to Arawn. However, he was stopped on the way by his nephew Xander.

"Uncle Sanders!" shouted the boy, running over to give him a hug. "I was looking for you everywhere!"

"I . . ." Sanders started thinking about possible answers to his eleven-year-old nephew.

But he was saved the effort when he was interrupted by Lady Calanthe, Xander's mother.

"Sanders!" Her ringing voice echoed within the hall. With quick steps, she approached him. "Where have you been?" asked the duchess, her words full of worry.

Sanders lowered his head like a guilty child, saying, "Sister, I . . ."

"We haven't seen you since Father's leave!" Xander added, cutting his uncle's words.

Only then did Calanthe look at his son to give him a reprimand.

"Prince Xander, where are you supposed to be right now?" she asked in a stern voice.

"Lady Mother, I . . . I am sorry. I am leaving!"

Unwillingly Xander left the elders and followed his mentor, who was waiting for him several steps away. Calanthe looked at Sanders, her eyes filled with worry and anger.

How fool could a prince be to disappear from the palace without saying a word? Why on earth do these men behave like careless kids? thought the duchess, looking at his brother-in-law.

"Go to the Red Hall!" ordered Calanthe at last. "The king will be mad at you if you miss the council!"

Sanders bowed to his sister-in-law and rushed toward the Red Hall. Arran followed him till the doors of the hall. Although Arran Cassell belonged to one of the respectable houses of the kingdom, his rank did not allow him and the other members of his house to attend the royal council. The guards at the threshold opened the door for Prince Sanders, and all Arran could do was wait for his friend outside the main council hall.

When Sanders entered the hall, the lords of the most influential houses of the kingdom were loudly deciding the future relationship with the representatives of the centenarian world. Sanders said nothing but stood next to Keon, who welcomed him with a silent nod.

"Your Majesty, it would be better to wait for the message from the marshal," Clive Lander stated his opinion to the king. "Alexey

Lyov always sided with us when it concerned foreign relations. Always! I believe he will be able to persuade Tsar Michael to support us in protecting the northern lands. They know their own lands better than our forces. We'll just lose time and men by sending the army to the fortress in Dolorem. Besides, we must protect our borders within the Mediterranean!"

"I agree with what Lord Clive Lander said," Tiergan Damen interrupted the words of the one he always despised. "The Russian Boyars won't let the centenarians take away what belongs to them. Apart from that, everyone knows that the braaf army is planning to march to Vatika under the command of the centenarian king's brother in a few months. If ten thousand warriors of the enemy cross the border, we will be doomed without our army and the support of ally countries, Your Majesty . . ."

"What if Michael fails or refuses to serve me as his grand commander?" Arawn frowned. "We can't lose the north at any cost. Otherwise, we'll fail the war against the centenarians."

"Your Majesty . . ."

"Did you receive any news from the Turks?" Arawn asked his brother, Tomaso.

"We are still waiting for a response from Şehzade Ibrahim. Rumors are spreading about the sultan's condition, despite the palace people denying it."

"My king!" Lord Harvin Calhoun, who was observing the council behind the lords, stepped forward. "With your permission, I would like to speak my opinion," said the head of the royal armed forces.

Arawn made a sign to Lord Calhoun to continue his speech.

"At the moment, over a thousand armed men are gathered on Crete Island. With your order to improve the island's reinforcement, we can increase the number of our troops. Since the king's safety is above all, allow us to increase the provisions and arm the fleet. They will protect our borders in the Mediterranean until we receive the support from the Turks."

"I am afraid I must disagree with the words of Lord Calhoun, Your Majesty!" Raymond Stavros opposed Harvin Calhoun. "We can't send all the sons of Rhodareen to far lands. We need an army to protect our home. We don't know when the war will start and where it will begin. Besides, we haven't received any news from Perle de la Mer yet."

"I understand your worries, Lord Stavros," added Gregory Magus. "Yet I daresay that Lord Harvin Calhoun is the most experienced warlord of the kingdom, and I support his opinion. The youngest Ulyses had been noticed in east Al-Jaghbub recently. He went south with his armed men, probably to meet the special warriors. Our undercover men informed us about the great movement in the Ituri rain forest near Mount Hoyo. Soon, the braafs will stop waiting and come into action. We must strengthen our forces in the Mediterranean."

"We can't separate the army!" Lord Stavros tried hard to keep his manners in front of his king. "What if the neighboring countries decide to use this opportunity and steal the power? We may lose the war against the centenarians without even starting it."

"The war hasn't started yet!" Tomaso Layland, who was listening to the arguments of the noble lords of Rhodareen, said and looked at his brother. "My king, I agree with the other lords that we must prepare ourselves for an unpredictable future. Our duty is to protect Rhodareen and all people living within it, as well as the people living behind the walls of our kingdom. But rushing won't do anything better. It will be right if we try to talk to the centenarian king and understand what exactly he wants."

"Lord Tomaso Layland," Raymond Stavros said, giving Tomaso a stern look.

As a cousin of the late queen Ellinor, and the only heir of one of the most influential houses of the kingdom, Lord Raymond Stavros was never afraid of speaking his opinion openly against the king or the other royal members.

He continued, "Haven't you read the message that came from the Dolorem fortress? Or didn't you see the body left at our gates?"

"I did . . ."

"Then why are you still siding with the centenarians? Is it because of your loyalty to your king or to your daughter?"

"Lord Stavros!" Tomaso yelled as he couldn't hide his temper anymore.

"Enough!" with a loud shout, Arawn silenced the other two.

He kept watching his brother in silence before concluding the council.

"Lord Harvin Calhoun is charged with the reinforcement of the Crete Island. My first adviser will negotiate with the Republic of Venice to begin the process and support Lord Calhoun with everything needed."

Tomaso said nothing to his brother's words, and Lord Calhoun nodded to show his agreement.

"Prince Keon will be in charge of the military division on Crete Island," continued Arawn. "Lord Gregory Magus will visit Constantinople in person to observe the situation in the Turks' land and persuade the sultan to support Rhodareen against the braafs. Inform our people in Juba, Isiro, and Malakal. Ulyses should never reach the burning lands of Ifrane. I order them to bury every braaf under the desert. Also, send riders to Khanates. We need more allies close to the borders of Dolorem, as we can't rely on the Russian tsar only. We can't let Dolorem fall. The chief treasurer, Lord Dallin, will prepare the report regarding the royal resources and the estimated costs for the war. Everyone is free for today!"

All the lords bowed to their king before leaving the Red Hall.

"Tomaso!" Arawn called for his brother. "You'll stay!"

Before everyone could leave the hall, Tomaso Layland approached his son and ordered him to wait for his father in his chamber. When the doors were closed at last, only Arawn and his brother were left in the Red Hall. Tomaso waited for Arawn to start his speech, afraid of what to expect from his elder brother. The stern look of Arawn bothered Tomaso.

"You haven't received any messages from Isabelle, have you?" asked Arawn at last.

Tomaso shook his head. "No, not yet."

"Be reasonable! Leon is the one who wants to start the war. He broke the agreement. I wish no harm to Isabelle."

"I know . . . ," Tomaso agreed with the king.

"Don't fail me, brother."

Tomaso just nodded to Arawn's request.

"You can leave," said Arawn as he wished to stay alone.

Tomaso rushed to his own room. All that worried him at that moment was his son, Sanders. When the chamber's doors opened, Sanders stood up to meet his father, only to get slapped on his cheek.

"You foolish boy!" Tomaso shouted at Sanders in anger. "How dare you disobey my order!"

"Father, I am sorry," Sanders apologized in a low voice, his cheek turning red.

"Sorry? Why, is it because you feel regret, huh?" Tomaso asked with irony.

He unlatched the sheath of his sword from his belt and went to the table, throwing the sword. His shaking hands missed, and the sword fell to the floor. The loud sound of the metal ringing echoed around.

"Damn it!"

"Father," Sanders said, approaching Tomaso and putting his hand on his shoulders supportively, "please explain to me what is happening."

Tomaso shook his head.

"You are aware of something that no one else knows. What is it? I must know. Tell me . . ."

"What you *must* do was obey me and stay in the palace! But you ran away! Where did you go? And where is my servant?"

Again, Tomaso could hardly hide his temper. He took a glass and poured old Irish wine into it.

"If I find him, I'll cut his dumb head off . . ." he murmured before taking a sip.

"Leave the servant alone. Don't change the subject! You are hiding something from me. From all of us!" Sanders raised his voice. "There was something about Perle de la Mer. And there is something about this turmoil. I know. Is it related to Isabelle? Did something happen? Please tell me what happened."

"I don't know." Tomaso sighed.

"No, you know!" Sanders shouted impatiently. "Tell me for Isabelle's sake! Anything . . ."

"I don't know what happened to Isabelle! And I don't know what happened at the fortress." Tomaso could hardly hide his tears. He was too scared for his children's lives. "I had been threatened with your lives. I didn't want to send you to the island to protect you."

"Who threatened you?" asked Sanders, his face turning red with anger.

"I don't know. Darragh is working on this," said Tomaso.

Darragh Rafferty was Tomaso Layland's most loyal servant and personal guard. Tomaso could trust only him.

"Soon, he will find out."

"What was the threat?" Sanders asked his father. "What did they want?"

"I am not sure. Whatever it is, they probably don't want me to mess up. I have been warned. There is no request or demand yet."

Tomaso hit the table with his fist. How weak and vulnerable he was in front of his unseen enemy.

"What about Dolorem?"

"The two divisions sent to the valley didn't return. The watchers traced the centenarians in the mountains, and they were gathering an army with Arimaspians not far from the fortress. Our men are worried about a possible attack from the north."

"They had to pass the control over the Riphean Mountain to the people . . . ," Sanders said, wondering.

"Leon betrayed us!" Tomaso stated with anger.

"What are you going to do, Father?"

Again, Tomaso shook his head at his son's question.

"Until Isabelle is completely safe, I can't act thoughtlessly. I must be careful. Arawn must not know about the threat. He will not spare Isabelle for power."

"What if Leon makes you choose between them?"

"Whatever happens, Arawn should not doubt you, son. Show your king your undoubted loyalty. I'll take all the burden."

"I won't let that happen—" Sanders wanted to object to his father.

But Tomaso cut his words, "Don't even dare! Watch your every step. Don't be foolish. Don't trust anyone. Even Keon. One day, you may become my only hope for survival. And the only hope for Isabelle!"

"Father . . ."

"Promise me!" Seeing the sign of hesitation in Sanders's eyes, Tomaso had no choice but to force his son to promise.

"I will never fail you, Father!" Sanders assured his father at last.

Even though he was totally unaware of what he could do, or what he would have to do in the future, Sanders decided to make a promise to himself to protect his family. And he made his promise in front of his father.

After sending Sanders away, Tomaso tried to cope with his thoughts and think about what he could do further. He had to be cautious. The king had already started suspecting him. When his brother asked him to linger in the Red Hall, Arawn asked Tomaso a few more questions regarding him and his son. Sanders's disappearance for several days didn't escape the king's attention, and Arawn demanded to send Sanders to Crete Island together with his second son, Keon. Tomaso knew . . . Arawn would put men to spy on him and his son.

The king didn't trust anyone. Tomaso could not deny the fact that from this very moment, not only Isabelle's life was in jeopardy. For Tomaso and his son, their safety as well was not promised not only within the walls of the palace but also beyond Rhodareen's borders. All Tomaso could do was wait until everything turned in his favor or against him.

About the Author

Dilobar Ortiqova was born in 1991 in Tashkent, Uzbekistan, into a writers' family. From early ages she participated in school contests with her poems and short stories and won the best poetess nominee within the Tashkent city in 2010. She studied Turkish literature at college. She received her higher education in Almaty, Kazakhstan. After graduation, Dilobar moved to Japan, and later to Singapore with her family.

Learning about beautiful and extraordinary cultures and lifestyles of different countries became an unforgettable experience. Currently, she enjoys living in USA. Dilobar speaks Uzbek, English, Russian, and Turkish languages. She loves literature and finds her peace of mind in writing.